Anatomy of an Alibi

Ashley Elston is the author of the million-copy-selling thriller *First Lie Wins* – a No. 1 *New York Times* bestseller and a Reese Witherspoon Book Club pick. She is the author of several young adult novels, including *The Rules for Disappearing* (a finalist in the Best Young Adult Novel category of the International Thriller Awards) and *10 Blind Dates*. Her work has been translated into 23 languages. Ashley lives in Shreveport, Louisiana with her family.

ALSO BY ASHLEY ELSTON

First Lie Wins

Anatomy of an Alibi

ASHLEY ELSTON

Copyright © 2026 Ashley Elston

The right of Ashley Elston to be identified as the Author of the
Work has been asserted by her in accordance with the Copyright,
Designs and Patents Act 1988.

Published by arrangement with Viking, an imprint of Penguin Publishing
Group, a division of Penguin Random House LLC.
First published in the United States in 2026.

First published in 2026 by Headline Publishing Group Limited

1

Apart from any use permitted under UK copyright law, this publication
may only be reproduced, stored, or transmitted, in any form, or by any
means, with prior permission in writing of the publishers or, in the
case of reprographic production, in accordance with the terms of
licences issued by the Copyright Licensing Agency.

All characters in this publication are fictitious and any
resemblance to real persons, living or dead, is purely coincidental.

Cataloguing in Publication Data is available from the British Library

Hardback ISBN 978 1 0354 2076 6
Trade Paperback ISBN 978 1 0354 2077 3

Offset in 11.98/19.26pt Adobe Jenson Pro by Six Red Marbles UK, Thetford, Norfolk

Printed and bound in Great Britain by Clays Ltd, Elcograf S.p.A.

Headline's policy is to use papers that are natural, renewable and recyclable
products and made from wood grown in well-managed forests and other
controlled sources. The logging and manufacturing processes are expected
to conform to the environmental regulations of the country of origin.

Headline Publishing Group Limited
An Hachette UK Company
Carmelite House
50 Victoria Embankment
London EC4Y 0DZ

The authorised representative in the EEA is Hachette Ireland,
8 Castlecourt Centre, Dublin 15, D15 XTP3, Ireland (email: info@hbgi.ie)

www.headline.co.uk
www.hachette.co.uk

For Dean

Alibi: A defense offered by a defendant who claims that he or she was at some other place at the time of the commission of the crime and therefore did not commit the crime charged.

—LOUISIANA STATE BAR ASSOCIATION

Anatomy
of an Alibi

CHAPTER 1

Aubrey

THE ALIBI
SATURDAY, OCTOBER 10

With a single nod of my head, the bartender reaches for the bottle of gin. The crowd has steadily increased in the forty-five minutes I've occupied this barstool, and I'm thankful the place was relatively empty when I arrived. These old wood floors really sell the honky-tonk vibe, but they practically attacked me the second I walked into the room. I nearly took out a waiter and his tray of drinks, along with a couple of patrons whose only mistake was being too close to me when my three-inch heel got stuck between two boards. There are a few things I'll miss from my time here, but these shoes aren't one of them.

The second Negroni of the night appears in front of me. "Wanna order food?"

Glancing at the bartender's name tag, I say, "No thanks, Ray. Just drinking tonight."

He moves to the cooler and pulls out two Ultras for the girl who has wedged herself between my seat and the one next to me while I brace myself for that first sip. I get a thimbleful down without cringing. An improvement.

"You sure I'm making it right?"

I have Ray's full attention, the two beers forgotten in his hand. Maybe I wasn't as composed as I thought I was.

When I ordered my first cocktail, he was surprised by my choice. This crowd looks like they lean more toward well drinks and shots when ordering hard liquor.

"Yes, it's just right." And it's made exactly the way it should be. It's not his fault I hate gin. I lift the glass and take a healthy swig, praying I don't have to wobble my way to the ladies' room to throw it back up.

He seems satisfied and turns his attention back to the girl, exchanging the two bottles for some crumpled bills.

Tapping my phone screen, I see it's only been seven minutes since the last time I checked. I need to stay at least another hour. If only I could stir my drink in the same way I would push unwanted food around my plate so I could spare Ray's feelings.

The couple on my right drops a few bucks on the bar before taking their leave, but the stool next to me is only empty for a second or two.

"Miller Lite," the man says when Ray asks for his order.

He takes a deep drink as soon as it's set in front of him. "What a fucking day," he mumbles to himself, then runs a hand down his face.

God, do I know that feeling. I could say the exact same thing about the day I've had. I know what was rough about mine, but I'm biting my tongue so I don't ask him about his. I remind myself I didn't come here for idle chitchat with strangers, no matter how antsy I am for this night to be over.

The man turns in my direction as if summoned by the questions slamming against my tightly closed lips. His gaze sweeps across me, and I pull my hand off the bar and bury it in my lap before he has a chance to spot the rather large diamond solitaire and platinum band on my left ring finger.

Instead of analyzing the motive behind that impulse, I swivel around on my stool. My back is to the bar as I take in the scene in front of me. Smoke clouds the already dim lighting, making everything look a bit hazy.

It's only a few seconds before he mirrors my move. There's at least a couple of feet between us, but sitting here like this, next to him, feels oddly intimate.

In desperate need of a distraction to pass this last bit of time, I lean toward him and ask, "Have you heard this band before?"

Spotlights highlight the trio of instruments on the tiny stage in the corner of the room. The band finished setting up just after I arrived but has since wandered to the end of the bar, where they've held court with a group of girls here for a bachelorette party. From the looks of it, it doesn't seem like *Live Music* will happen anytime soon.

"I haven't." His voice is deep and rich. Nodding toward the three pool tables at the other end of the room, he says, "Most people come here to play pool and drink, not listen to the band." There are lines of stacked quarters down the side rails of each pool table staking claim on future games. Looks like you've got to get here pretty early if you want a chance to play. He adds, "Gary, the owner, has the worst taste in music, so I wouldn't get your hopes up that they're any good."

I steal peeks of the stranger next to me while he watches the game closest to us. We look like we're about the same age, so I'm guessing he's a few years shy of thirty. He's attractive but still seems approachable, which is the best combination. His deeply tanned face and rough hands tell me he doesn't work in an office, but the pressed button-down says he likes to look good when he's off work. No wedding ring. Nice watch. Altogether, it's a pretty good package.

He eyes the drink in front of me. It's still mostly full but clearly watered down now that the ice has melted and a river of condensation has soaked the napkin under my glass.

"You want something else to drink?" He angles toward me and I do the same until we're almost facing each other.

"I can't order anything else," I say with a shrug.

His head tilts as he analyzes my words. "But I can order something else for you." It's not a question.

My eyes fall on the bottle resting in his grip.

The man raises his beer and holds up two fingers. I can't look at Ray when he sets one down in front of me. Once he's moved on to his next customer, I ditch the cocktail and grab the beer, but before I can take a drink, he taps the neck of his to the neck of mine. "I hope this is more to your liking."

I've never been so happy to cleanse my palate. I blot my lips with the paper napkin after I take a long swig. "Thank you for the drink."

His stare holds mine while I silently recite *This is not why you're here!* over and over. I shouldn't be talking to this stranger. Letting this stranger buy me drinks.

"I really want to say *You're not from around here*, because I know everyone from around here, but I realize it's the absolute worst line."

A laugh escapes me before I can stop it. "Yeah, don't say that," I say, even though he already did.

This is where I should mention Ben.

But I'm tired of talking about Ben. Ben and his high-profile cases. I'm over explaining how a wife can get really bored when her husband spends more time at the office than at home. And as soon as I mention Ben, this man's gaze would search for my still-hidden left hand. His eyes would move to the diamond earrings and the Chanel purse hanging off the back of my stool, then to the smoky eyes and red-stained lips that match my dress perfectly. I can already anticipate the change in his demeanor after he has summed me up with such a quick appraisal: what a spoiled brat I must be.

So I don't mention Ben or demanding clients or big court cases.

The stranger next to me doesn't offer his name, nor do I offer mine. Maybe there's a woman he should mention but chooses not to as well. Maybe we're both enjoying a few minutes in which we could be anyone other than who we're supposed to be.

"I'm calling your bluff that you know everyone here."

His eyes light up. "Try me."

I swivel back around toward the crowd and he does the same. My eyes sweep across the room until they land on a middle-aged man in faded jeans and a black leather biker vest covered in patches. No shirt underneath, just the vest. It's not a bad look, but in my opinion the arms need to be droolworthy to really pull it off, and sadly, his are not. I lean closer and try to point at my target without being too obvious. "What's that guy's name, and tell me one interesting fact about him."

The space between us shrinks even more. He laughs when he sees who I'm asking about. "Ah, we're starting out with an easy one, I guess. That's Kenny Hudson. He manages the bakery on Commerce Street. While you would think there's a Harley in the parking lot with his name on it, he actually drove here in a beige Corolla. He bought that vest on eBay. A couple of guys roasted him the first time he showed up wearing it, and he retaliated by taking his apple crumble off the menu for the next week. No one has said anything to him since."

I can't stop the laugh that started somewhere in the middle of his description of Kenny. "I don't believe you."

He shrugs one shoulder. "It's a mean apple crumble." His face is close and the corner of his mouth is kicked up in an adorable little smirk. "Maybe that's what brought you to town? Kenny's world-famous apple crumble?"

The smile on my face feels permanent now. This guy is ridiculously charming. "Okay, game on." I scan the crowd once more. "What about the woman leaning against the jukebox?" She's got her back to the machine and seems oblivious to everything and everyone around her while endlessly scrolling on her phone.

"Oh, that's a sad tale for sure," he says. "That's Frieda von Samsung."

I almost spit out my beer. "Did you just say Frieda von Samsung?"

"Yeah, she's the missing heiress of the Samsung empire. But she's an Apple girl at heart so she ran away and has been in hiding here ever since, so she can live in peace with her iPhone." He leans a little closer. "Did you come here to find Frieda von Samsung so you could collect the reward?"

I'm not even trying to hold my laugh back. "You caught me. I have been tracking Frieda since she fled from home."

The next thirty minutes fly by as we move from person to person, each description more and more absurd. And each one ending with his increasingly far-fetched guesses for why I'm here. The band has finally started playing, and by the second song the dance floor is about half full, even though this *is* the worst band I've ever heard.

"Had high hopes for this band but it looks like Gary's taste hasn't gotten any better," he says, nodding toward the guys onstage.

"Oh, I hate to hear that." I give him a small frown. "I'm their manager. Cheese Freedom has a lot of potential. I'm determined to make them the next One Direction."

For a split second, I've caught him off guard, then his mouth stretches into a smile, and I have to admit he's not only charming, he's devastatingly handsome.

"Just for that, you're going to have to dance with me while Cheese Freedom destroys this Tom Petty song."

Before I can even consider whether to take him up on his offer, my screen lights up with the alarm that was set earlier, and I'm reminded very quickly my day isn't over just yet. I swipe it from the bar and turn it off, then flag Ray down and make the universal sign for the check.

"You're going already?" the man asks once we're both turned back toward the bar.

"Yes, I'm sorry." It's been fun killing time flirting with him but I need to go.

Ray hands me my bill and I give him a credit card without looking at the total. When he returns, I scribble a generous tip on the slip and sign across the bottom line.

Sliding off the stool, I pray I don't roll an ankle so I can get out of this bar with some dignity still intact. Just before I step away, the man asks, "Can I walk you out?"

I'm shaking my head before he finishes his question. I give him a quick glance then say, "I needed to laugh more than you know, so thank you."

I make my way to the door in slow, steady steps. The second I'm outside, I strip off the heels and run to the car.

Once I'm inside, I crank the engine and stare at the clock on the dash as I idle in the parking lot. A couple stumbles into the passenger-side door, startling me enough that I let out a startled cry. The guy is pressing the girl right against the window, and his hands are pushing up the back of her shirt. This cannot be happening right now. I knock on the glass loudly, spooking them like they did me. They both lean down to look inside the car then give drunken waves before finding another spot to continue their make-out session.

Stopping here for a drink was really not a great idea. I put the car in drive. This won't be my problem for much longer.

CHAPTER 2

Aubrey

THE ALIBI
SATURDAY, OCTOBER 10

At this hour, it's a quick drive back to the gas station, the same one I stopped at just twelve hours ago on my way into town. The foggy mist that has settled around town distorts the glow of the neon lights that edge the overhang above the gas pumps, giving the night an eerie feel. My time at Chantilly's was a nice distraction, but the unease I've had most of the day is back. I grab the plastic bag from the passenger seat, drop the phone inside, then hop out of the car.

It's more crowded than I thought it would be given the hour and the size of this town. The haze plays tricks on my eyes as strangers seemingly slip in and out of existence as they step into the darkness.

The bright fluorescent lights are a shock when I step inside the store, causing me to squint as I make my way to the small public bathroom.

I must have beat her here.

Once I've dropped the plastic bag on the closed toilet lid, I pull the lever on the towel dispenser next to the sink until I have five or six sheets. Carefully, I form a small square pattern big enough for me to stand on so I'm not barefoot on the dirty floor.

It's a juggling act to change from the dress and heels to a graphic tee, joggers, and flip-flops, but I manage it without moving from my paper towel island.

I run one hand down the long light-brown hair before I pull off the wig and cap, causing my own nearly black hair to fall into place just above my shoulders. The dress, shoes, and wig go back in the bag. As soon as everything is packed away, there's a soft knock on the door.

Opening it slowly, I peek outside.

Here she is. Camille Bayliss.

It's a tight squeeze, but we both manage to fit inside.

And now the question I've been dying to ask all day. "How'd it go?"

"Not the way we hoped."

My head tilts as I study her. "If not the way we hoped, which way was it?"

Her lips purse as she considers how to answer me. "I was unsuccessful."

Before I can question her further, she asks, "What about with you? Any problems?"

"All good on my end." I pause, then add, "You didn't find anything?"

She shakes her head but offers no other excuse or explanation.

There's so much neither of us is saying, and we both know it.

I rock back and forth on my feet. This space is too small for this conversation. "What happens now?"

Camille takes a deep breath. "We'll try again. Just need to figure out when."

She's lying. I can see it on her face. Something changed for her today, and I wish I knew what it was.

"Here," I say, holding the plastic bag and purse out to her. I have no desire to keep the dress and heels even though I'm sure she doesn't want the clothes back. She takes them both, then holds out her right hand, but I don't know what else she wants from me.

"The rings."

As soon as she says it, I feel the heavy weight of them. "Oh, yeah, I almost forgot." They are surprisingly easy to pull off given how trapped I've felt by them. I drop the engagement ring first, then the wedding band, into her outstretched hand. She stares at them for a few tense seconds then shoves them on her finger.

"Phone and keys?" she asks.

"Keys are in the purse, phone is in the bag." I'm ready to get out of here. But I need her to think we're still on the same team even though we're far from that now.

"You ended up at a place called Chantilly's instead of the one I picked out?" Camille asks it like a question but it's not.

The mystery man's smiling face flashes in my mind, but I push it away as fast as it appeared. "Yeah, didn't figure it mattered where I had a drink." I force my lips shut before I apologize for the change of plans.

She watches me for a second or so, then nods. "Sure, no problem. I noticed a couple of other detours too. You sure everything went as planned?"

My turn to lie now. "Yes. Just got a little turned around. Figured it didn't really matter as long as I was in St. Francisville."

Camille clutches the bag close to her chest. She's as ready to get out of here as I am. "Key to the other car is in the ignition. Head home, and I'll reach out in a few days and we can make a new plan."

She ducks out of the bathroom, and I wait a minute or so before doing the same.

Camille and the Range Rover are long gone by the time I make it to the parking lot, but the same old Honda I drove here from Baton Rouge is waiting for me.

Our plan was to create a clear and unwavering digital trail that started at noon and ended just before midnight. Every move planned out in advance.

But that carefully painted picture wouldn't tell my story. It would tell the story of Camille Bayliss, wife of Benjamin Bayliss.

Camille needed the ability to move around without being tracked and monitored by her husband. Ben has been hiding a dirty secret for years, one that affects us both, and it would be impossible to get proof of that while he watched her every move in real time, as he was apt to do.

So he would watch my every move instead.

Ben would see the exact location of Camille's phone as well as the Range Rover, thanks to the handy Journeys feature. And because Camille is Camille, there would be multiple purchases that would generate notifications from their bank, matching the stack of credit card receipts sitting in the bottom of her Chanel purse.

And for the most part, that's what happened.

Not sure what the new plan would entail, but there's no way I'd trade places with her a second time. There was a moment when I needed her more than she needed me, but not anymore.

I used my time as "her" today to make sure of that.

It's not a long drive home, but it feels like it takes twice the time it should. I park the Accord in a lot not far from downtown, the same lot I picked the car up from this morning. I'm hesitant to leave the keys under the mat. Just because the car is older than me doesn't mean someone won't steal it, but I do as Camille instructed.

This isn't my problem any longer either.

None of the belongings in the Range Rover were mine, just as there is nothing of mine in the Honda.

It's a short walk down the main road to my neighborhood. Wearing designer clothes and driving a luxury car while using a credit card that probably doesn't have a limit makes the reality of my life hit a bit harder when I turn onto my street. It's a decent enough place to live, but it's also not the coveted gated communities on the outskirts of town.

It feels like every step I take requires more energy than I have. The last twelve hours have completely drained me. It was mentally exhausting juggling what I was supposed to do as Camille while hiding what I wasn't.

But hearing that she was unsuccessful makes all my efforts worth it. Today may have been a bust for her, but it won't be a bust for me.

The closer I get to home, the slower my steps grow. The last couple of weeks have been an emotional whirlwind, and now I'm feeling the crash.

By now, Camille is probably back at her hotel, sound asleep, while I trudge up my driveway. The brightness of the full moon casts a deep shadow of our house, blanketing the front yard in darkness. It's quiet enough that I can almost hear the creaks and groans of a structure that is too old to be burdened with so many residents. Once home to a single family, it's since been chopped up to create four separate units. It's only a matter of time before the seams burst.

This is basically a boardinghouse that no one ever leaves. Being set up the way it is, this property should attract renters who only need something for a short period of time—people stuck between their pasts and their futures.

I left my spouse but we're not divorced yet.

I got fired from my job and haven't found another one yet.

It's the "yet" that's the dangerous part. The hope that living somewhere like this is temporary, and a positive life change is just around the corner.

A positive life change that you'd go to great lengths to achieve, like I did today.

I moved into this house years ago because it was all I could afford, and I haven't saved up enough money to move—*yet*. Pretty sure everyone who lives here would say something similar.

This is not a forever kind of home, but that's what it has somehow become.

My unit has its own exterior entrance at the back of the house, but seeing the light on in the kitchen has me moving to that door instead.

I twist the knob and push it open.

I see a handful of faces staring back at me from the scarred wooden kitchen table. Everyone is here.

"Any luck?" I ask.

Deacon shakes his head and says, "No, he's still there."

"Okay, it's on to plan B."

CHAPTER 3

Hank

AFTER THE ALIBI
SUNDAY, OCTOBER 11

My tires squeal as I make the turn. I'm driving faster than I should on a residential street on a Sunday morning since there's bound to be kids out, but I'm in a panic. It's one of those perfect, crystal-clear, blue-skies kind of days where you're looking for any excuse to be outside. Cars are being washed in driveways, weeds are being pulled from flowerbeds, and there's a lemonade stand set up even though we're well into October.

But this is the calm before the storm. Everyone I pass is completely unaware that their peacefulness is going to be shattered.

Just like mine was shattered when I received that frantic call seven minutes ago.

Slowing down just enough that I don't take the turn on two wheels, I pull into the driveway.

My truck screeches to a stop, and I see her waiting for me exactly where I told her to. Looks like I'll have a few minutes to talk to her alone, and it won't be nearly enough time.

Camille is sitting on the stone steps that lead to the massive wooden front doors of her house, her arms wrapped tightly around her legs. Her hair is pulled back from her face, and she's bathed in the midmorning light, making it easy to see how pale she is.

I'm in front of her within seconds, dropping down to a crouch.

"Hank . . ." Her voice cracks when she says my name.

There are trails of watery mascara down both cheeks and her nose is running. She ducks her head toward her shoulder, wiping her tears on the sleeve of her button-down, only for a fresh wave to take their place.

"Is anyone else here?" I nod in the direction of the 1970 red Mustang that's parked in the overflow parking spot near the garage. It's hard to miss and also very out of place.

She looks over her shoulder at the car and stiffens slightly. "No. That . . . was here. There's no one else here."

Her answer begs more questions, but I let it go for now. "Wait while I check inside."

She grabs my arm, her eyes wide. "No . . . don't go in . . ."

I take her hand in mine, giving it a quick squeeze. "I'll be right back." I press down on the handle with my elbow then use my shoulder to push the heavy door open.

The smell hits me first. My throat tightens as I pull my shirt up to cover my nose. The sight that greets me once I'm inside almost brings me to my knees. It's as bad as she described. I take one step, then two, but stop before entering the home office just off the foyer.

Ben is lying on the floor, and the purplish-gray tint of his skin tells me he's been dead for some time.

It's not easy to look at what happens to a body in this condition. Even though it's clear there's nothing to be done for Ben, I move closer. The blood looks like it poured from some opening in the chest before soaking into the rug underneath him, but without touching him, it's impossible to tell whether a bullet or a blade or something else caused the damage.

A wave of grief rolls through me but I force it down, locking it away to be dealt with later, when Camille isn't falling apart outside and the cops aren't racing this way.

It's hard to pull my gaze away from him, but I need to make the most of my time before the police arrive since I won't be allowed inside once they get here. I scan the room, taking it all in, try to see what's in front of me objectively.

Ben's desk is a large ornate piece that is the focal point of the room and he's on the floor next to it. I try to imagine the steps that led him to this spot. Imagine him alive in this space. His desk chair is pushed back, so he could have been seated and then gotten up and rounded the corner from the right side, leaving the seat turned in that direction. But he didn't get much further than that.

There are two smaller chairs in front of the desk for guests, and the one closest to Ben is on its side. Was someone sitting there and knocked it over in their rush to meet Ben head-on? Other than that, everything else in his office seems intact. Nothing looks rummaged through or noticeably out of place, but I do spot several client files on his desk. Ben may be gone, but his clients are still protected under privilege. There's no murder scene exception that allows the cops to look through any of that information, so I make a mental note to deal with that when they get here.

There is a credenza behind Ben's desk, against the back wall of the room, where his laptop sits open but dark. The bookshelves on the far wall are in order, and the cabinet doors that hide his bar setup are open. The crystal decanter that I know from firsthand experience contains some of the best bourbon I've ever tasted is pulled forward from its usual spot. I glance back at the desk for the glass he must have used to pour a drink but don't see it. Another step further in the room and to the left, I find it behind the desk on the floor, still intact but on its side.

I take one last glance at Ben before I back out of the room.

What the fuck happened in here?

There will be time to mourn him later, but right now I need to see about Camille.

Exiting the house, I sit on the step next to her. "Tell me exactly what happened when you got home." Her eyes are glassy, like she's not really seeing me. Hearing me.

She draws a ragged breath. "I came in through the garage door like I always do. Called out for Ben. Went looking for him . . . and then I . . . I saw him. On, on the . . . floor." She turns and looks back at the house. "I called 911. They wanted me to stay on the phone, but I was scared. I knew how close you were. Ben . . . Ben always said I could call you if there's an emergency. So I called you. Then came out here. Like you said."

The sirens in the distance tell me we are almost out of time. "He was right. The police are going to ask you a bunch of questions so they can find who did this to Ben. Answer them honestly. But don't guess at anything. Don't assume anything. Don't agree to something they say if you don't think it's correct. If there's something you can't answer or don't think you should answer, look directly at me. I will take it from there. Don't worry about what that looks like. Better to be safe now than sorry later." We're staring at each other. I'm throwing a lot at her and I'm hoping most of it is sinking in. "Okay?"

She nods.

"I need to hear you say *okay*."

She nods again and then utters a faint "Okay."

"You just got back to town? Just now? Right when you called me?"

Her bottom lip quivers and some of her hair falls loose from the clip holding it back, but she ignores it. "Yes. Just got back. Just now."

I squeeze her arm. "You're doing good. We'll figure this out. But for right now we've got to get through the next few hours, okay? Did you touch anything in the office? Was there anything out of place inside?"

"No . . . I don't think so . . . just set my stuff down in the kitchen . . . went looking for Ben, and then I saw . . ." She can't finish the sentence.

"That's good. You're doing really good." She's not far from shutting down completely.

When the first cop car pulls into the driveway, she falls into my side, sobbing.

There's so much I don't know about what happened here, but my first priority is her. That's what Ben would want. I can unpack the rest of it later.

Two officers exit the vehicle and jog toward us, their right hands resting on their firearms. It sounds like there are a dozen more sirens racing to the house. I imagine all the neighbors are edging their way toward the street to get a better look, although in this neighborhood it won't be easy for them to see too much since the houses sit so far apart.

One of the approaching cops stays a few feet back while the other stops just in front of the steps.

Keeping her tucked under my arm, I pull us both up to standing, making sure my free hand stays loose by my side. Based on the wild eyes, these two haven't been on the force long, so no need for nervous, twitchy fingers to decide I'm a threat. The new arrivals are exiting their vehicles but keeping some distance.

"We're responding to a 911 call that there's been a break-in and possible homicide," says the officer closest to us. If I wasn't holding on to her as tightly as I am, Camille would have hit the ground when he said "homicide." I angle my body in a way that puts me closer to him while also sliding her somewhat behind me. We're one step above so I'm towering over him. I'm a big guy and have no problem using my size to establish some dominance when needed, like right now.

"I'm Hank Landry." I see recognition flicker across both their faces. "My client just arrived home from being out of town and discovered the victim." It's a conscious choice to call her "my client" instead of using her name.

A handful of cops are a dozen feet behind these two, waiting on orders. An ambulance barrels into the yard, with little care for the grass or flowerbeds, since the driveway is now full of cop cars. The level of response this call has received is not lost on me.

"Is there anyone else inside?" he asks.

"Not that we're aware of, but neither of us has checked the house."

Within minutes, every cop swarms inside except for the uniformed babysitter instructed to watch over us. The EMTs wait off to the side, but once they're told there's nothing to be done for Ben, they'll pack up and leave.

While we wait, all I can think of is how much Ben would hate all these people in his house. This place was on the market for less than a day when Ben scooped it up. It didn't matter that it was old and dated, because a lot this large in the heart of Baton Rouge made up for it. He and Camille spent more than a year remodeling it with a team of designers. Ben sat in on every meeting, and every decision, no matter how small, had to be approved by him. He was obsessed with each little detail, making sure he had the best of the best, the way only a poor kid turned rich would be. He talked about this house like other guys talk about fixing up an old car or getting their duck blind ready for hunting season. If I heard him say "French Provincial style" once when describing the aesthetics, I heard it a hundred times.

Now, the meticulously maintained landscaping is being trampled just as I'm sure the expensive rugs inside are.

The crowd grows. Nosy neighbors have walked down the street and are standing in groups of twos and threes on the edge of the yard in front of the house. I'm sure the cops will talk with all of them, but I'd be surprised if they get any useful information. The dozens of live oak trees and the mature landscaping will make it damn near impossible for the neighbors to provide any real insight since it's difficult to see from one house to the other through the thick foliage.

I scan person after person looking for the detectives, the ones in plain clothes I know will turn up eventually. The first conversation will be the most important, and I'm not wasting it on some pimply-faced rookie. Finally, I see a familiar face walking toward me.

Detective Sullivan joins us on the steps, and I raise my right hand to shake his. "Sully, good to see you, but wish like hell it was under different circumstances."

"I was just about to go off shift when I caught this call. Didn't realize whose place this was till I pulled up and saw you two." He's talking to me, but his eyes are taking everything in, especially the way Camille is clinging to me.

Shouts of "all clear" filter through the front door. A few cops head back out, one of them pulling Sullivan aside, catching him up, while the other tells the paramedics they aren't needed. There's no saving Ben.

Sullivan steps away and whistles loudly. Everyone in uniform stops and gives him their full attention. "Lock it down."

And then they're all on the move again. One of the cops produces yellow police tape and begins to unroll it.

The Bayliss home is officially a crime scene.

CHAPTER 4

Hank

AFTER THE ALIBI
SUNDAY, OCTOBER 11

Sullivan makes his way back to where we're still waiting on the front steps while the cops establish a perimeter to control access to the scene. "I'm going to ask that you wait here."

I nod then add, "Ben had a habit of working from home so I will need to take possession of any client files that may be inside." I don't tell him I'm already aware they're present.

"Okay, give me a few minutes to check it out."

He steps inside while Camille and I sink back down on the steps. Neither of us speaks and we barely move. The weight of what happened here feels like it has settled in every part of me.

After about ten minutes, Sullivan pokes his head back out. "Hank, sign in that you're entering the scene and I'll escort you inside. I'm going to ask that you not enter the office. You can witness the collection of the files from the surface of the desk, and I will hand them over to you."

When I step away from Camille, she panics. Squeezing her shoulder, I promise, "I won't be gone long but I need to take care of this. Sit here and I'll be right back."

She drops back down, clearly uneasy being left alone.

The officer at the door takes my information, noting the time I entered the house, then hands me some of those paper booties to put over my shoes, just like everyone else inside the house is wearing so they don't contaminate the scene. It's only a few steps until I'm at the threshold of Ben's office, and it's not easier seeing Ben's body a second time.

Sullivan goes around the far side of the desk, avoiding Ben. There is an open folder on the desk, and he's scanning the pages that are in clear view but there's not much I can do about that. He's working with me here when he could make this difficult.

"Not everything here is a client file," he says, as he closes the folder and begins stacking files in his arms. I spot a FedEx envelope and some other papers that he leaves behind. Then he grabs the stack of folders from Ben's briefcase. I make a mental note that the folder that was open, and probably what Ben was working on before he died, is on the very bottom.

I take the stack from him and he escorts me back outside, trusting he hasn't left anything behind.

"I'm gonna need to ask you both some questions," Sullivan says once we've exited the house.

Camille jumps up the moment she sees me.

I gesture to the side yard, using my free hand. "There's a seating area over there where we can talk. My client needs to sit down."

His left eyebrow arches. "Client, huh? Aren't you a little too close to all this?"

Camille doesn't move or speak. She barely blinks. "For now, I'm her attorney."

"I'll follow you." We step out into the yard and through the gate in the iron fence.

There's a small outdoor couch and a couple of chairs tucked into a manicured pocket of the side yard. It's one of those areas only a designer would think of creating. I can't imagine choosing to sit here when you could be hanging out by the pool instead. But it suits our purposes today.

I direct Camille to the couch and take a seat next to her, putting the stack of files on the side table, while Sullivan takes the closest chair.

He pulls out a small notebook and pen then turns his attention to her. "Mrs. Bayliss, I need to ask you some questions. Can you please tell me the events that led up to you finding your husband's body in his home office?"

She takes a deep, gulping breath. "I just got back from a weekend away. His car. His car is here. I knew he was here because of his car. And then I . . . I saw him. On the floor. And the blood. I screamed. I think I screamed." She swallows hard. "And then I thought maybe he was okay—you know how sometimes you can bleed a lot but it's not really that bad and maybe that's what happened to Ben, but then I moved closer and I could see his face and I knew . . . I knew . . . it wasn't that . . ."

She's gone from barely speaking to vomiting up words, and I wonder what Sullivan's thinking. Does he think she killed her husband?

The police always look at the spouse first. No matter what. And then they look at who else has the most to gain by the victim's death. After Camille, the next person in that line would be me.

As his law partner, I will gain the most from Bayliss and Landry Law Firm becoming just Landry Law Firm. I don't need to give the police even the smallest crumb to suspect either of us as the perpetrator of this crime, which is why I'm glad Sullivan took this call. He's tough and has a reputation for not jumping to easy conclusions. That's what I need right now—an open mind.

"Let's take it step-by-step, Mrs. Bayliss. Can you tell me where you were this weekend? You mentioned coming back from out of town."

She wipes away her tears. "I was in St. Francisville."

St. Francisville is a quaint small town about half an hour from Baton Rouge that tourists flock to every weekend. There's always some sort of festival involving food or art or music, and it's also a regular stop for the riverboat cruises that sail up and down the Mississippi River.

She's fidgeting. Pushing her hair back behind one ear. Rubbing at the mascara smudge that transferred to the back of her hand after she rubbed it across her face.

Sullivan is seeing everything I do. Taking mental notes right along with his written ones. "Did you travel alone?"

Camille nods. "Yes. Ben booked a room for me at the inn there. I have an Instagram account where I post about food and old restaurants . . . I travel around looking for content. Ben knows I like to explore little towns in the area and books me trips when he's going to be out of town or busy."

"Was Ben out of town or busy this weekend?"

"Out of town."

"Where did he go? And do you know when he returned home?"

I jump in to answer. "Ben and I went to New Orleans late afternoon on Friday for a continuing ed seminar on Saturday morning, since we both needed a few more CLE hours before the end of the year. We had planned to stay last night too and go to the Saints game today, but Ben said he needed to get back so we left yesterday when the conference ended."

"What did he need to get back for?"

I shrug. "He said work. I didn't press for details."

"What time did you get back to Baton Rouge?"

"A little after one p.m. yesterday."

"Where did you go when you got back? Your office?"

"No, we came here," I say. "My car was here since I rode with Ben."

"Did you go inside when you arrived?" Sullivan asks.

I shake my head. "No. We talked for a moment in the driveway then I left."

Sullivan looks at Camille. "Did Mr. Bayliss let you know he was coming home early?"

She shakes her head. "No."

This surprises me, but I don't let it show. Why wouldn't Ben have told her?

He makes some notes. "Can you tell me what you did while you were in St. Francisville?"

"What I did?"

I lean closer to her and say, "Just give him a rundown of your time there. Where you ate, stores you visited . . . he just needs a clear picture of the weekend."

"Yes, of course. Friday night, I had dinner at Restaurant 1796. Saturday, I walked around . . . there was a festival. Did a little shopping." She gestures vaguely at the house. "The bags . . . all my stuff . . . is still in my car." A sob escapes and she has to clear her throat before she can continue. "They had a pumpkin patch set up. Stopped at the feed store to buy some fall plants. Mums."

"Anything else?" Sullivan asks.

She considers his question and adds, "I had dinner at the Waterfront

Grill then stopped for a nightcap at"—she pauses as she wipes away fresh tears—"at Chantilly's. Wasn't quite ready to call it a day and it wasn't far from where I was staying."

Sullivan nods. "Any chance you kept something that shows you were there?"

"Yes, of course. I have all the receipts in my purse in the car." She hesitates a moment, then stands up. "I'll just . . . I'll go get them for you."

Camille leaves to retrieve her bag and Sully gives me a curious look. Does he also think it convenient she's ready with a stack of receipts? It's almost as if she spent yesterday preparing for the alibi she'd need today.

CHAPTER 5

Camille

THE ALIBI
SATURDAY, OCTOBER 10

The clock starts now. It seemed impossible that I could find a way to move around without the prying eyes of my husband following my digital trail, but somehow I've managed to become a ghost. No phone to show my location, no smartwatch to record my raised heart rate and steps taken. Even the car I'm driving was picked because it doesn't have a fancy navigation system to track and report back every mile I've covered. I bought this beat-up Honda Accord with cash a few days ago, which felt like an extreme move at the time, even though I plan on selling it as soon as we're done. Aubrey doesn't own a car, and I couldn't rent one without the credit card charge alert popping up on Ben's phone, so there weren't many other options. But extreme or not, it's exactly what I need to get me back to Baton Rouge undetected.

Ben wasn't always this obsessed with tracking me. It was a gradual thing. Seemed innocent enough at first since I could see where he was at any given moment as well. I just never thought to check it as often as he did. And I really don't think he's trying to catch me doing something wrong or cares how much I spend at the grocery store. Ben loves control, and technology helps feed that monster. Every single move I make is only an app away.

It was only twenty-four hours ago that I was home with Ben. I kept him company while he packed his duffel bag for his weekend in New Orleans. He had taken the afternoon off from work, and his charm and playful demeanor were at an all-time high, as if that would distract me from the fact that he was lying about his plans.

We made small talk as he moved between the closet, the bathroom, and the end of the bed, where his open suitcase sat. He gave me a brief rundown of how he would spend his time away, while I sat perched on the chaise longue tucked away in the corner of our room.

There have been a dozen times when we shared a similar moment in the past—him packing while I watched—and I always believed he was going to be where he said he was.

But not this time.

The road out of St. Francisville is a straight two-lane divided highway with only the occasional house or trailer and the random industrial plant that supports the local oil-and-gas industry. It's a boring drive, and my mind drifts to the events of the last few months that led me to take such a drastic move as allowing a woman I barely know to pretend to be me.

I had a feeling something was wrong in my relationship with Ben. Looking back, I think that feeling had been there a long time. It sat like a pebble in the pit of my stomach. Small enough to brush off at the beginning, until it began growing. And growing. Over the years, that pebble turned into a stone that weighed me down. Slowed my steps. Even though there wasn't anything in particular Ben did that made me start to doubt him, I couldn't ignore the feeling any longer.

But deciding to finally do something about it is much simpler than actually doing it.

I'm not proud to admit it, but leaving a marriage is a lot easier said than done if it will result in a drastic change in lifestyle. Any money I have is tied to Ben, and thanks to the "bad behavior" clause in our prenup that my father insisted on, access to that money requires proof of infidelity, abuse, gambling, or any criminal wrongdoing. Dad promised this would protect me, but all it's done is strengthen the chains that bind me to Ben.

Ben didn't become one of Baton Rouge's best defense lawyers by accident, so I knew it would be a challenge to find something to prove what my gut was trying to tell me. So I went on the hunt for anything that would fall into one of those categories. I was limited to his home office, and I knew the chances that I would find a proverbial smoking gun were slim. And I didn't. But once I got started looking through his things, I couldn't stop.

Ben had his obsession and now I had mine.

I went through the drawers on his side of the bathroom. The glove box and center console of his car. His pockets after he put his pants in the hamper. His wallet. Ben always says that the first thing any cop or prosecutor looks at is the suspect's phone, so even though I knew he wouldn't have anything there for me to find, I looked anyway. And found nothing. Absolutely nothing no matter how hard I searched.

Finally, I had to admit to myself that I was no longer scared I *would* find proof he was doing something wrong. I was scared I *wouldn't*.

And maybe that feeling in my gut was more about me than him. It wasn't about Ben and what Ben was doing. It was about me wanting out and not having the courage to leave him.

There was a time I loved Ben. Madly.

It was the young, chaotic kind of love. Where every touch is new and exciting. Every emotion consuming. Every experience is a first.

Ben and I are from the same small town and started dating our senior year of high school.

In the beginning, my parents didn't approve of him. But somehow Ben won them over. Instead of trying to pull us apart, they began pushing us together. The fire that probably would have burned out on its own was stoked by everyone around us. He proposed the night of his law school graduation, to the utter delight of my parents and his. I got swept up in the moment and set aside any reservations I might have had.

We had big moment after big moment: graduations from high school, then college, and finally law school for Ben. Then the big, splashy wedding that took a year to plan. But when the dust settled, it was clear Ben was at the start of a new and exciting career, while I was expected to be just like my mother—a dutiful wife who volunteered for worthwhile causes and joined the boards of charitable foundations.

And somewhere along the way, those flames had turned to dying embers, and no amount of gasoline would bring them back.

By the time I realized I'd made a mistake, it felt impossible to do anything about it. I had no idea how to even begin to break the rules I'd followed my entire life. My dad gave me a charmed, privileged upbringing, then passed the torch to Ben. I had been conditioned at an early age to believe that if someone provided you a nice life then they were owed the right to make every decision as to how you lived it. My parents wouldn't agree to help me leave my husband unless I had a very, very good reason. To them, marriage was until death. You rejoiced in the good times and suffered through the bad, but you never quit.

I think back to the one time I tried to talk to Mom about how I was feeling. I was staying with them while Dad and Ben were away on a hunting trip. We were at the breakfast table when I told her I didn't want to stay married to Ben.

Her response left no room for argument. "What on earth are you talking about. Of course you're going to stay married to Ben. You're not going to humiliate your father and me by becoming a divorcée." By her reaction, you'd think I'd just told her I was about to work the pole at one of the strip clubs on Bourbon Street.

I knew in that moment there was no chance my parents would support me financially if I left him.

So I stayed, and Ben made plans for us, a timetable for our future with benchmark goals. He never once asked if these were goals I shared.

Open his own practice. *Check.*

Hit his annual income goal. *Check.*

Build or buy the perfect house. *Check.*

Start a family.

It's no coincidence the moment he mentioned that next step was when that feeling in my gut began to grow.

Once the house remodel was finished and the perfect pieces of furniture graced every meticulously designed room, I knew he'd be anxious to check that next box. While I may feel stuck now, it would be nothing compared to when we had kids. My search through Ben's things was fueled by the desire to find . . . anything . . . that would force me to act.

Something I could hold up to him, to my parents, and say, *See this? This thing he did? This is the reason I have to leave him.* Something that would trigger the clause in our prenup.

So I continued my search.

And then one night I got lucky.

I shift in my seat, my memories scattering as I'm forced to concentrate on the road now that the traffic has picked up. The exit for the interstate that will take me back to Baton Rouge is quickly approaching. It's been twenty minutes and there's only about fifteen more to go until I'm home. I check the time. Everything is still on schedule. By now, Aubrey should be at the festival in the park next to the St. Francisville Inn.

I lose a little time as I battle the ever-present Baton Rouge traffic. A few notifications have popped up on my iPad, which is sitting on the passenger seat, but a quick glance tells me all of them can wait. Although I had to leave my phone with Aubrey since that's the device Ben tracks, I didn't trust her enough to let her into my phone or handle my communications. I'll take care of that myself with my iPad.

Finally, I'm pulling into the lot of a small market on Perkins that's close to our street. While it's not perfect, I decided I would stash the car here and jog to my house. Our street is off one of the busiest roads in the heart of Baton Rouge. Some houses in our neighborhood can easily be seen from the road, while others, like mine, are tucked much further back, the live oaks and dense foliage screening it from the street. But all of us have privacy from one another.

There is more traffic on our street than there should be, given how few of us live on it, but it's a cut-through of sorts between two busy areas that has been exploited more and more over the last several years. Ben has even drafted a petition to the city to have one end blocked off, making it a dead end, but it will take more than the full support of the residents to pull that off.

While the constant flow of cars won't make anyone think twice if this old Honda drives by, the same can't be said if I park it on the street in front of a neighbor's house. I put on an LSU ball cap and oversize sunglasses before I exit the car, then start off toward my house. Even though I'm parking in a place I'm allowed to park and going to a house I have every right to enter, it still feels like I'm breaking the law.

I jog past the first few houses with a steady pace and a watchful eye to see if anyone who may recognize me is out and about. We socialized with our neighbors on a few occasions right after we moved in, but Ben and I both found it to be more exhausting than entertaining.

The first question every woman asked me was: *When are you starting a family?* Really, it was the only question anyone asked me. They took my vague answers as an invitation to give me their thoughts on the subject. And when they weren't talking directly to me about procreation, every other conversation was about kids and schools and after-school activities and sports for kids and kids and kids.

Ben didn't have it quite as bad as I did, but he did complain that most of the questions directed toward him had to do with the high-profile cases he was in the middle of defending. Apparently, they would know of at least one of Ben's clients in a six-degrees-of-separation kind of way and wanted whatever juicy details he would give them.

Both of us began to gently brush off future invitations. It was one of the few things we agreed on lately.

As I approach my driveway, I take one last quick look around then increase my pace. Don't need anyone being a Good Samaritan and calling the cops about an intruder.

As soon as I know I'm hidden from view, I slow to a walk and study our house as if I'm seeing it for the first time. It's a gorgeous structure made of rough-cut stones, with a steep slate roof and copper gutters, painstakingly remodeled to its former glory. A house anyone would love to have. A house that could grace the pages of *Southern Living*.

But that's the problem.

Ben wanted it to be a showplace, so every piece of furniture, every picture on the wall, every book on the shelf was chosen by an interior designer. While I was involved in the process, he got final approval. The end result is beautiful, but there is nothing inside that reflects my personality or, really, Ben's either.

It could belong to anyone.

During my soul-searching, I realized I'm no different from the achievements that hang on his wall and line his shelves. A trophy wife in every sense of the word.

I know what I want out of today. I want a way out. And just because I'm more self-aware than I've ever been, that doesn't mean I'm not terrified of slipping back into the role I've played my entire life. My father and my husband have had years to shape me into the woman I am today, one who does what she's told, one who doesn't go against them. Today, I'm hoping for something that will balance the scales. Evidence of his bad behavior that will speak louder than I ever could.

Aubrey thinks we're in this together, and that whatever I find I will share with her.

And I might. Ben has lied and hid things that have hurt us both.

But . . . I also might not. The only people who need to know what he's done to trigger the prenup clause are my family and our divorce lawyers.

I'm hoping I'm strong enough to leave him, but I'm not sure I'm strong enough to weather the inevitable scandal that would roll through this city if what he's done is made public.

Is this fair to Aubrey?

No, it's not. And I feel really bad about that.

But as Ben likes to say, "Fair is where they sell cotton candy."

CHAPTER 6

Camille

BEFORE THE ALIBI
THURSDAY, SEPTEMBER 3

My phone vibrates with an incoming text from Hank.

> Heads up! Dropping Ben off in five
> He's hammered
> Also he bought some hunting trip to Argentina

It's late. Close to midnight. I must have dozed off while I was waiting on him to get home from the Ducks Unlimited banquet. After liking Hank's first message, I throw off the covers and head downstairs in case he needs any help getting Ben inside.

Part of me is pissed I'm having to deal with this in the middle of the night, but mostly I'm struck by how out of character this is for Ben. He isn't a big drinker. It's not that he doesn't drink, he just keeps a strict limit on the amount.

But over the years I've realized the lack of drinking is more about control. Ben likes control, and getting drunk makes him lose it. When he drinks, he speaks more freely. Drops his guard in a way that makes him vulnerable.

I'm more curious about what brought on the loosening of his usual ironclad control than I am bothered to have to tend to him in this condition.

By the time I make it to the kitchen, headlights flash across the room as Hank pulls up the driveway. I open the side door and watch Ben struggle to get out of Hank's truck. It's a massive vehicle, very different from the sleek SUVs Ben prefers. It suits Hank, though. The DU event was his idea. It's an annual dinner where duck hunting enthusiasts raise money to support wetland conservation. There's always lots of things to bid on during their live auction, including, I guess, hunting trips to Argentina. Ben isn't much of a hunter but has been known to go on trips for either the social or business networking aspect. He was less than enthused to attend, but something must have changed his mind when he got there because he's all smiles now.

"Cammie! Want to go to Argentina and shoot some ducks?"

Ugh. I've made it very clear how much I detest that nickname.

"Not particularly." I look at Hank, who has grabbed Ben's briefcase from the back seat of his truck and is steering Ben toward the door. "I should make you take him to your house."

Hank lets out a deep laugh, the kind that makes you want to laugh too. "Not on your life, *Cammie*. He drank enough Scotch that it's likely to come back up at any moment."

I elbow him in the side when he passes by me to get Ben through the door and he just laughs again. Ben's eyes are glassy and his cheeks red. He is in rare form and has completely zoned out. As soon as he's close enough, he falls into my side. His arms wrap around me while he buries his face in my neck. Yeah, drunk Ben is very different.

Hank steps away, holds Ben's briefcase up. "I'll just put this on the counter."

By the time I maneuver Ben to a chair at the kitchen table, Hank is shutting the door behind him.

"Sit here. I'll get you some water and Advil. Did you eat anything?"

I step away but he pulls me back, causing me to fall in his lap. His hands slip under my shirt and his mouth moves to my neck, giving me sloppy kisses while he feels me up. "Don't go."

Ben is rarely affectionate. At any other time, this attention might be nice, but not when I'm worried he's going to vomit all over me.

"What brought this on?"

"So stressed out." His hand edges to the waistband of my pajama bottoms. "Fucked up and now everything is fucked."

I stiffen in his arms but he's too far gone to notice. "What did you do?"

"Fucked up."

Running a hand through his hair, I try to stay calm. There's a glimmer of hope at his admission, since I had all but given up on finding evidence to use against him.

"We can fix whatever it is, but you have to tell me so I can help."

He pulls me in closer so his head can rest on my shoulder. "I'm gonna fix it. Got a plan. After, we'll go to Argentina then come home and start making babies."

I scoot off his lap and he almost falls on the floor before catching himself at the last minute. Making babies is the last thing we're going to talk about.

"I'll fix you a sandwich. The bread will hopefully soak up some of the booze." My sharp tone is also lost on him.

Ben leans back in the chair, his legs stretched out in front of him. His head is tipped back and his eyes are closed. He's not far from passing out. There's a good chance he won't remember any of this tomorrow.

I move to the cabinet and grab a glass and fill it with water, then pull the bottle of Advil from the drawer. Just as I'm shaking two pills out, I glance at his briefcase where Hank left it on the counter.

And the first thing I notice is that the little brass latch is in the up position. It's unlocked.

That briefcase is never unlocked.

My eyes flick to Ben and then back to the briefcase. If I am ever going to have a chance to see what he hides inside, it's tonight.

Making sure I don't lose this opportunity, I start moving with intention. Sandwich forgotten, I hand him the pills and water. Then help him upstairs. It's painstakingly slow since he misses every other step while also still trying to get a hand down my pants. The second his head hits the pillow, he's snoring.

And I'm racing back downstairs.

I stare at the briefcase a few seconds before I flip it open. There is a stack of files and papers, and I lift each one out, studying it carefully before putting it face down on the counter next to me. Once I'm done, everything will go right back inside in the same order so there's no way for him to know I went snooping.

The only sounds in the house are the hum of the air conditioner and the rustle of paper, which makes this feel more stressful than it should. After about every third piece of paper I pull out, I check over my shoulder to make sure he's not behind me. He's already admitted he "fucked up." Now I just need to discover what that *fuck up* is. When I think there's nothing here to give me any clue, I finally find something.

It's a bar napkin.

There's a logo in black in the bottom corner that says DOUG'S TAVERN.

It's the words on the napkin that give me pause.

A woman's name: Aubrey Price, followed by a phone number and address written in handwriting that isn't Ben's. I pick up my phone, searching both the bar's location and the address on the napkin. They're fairly close to each other; both are in a part of town I don't frequent.

Next, I type the woman's name in the search bars of my social media accounts. I find her easily enough, confirming I have the right person when I see her last post is a picture of her behind a bar, bottles of bourbon in both hands as she pours drinks. Doug's Tavern is tagged as the location.

Aubrey looks to be in her midtwenties. Shoulder-length dark hair. Maybe black but it's hard to tell in the low lighting of the image. She looks slim and petite behind the bar, her face lit up in a big smile. Someone who's probably fun on a night out.

Anger bubbles up inside me as I take a picture of the napkin before carefully putting everything back into the briefcase the way I found it.

Before, my obsession felt unfounded. Now, I feel vindicated.

CHAPTER 7

Aubrey

BEFORE THE ALIBI
WEDNESDAY, SEPTEMBER 9

I hate working on nights like this. Doug's is close enough to campus that we get some college kids, but we're also popular with the young professionals looking for a place to get a cheap drink and play a little pool after a long day at the office. It's usually busy enough that my shifts fly by, but not tonight. Rain pelts against the metal roof and the thunder is loud enough to rattle the windows. It's basically a ghost town in here, but Doug won't let me close early since three people braved the weather to hang out.

So I refill the occasional drink and clean an already spotless bar and stare at the clock as it moves in slow motion.

Just as I'm about to announce last call, the door opens and a gust of wind propels a woman inside. She struggles to keep the hood over her head while the bottom of her raincoat whips and swirls around her legs, making her stumble. She pulls the door shut and faces the room. We're all staring as she stands there with water rolling off her, puddling at her feet.

When she realizes she has our undivided attention, she dips her head and draws her shoulders inward as if trying to hide. The three guys at the bar track her as she moves into the room, picking a stool as far from them as possible. I slide a napkin down in front of her as soon as she's seated.

"What can I get you?"

She runs her hands across her face and droplets of water sprinkle the bar top. "Negroni."

I raise an eyebrow but she misses my look of surprise and instead focuses on brushing water off the sleeves of her jacket. If she's trying not to bring attention to herself, she's doing a terrible job.

I make her drink then set it in front of her. "Six fifty. And it's last call."

The woman digs in her purse and hands me a ten. "Keep the change."

I nod, thanking her for the tip, then grab a mop to take care of the trail of water she left in her wake.

The woman sips at the drink, never removing her hood. She looks ridiculous. Both hands are gripped around the glass, and it's hard to miss the giant rock on her left hand. One by one, the other patrons leave until it's only the two of us left. I glance at the clock and then at her glass. It's still half full.

Wiping down the bar, I edge in her direction. "We close in ten."

She nods but doesn't make any move to leave or finish her drink.

I turn on the main light and cut the music, hoping she gets the hint.

The woman's eyes are red rimmed and tired looking. Whatever she's going through is taking its toll. Her bottom lip quivers, and I pass her a handful of napkins as I see the tears form in her eyes.

"You okay?"

She lets out a frustrated laugh. "No. No, I'm not okay." Then she takes a deep breath as if she's trying to pull herself together. Finally, she raises her head and looks at me. "I had this whole speech worked out and honestly there's no real way to ask you this without it being really awkward, but are you having an affair with my husband?"

I stand frozen in front of her. "Who in the hell is your husband?"

She finally pushes the hood back and her long brown hair spills around her shoulders. "Benjamin Bayliss."

Wait. I know that name.

But not because I'm sleeping with him.

My arms cross in front of me. "Your husband is that big-shot lawyer, right?"

She gives me a slight jerk of her head, letting me know I'm thinking of the right guy.

"I've never met your husband and have no idea why you think I'm sleeping with him."

I feel bad for her. It's clear this has hit her hard, but it's absurd she's here accusing me.

She rolls her lips inward, watching me, as if she's trying to decide if she believes me.

It's a long minute before she says, "If you're worried about telling me, I wouldn't blame you for it—this would be totally on him. I just . . . want to know. I *need* to know."

Funny thing is I believe her. She came in here thinking I'm screwing her husband, but there's no anger directed toward me. Just sadness and genuine curiosity. "I swear, I don't know him."

She shakes her head slowly back and forth. "I don't understand. He knows you. Your name. He was here last weekend."

My forehead scrunches. "He shows up at this bar and you automatically think he's screwing around with someone here?" I gesture to the empty room. "I know it doesn't look like it, but when the weather's not so shitty, we get pretty packed in here." I pause a moment, then say, "He may be cheating on you. He may even have met them here, but you have no reason to assume it's me."

She raises one eyebrow. "If he had just come to this bar, I would agree with you. But I found this." She pulls out her phone and taps on the screen, then turns it to face me. I step closer to get a better look. It's a picture of one of our bar napkins with my name, phone number, and home address. "This is where you live, right? I did a little . . . research. You live there with a few other people. And according to the travel history on his car, he's been there too."

My mouth drops open in shock as my mind spins, trying to understand what is happening right now. "There's no reason he should have been to my house."

We stare at each other, and I see the first signs on doubt creep into her features. She was so sure her assumptions were correct until now.

"What's your name?" My question takes her by surprise.

"Camille."

"Camille. Call him. Get him on the phone and put it on speaker. Let's ask him why he has my name and number and address and why he's been to my house when I've never met him in my life."

She looks stunned. "What?"

I'm pissed. How dare she come in here, hurling accusations at me like this. "You heard me. Let's not screw around. We're gonna get to the bottom of this."

She stands up abruptly, almost knocking her stool over. "I'm not calling him. I can't. He can't know I'm here."

I'm shaking my head. "Oh, no. You came in to get some answers so let's get some answers."

The color drains from her face, and I feel a little bad because she's clearly scared at the thought of him finding out she's here. But not bad enough to let this go.

"Look, I'm not trying to get you in trouble, but I'm also not going to be accused of something I haven't done. It's clear your husband is up to no good and it somehow involves me, so we *are* going to ask him about it."

Camille pulls her purse close. "I made a mistake coming here. I obviously misunderstood."

"And I'm misunderstanding why he has my name and personal details! Why he's been to my house!"

Camille runs a hand through her hair. "I must have seen work information and assumed it was personal. I believe you when you say you don't know him. This must have something to do with one of his cases. I'm so very sorry for bothering you."

My spine straightens when she mentions his cases.

"You think this is because of a case?" Because there's only one case my name would ever be associated with and it's an old one. "Does this have anything to do with Paul Granger?" Paul was convicted ten years ago, but in his recent letters he's told me he's trying to appeal his case.

"Who did you say?" she asks, her voice just above a whisper.

"Paul. Granger."

If I thought she looked pale before, it was nothing compared to what she looks like now.

My head tilts to the side while I study her. "I'm guessing my name didn't ring a bell, but it's clear Paul's did." She doesn't say anything, but her eyes get big, so I push a little further. "Maybe you should do a quick search and see how we're connected."

We're both startled when the door opens again. Deacon steps inside and glances from Camille to me and back at Camille. It's obvious he's walked into a tense situation.

He shuts the door and moves closer to the bar. Deacon is one of my housemates and can be very intimidating, especially if you don't know him.

Camille takes him in then takes a step back.

He's a big guy, but there's a natural look to his size. Muscles that come from work, not working out. His dark hair and tan complexion are a gift from his mom, who came here from Cuba when she was just a little girl. He works for his cousin, Chris Ricci. I know Chris owns a few bars, I know Chris is a bookie, and I know there's a lot more I don't know when it comes to Chris and his business endeavors. I'm not even sure what the extent of Deacon's job duties are, but picking up on comments he's made, I'm convinced collections is a big part of it.

Deacon usually swings by near closing to offer me a ride home so I don't have to walk, especially on nights like tonight when the weather is so bad.

"Aubrey, you good?"

I give him a quick nod. "I'm good."

"I'm so sorry I bothered you." Camille walks quickly to the door, making a wide berth around Deacon, then disappears into the night.

"What was that about?" Deacon asks.

"I'm not really sure." I lean back against the counter, still a bit stunned by what just happened. "You know a lawyer named Benjamin Bayliss?"

Deacon shrugs one shoulder. "Heard about him but don't know him. He's the guy you want if you're staring at serious time. Word is he can get you out of just about any charge." He watches me a moment, then asks, "Why?"

I nod toward the door Camille just fled through. "That was his wife. Accused me of sleeping with her husband."

Deacon's eyebrows shoot up.

Holding my hand up, I add, "Before you even ask, no. I've never even met him."

"So what made her think that?"

"She found one of our bar napkins with my name, number, and our address. Says he's been there according to the travel history on his car, whatever that means. I told her to get him on the phone so I could ask him about it and she panicked. Walked it back by saying she must have misunderstood. That he must have had my info because of a case. I asked her if it was Paul Granger's and she flinched."

Deacon's eyes widen. "You think he's taking Granger's case?"

I shrug. "No idea. But if he is, why would he be checking on me?"

Deacon walks closer to the bar then takes the stool she just vacated, whipping out his phone. "Gonna text the house group chat and ask if anyone knows him. Seen him lurking around."

My phone vibrates in my back pocket when his text comes through. At this hour, there's a good chance we won't hear back from everyone until tomorrow.

I can't stop the shiver that rolls through me. "Let's just get out of here."

Deacon has been here enough at closing that he helps me get everything shut down and locked up in record time. Thankfully the rain has stopped by the time we pull into the driveway at home.

When I go to open the door, I notice he doesn't get out. "Are you not coming inside?"

He shakes his head. "Got one or two things to finish up before I'm done tonight."

"I should be mad you left work just to bring me home, but I'm very glad you did since the weather was so awful. Very sweet of you."

He ducks his head since he's terrible at accepting any sort of compliment. "Lock up behind you. We'll talk in the morning about the Bayliss woman's visit."

I jump out of his car and step carefully through the yard, trying to avoid the landmine of puddles.

"You're home later than usual."

Spinning around with my hands clutched to my chest, I spot Serenity, another one of our housemates, sitting in the dark on an old wrought iron chaise. She's using an upside-down orange Home Depot bucket as a side table to hold her cocktail and ashtray.

"You scared the shit out of me," I say.

She lights a joint, and the glow from the flame illuminates her face for a few seconds, long enough to see this isn't the first one she's smoked tonight. Her hair is a mess and her gaze unfocused.

"How long have you been sitting out here?" I ask, moving closer to her.

She raises her hand, offering me a hit, but I wave her away. It wouldn't be the first time I smoked with her but tonight's events have me feeling it's important to stay sharp.

"Ever since the rain stopped. Was going crazy cooped up in the house. Shane and Eddie were working late in the garage."

I drop down on the end of the chaise. I'm in no rush to get to my room since I'm still so keyed up from Camille's visit. I'll give myself a few minutes to sit in the dark while the pungent smoke floats in the air around me.

"You upset? Why?" Serenity asks. She's squinting one eye at me as if that's the only way she can focus.

I twist around until I'm fully facing her. "How can you tell I'm upset?"

"Your aura is dull and sad looking."

I roll my eyes. "You know I don't believe in all that."

"Does it have something to do with Deacon's text about that lawyer?"

Drawing my legs in close, I wrap my arms around them. "Kinda. Yeah." I'm sure I'll end up telling her the whole story at some point, but right now I don't feel like getting into it again.

Serenity curls her lip. "Tried to hire him not long ago. Called his office and left a message. Wanted to see if he would take my case. But no one ever called me back." Her head tilts back as she stares at the night sky.

"What case?" She had some legal issues a while back, but I didn't know she had any active charges.

"Shoplifting."

"Oh." I leave it at that even though I'm kind of dying to know what she stole.

"I know that snotty wife of his, though. She's a real piece of work," Serenity adds.

There's no stopping the startled cry that flies out of my mouth. "How . . . how do you know . . . her? The wife?"

"She came to my yoga class Monday night." I wait for more. But that seems to be all she plans to say.

Was this the "research" Camille was alluding to? "How was she snotty?"

She looks at me, takes another long drag, then blows the smoke out slowly. For a few seconds, she's hidden behind the white cloud. "I get a lot of women who come to my class once and never come back. Same ones who have the expensive mats and the fancy water bottles and the high-dollar yoga clothes. My classes aren't the classes they're looking for."

"What do you mean?"

"They want the yoga body but not the yoga mind." Her eyes close and she leans her head back again, the lit joint forgotten in her hand. It continues to burn, inching closer and closer to her fingers, so I snag it before she burns herself, then gently put it out, making sure to salvage the tiny bit that's left.

Serenity teaches at a place called Goddess Divine, not far from the bar. It's an old house turned into a business that sells everything from crystals to incense to chakra beads and offers not only yoga classes but also palm reading and massages. By the way Camille was dressed tonight, I would think she'd stick out there. Goddess Divine would not be her scene.

Don't get me wrong, Serenity is probably an amazing teacher, but she's unconventional. She's a free spirit who doesn't care what anyone else thinks and will let you know it. It wouldn't surprise me if part of her class involves beating drums and writing down your intentions before lighting them on fire. Based on my impression of Camille Bayliss, Serenity's classes seem like they would be too hippie for someone like her, who would be dressed in head-to-toe Lululemon.

Just when I think Serenity's completely passed out and I'll have to wait for the rest of this story, she says, "But she came back yesterday even though I know she hated being there. It was all over her snotty face."

There are a million questions on the tip of my tongue, but I can tell Serenity is done for the night when a quiet snore slips past her lips.

I stare at her for several minutes, trying to fit this new information into what I learned.

Ben Bayliss had my personal information on a bar napkin and his wife is searching for answers despite being terrified he'll find out.

She said he's been here. At our house.

Even if all this is about Paul in some way, Ben Bayliss should never have come here.

CHAPTER 8

Hank

AFTER THE ALIBI
SUNDAY, OCTOBER 11

By the time I finally leave the Bayliss house, the sun has set. I'm tired. I'm hungry. I'm confused. And grieving my friend and partner.

Camille's brother, Silas Everett, and his wife, Margaret, showed up not long after Camille fished those receipts out of her purse and handed them over to Sullivan. Sullivan allowed her to take the bags she had packed from the weekend out of her car but wouldn't let her back in the house. I'm not sure she would have gone in given the option.

Until the police are done with her house, she'll stay with her parents in Corbeau, a small town that's only about twenty minutes from St. Francisville, the town she just returned from. Silas put her in his truck, nearly taking out half the paps when he peeled out of here. Margaret followed behind in Camille's car, so she'd have it there.

Sullivan will want a formal interview soon. The only reason he didn't push to do it today was both Silas and I agreed she wasn't in the right state of mind to answer any more questions. He wasn't happy about it, but he wants her willing, and I all but assured him she wouldn't be helpful if he forced her to continue.

Sullivan left hours ago, I'm sure chasing down leads even though he wouldn't give me any details. The police will keep their opinions to themselves until they're ready to go public. I stayed until the coroner took Ben's body away. It just didn't feel right leaving while he was still there, on the rug stained with his blood.

There's still one cop car in the circle drive close to the house and another one out on the street. They killed the sirens and lights hours ago, but their presence is to deter the onlookers who continue to cruise up and down the street. I back out and wave to the officer stationed there to keep the media at bay. They showed up almost as quickly as the cops did.

Because of Ben's notoriety in this town, the media isn't going to back off this story anytime soon. The best we can all hope for is that this case doesn't linger unsolved for long and the cops are able to catch his killer.

I can't imagine what Camille is going through right now. She and Ben have been together a long time—since they were teenagers. Ben had mentioned a few months back that he was ready to try for kids now that the remodel was finished. And now he's just . . . gone.

Sullivan won't cross my or Camille's name off his suspect list right away. It's just the way things work, and I can't even be mad about it. You always look at the spouse first. History tells you the odds are in favor of them being the killer. I can't see it with Camille, though. That devastation, that fear, that grief were real.

But I can also admit I'm looking at this through the eyes of a friend, not a lawyer or detective. If she did it, she's a hell of an actress. Solid Oscar performance.

I see Camille as the woman who has been trying to set me up on one blind date after another. The woman who always brought me lunch anytime she brought it for Ben. The one who makes sure to include me at every holiday, knowing how hard those occasions are since my parents passed away, one right after the other, a few years ago.

Camille has become a friend.

I want Sullivan to do his job the right way and cross off everyone who didn't do it, including Camille, including me, so he can focus on who did kill him. But I'm prepared to step in if he tries pinning this on either one of us if no other leads pop up. I know there's going to be a lot of pressure on him to close this case.

Even though I should go home, shower, pour a drink, end this fucking day, I head to the office instead. The eight a.m. staff meeting tomorrow is going to be brutal and I need to be prepared.

It was important I notified our employees about what happened to Ben before they heard it on the news. While I waited for the coroner to arrive, I took a minute to write the hardest email I would ever have to send. Sully told me they are keeping the details from the public for now by just saying Ben was found dead, not murdered, so I told them what I could.

Thankfully traffic is light this late on a Sunday and I make it to the office in good time. I park in my reserved spot and stare at the illuminated sign attached to the side of our building: BAYLISS AND LANDRY LAW FIRM. It's like a punch in the gut.

Ben and I met freshman year at LSU. We were similar in a lot of ways—two white-trash kids from small towns, both attending school on scholarships—his academic, mine athletic. He knew on day one he wanted to be a lawyer. Hell, he probably knew it way before then. Not me. I had my eyes on the NFL and signing bonuses and the dream of one day making it to the Hall of Fame.

I dump my dirty clothes out of my gym bag then fill it with the files I took from Ben's home office so I can bring them inside. Opening the back door to the office, I turn off the alarm, then reset it once I've locked myself inside. The images of Ben are still fresh enough that I'm taking precautions I haven't before.

Whoever killed him is still out there.

Is his murderer someone who has been in this office? Someone Ben knew? Or was it random—a burglary gone bad?

Can't go down that rabbit hole right now. It's a waste of time to speculate on what-ifs until I familiarize myself with every part of Ben's life and get details the police are willing to share once they comb through everything.

My office is in one back corner and Ben's is in the other. The entire center of the building is sectioned off for assistants and paralegals, the conference room and a small break room. Ben loved coming in after hours to work. He liked having the place to himself. The silence.

I hate it. Sometimes it's necessary, but I do my best work when this building is full of people and the noise level is something you can almost feel.

Instead of going to my office, I head to his, my limp more pronounced than I'd like. After spending most of the day pacing in Ben's front yard, my knee is throbbing.

At the time, I thought the injury during the LSU–Bama game my senior year was the worst thing that ever happened to me. I was living my best life as a starting running back for LSU until a gruesome tackle tore almost every ligament in my right knee. There was rehab and consults with specialists all across the country, but it came down to the simple fact that if I were to play again and reinjure that area, there was a good chance I would never walk again, so I walked away from the sport I loved while I still could.

A future with the NFL had been my dream since I was a kid, but being forced to reevaluate my life was a blessing in disguise. Was there a chance I would get drafted after my stint at LSU? Yes, but certainly not a guarantee. But once that was off the table, I had to come up with a new future.

Flipping the light on, I step just inside Ben's office but no further than that. It looks like he just finished for the day, leaving everything ready to pick up where he left off. There are framed pictures of him and Camille behind his desk, like a highlight reel of their time together. Images from college, their wedding, their honeymoon, the ski trip they took last winter. The wall next to his desk showcases his academic and professional achievements. His diplomas from undergrad and law school. The certificate showing he passed the bar. Awards and recognitions of service from a number of charitable organizations.

Ben went into private practice immediately after graduating law school. Early in his career, he represented a state politician, Representative Wells, who was accused of killing his mistress in a drunken rage. No one else wanted to touch that case after the DA announced he would personally be prosecuting it. It should have been a slam-dunk conviction for the DA, but Ben whipped his ass. And that single acquittal changed the trajectory of his career. At twenty-seven, he became one of the most sought-after lawyers in this area.

There are stacks of file folders along the left side of his desk and several piles on the floor. The weight of what happened and how it changes everything presses down on me.

But tomorrow will be soon enough to tackle the work ahead of me in this room, because tonight I don't have the strength to take another step inside.

Flipping the light back off, I shut the door.

I drop my gym bag with Ben's files on the couch in my office and head straight to the built-in cabinets along one wall, opening the center one that houses a small bar setup. I pour two fingers of bourbon in a glass and throw it back, relishing the burn, then refill my glass, taking it with me to my chair.

I have similar pictures and achievements on my wall, but I zone in on the one of the two of us the day I signed the partnership papers and joined this firm.

That was only two years ago. I took a different path out of law school by accepting an offer to join the DA's office. The first couple of years after school, Ben and I faced off in the courtroom: me prosecuting, him defending. We were evenly matched, both of us stacking up an equal number of wins and losses.

Ben pulled me aside after a particularly grueling trial where he managed to come out with the win and offered me a job. He knew I was getting burned out. The DA's office is full of lawyers trying to make names for themselves and move up the ranks. We were overworked, underpaid, and generally treated like shit. Ben's offer was good. Great even. Not only was the money a game changer but the idea of being my own boss was something I couldn't pass up.

It was strange the first time I sat on the other side of the room, defending a guy who had been arrested for grand theft auto. He said he didn't do it and I decided I would believe him. The not-guilty verdict felt unsettling. I was so used to dreading that outcome that it took some time before I was relieved to hear it.

Being on both sides has come in handy, though. I know how the prosecution works. How they think. The strategies they use.

And that's why I know Sullivan will be calling soon to request that Camille sit down for a formal interview. I need to clear my calendar and get everything in order so I'm next to her when she's questioned.

I push my empty glass away. "What the hell, Ben."

I'm not an overly emotional guy, but I feel like I've got at least a dozen different feelings rolling around inside of me—grief the strongest one.

Regardless of all the things Ben and I disagreed on or thought differently about, it's a punch to the gut he's gone. Not just gone . . . murdered. I can't wrap my head around it. Can't stop thinking about who would have done that to him and why. What's the motive? It's got my mind creating lists. A list of possible suspects. Was it a client Ben represented who was found guilty? Was it a client Ben repped who was found innocent and a family member or friend of the victim got their own form of revenge? Was it someone outside of our practice he had business with that ended poorly?

Was it Camille?

I'm surprised when that last question finds its way into my stream of consciousness. As much as I don't want to think about that possibility, I'd be a fool if I didn't at least consider it.

I force myself to focus on the work even though it is overwhelming to think about. More lists start to form. A list of his cases and whether it's best to absorb them into my already full workload or pass them off to another firm. A list of business ventures and assets Ben has and what needs to be done with them if I find I'm still listed in his will as the executor of his estate.

I move my mouse around to wake up my computer. First thing I do is pull up the folder we created in case of an emergency, opening the scanned document of the latest version of Ben's will, where I'm a little surprised to still be listed as the executor.

Once I've familiarized myself with his last wishes, I close out the document. I stare at the file folder that's sitting at the corner of my desk and decide one more drink won't kill me. With a fresh bourbon in hand, I pull that folder closer. I toy with the edge, trying to decide if I really want to look at it again while I'm in this headspace. Before I can think any more about it, I flip it open.

It's not any easier seeing it now than it was when Ben first gave it to me last week.

It's a single sheet of his letterhead that states he's officially starting the process of dissolving our partnership, confirming how screwed I am since he was the founding member. I would be forced out and not able to take any clients with me.

Or I guess how screwed I was.

Because he died before the dissolution went any further than this notice, it's like it never happened. And the firm is mine based on the agreement we made when we created the partnership.

And there's the other emotion that's been simmering underneath all that grief.

Relief.

CHAPTER 9

Aubrey

THE ALIBI
SATURDAY, OCTOBER 10

Camille drives off in the old Honda just as I get the Range Rover cranked. I've never owned a car, and today will be the first time I've been in, much less driven, one as fancy as this. I can't believe she's trusting me with it.

But trust is a funny thing. She didn't hesitate giving me her car or her platinum card, but her phone was a different story. I have to carry it around with me all day but it will remain locked. The trust doesn't extend to me reading her messages.

I get it, though. I wouldn't let her read mine either.

Before I back out of the parking spot, I remind myself of the schedule we mapped out last week at Doug's just before closing one night. First up, there's a festival being held in the park near the St. Francisville Inn, the hotel where she's staying. From noon to two p.m., I'm supposed to wander that area and buy things from three different vendors using her credit card.

I pull out of the gas station onto the main highway that runs through town, tugging on the wig when I see it's a bit askew in the rearview mirror.

But instead of turning right to head to the park, I turn left.

Camille doesn't know it yet but I'm going off script. She's got her iPad to answer her texts, so there's a good chance she can see the location of her phone too, and I'm sure she'll ask me about this later. And later is when I'll worry about that.

A quarter of a mile down the road, I'm at my new destination. It's a gorgeous October morning and the feed store parking lot is packed with trucks and SUVs. I drive Camille's car to the far-left side, pulling into one of the few open spots near a row of hunting stands for sale and pallets stacked high with deer corn.

The shiny red 1970 Mustang pulls in next to me, right on time.

He exits the car at the same moment I do.

I stand next to Camille's car while he walks toward me, a black backpack slung over one shoulder. "So much for trying not to attract attention."

He laughs. "You're the one who picked the busiest spot in town."

He's not wrong.

I look behind him, toward the Mustang. "Where's Shane?"

"We're meeting up after I leave here. You look weird with that wig on."

Rolling my eyes, I lean back inside the Range Rover and grab the key. "Love you too, Eddie."

Eddie puts the backpack on the hood of Camille's car and digs inside until he pulls out a small device. I hand him the key and he holds the two together, then pushes a button until it beeps.

"So that's all it takes to copy it? That little machine?"

Eddie jiggles the device once he's finished. "Only after a few modifications Shane made to it. But yeah, all I'm doing is sending the signal to unlock the car to this instead of the vehicle. And the code is recorded."

Eddie and Shane moved into the house about six months after I did. Both grew up in the foster care system. They were placed in the same group home when they were teens and have been together ever since. They have a special skill set: There's not an engine they can't rebuild, not a car they can't steal. As auto technology has evolved, so have they.

Now, they are retired car thieves. Mostly.

Camille would be furious if she found out that not only do my housemates know what is happening today but they're also helping make sure I don't get screwed.

Eddie hands me back the remote. "Let me get the tracker attached and then I can grab her garage-door signal if it's programmed to the car. There's a good chance once we're in the garage, the door to get inside the house won't be locked."

Yes, trust is a very funny thing.

Do I trust that if Camille is able to find proof of Ben's wrongdoing that she'll share it?

No, I don't.

So my housemates and I made our own plan that she doesn't know about.

And step one is to make sure we have access to Camille's car and home as well as knowledge of her location after I turn this car back over to her.

Eddie nods toward the Mustang. "Grab my phone from the car. I'll download the Range Rover app and connect to her car so we have that as well in case the tracker fails. Ben drives a Range Rover too, right?"

I nod. "Yeah, I think one just like this but black."

"How cute."

Once I've given him his phone, he goes through the steps to connect to her car. "There's a good chance their two accounts are connected and we can see where he is too."

I scratch at the wig. "This seems too easy."

Eddie shrugs. "The only easy part is getting through the door. I'm hoping it doesn't come to that."

"Thank you for helping me today. Tell Shane thanks too," I say quietly.

He stops what he's doing and looks at me. "We're a team. Ben Bayliss tries to screw with you then we're all going to screw with him."

For the first time today, a smile breaks out on my face.

Yeah, I may not trust Camille, but I sure as hell trust Eddie and Shane.

It only takes him a few more minutes and then he's done.

"Okay, I got everything I need."

I step close, hugging him tight. "Thank you again."

"No more thank-yous." He squeezes me back and ruffles the wig, making it slide across my head. "Want me to hang around until they get here?"

I shake my head. "No. I'm good."

Eddie makes a scene when the Mustang peels out of the lot, and I can't help but laugh.

Glancing at the clock, I'm guessing Camille has gotten to Baton Rouge and is close to her house. I turn the music up after I crank the car.

Just about time for step two.

CHAPTER 10

Camille

THE ALIBI
SATURDAY, OCTOBER 10

I let myself in through the side door that leads to the mudroom. Custom cabinetry lines one wall while a bench made to look old and worn runs the length of the opposite wall. Even though I know there's nothing recording my presence in this house right now while I make my way through the butler's pantry to the kitchen, I still avoid the areas the interior cameras would capture if they were working.

When Ben told me a few days ago the cameras were down, that was the only confirmation I needed that he would be meeting someone here. A "system-wide malfunction" meant there wouldn't be any alerts on my phone if someone walks up to any of our exterior doors, nor would there be any videos that could be used against him later.

He just didn't know he was making it easy for me too.

This house may be beautiful but it feels like a prison—one where the warden can check in on you whenever the need arises.

But not today.

Today I'll be the one watching, thanks to Aubrey.

Aubrey.

Oh, how wrong I was about her.

When I showed up to the bar to pressure her into admitting she was sleeping with my husband, I assumed I knew exactly what was going on.

But instead of getting proof of Ben's infidelity, I opened Pandora's box. Whether I like it or not, I'm stuck with Aubrey Price now.

Taking the stairs two at a time, I clear the landing on the second floor then head to the narrow door that hides the staircase to the attic. I spent the last few days stuffing an oversize storage container with everything I'd need today. The first thing I grab is the bag holding half a dozen small cameras and head back downstairs.

In the kitchen, I take my time powering them on and syncing them by Bluetooth to my iPad. After testing everything earlier in the week, I know the distance between the attic and the rest of the house is within range for the tablet to pick up each camera's feed.

Once I'm sure the batteries are fully charged in each camera, I scatter them around the house in places I think Ben could be when he gets here. I work my way through the downstairs: one in the potted plant that will show the driveway, then the kitchen, the dining room, his home office, the living room, and I finish upstairs, with one in our bedroom, just in case he has more planned today than I think.

Before I leave our bedroom, I stop and stare at the gallery of images hanging on the wall. Ben is classically handsome; he won the genetic lottery where all the parts and pieces are symmetrical and sized for the most pleasing results. He also has the ability to be exactly what he needs to be depending on the people around him. It's a gift that wins him both cases and friends. There's the image of us dressed up at DC Mardi Gras, him in a tux in what I call his Lawyer Ben look. Hair brushed back, not a strand out of place. Contacts in. No stubble. And next to it is one of my favorite pictures of us, taken last summer on vacation in Greece. He's in shorts, no shirt, on the deck of the boat we chartered to take us sailing. It's his Relaxed Ben look. Free of gel, thick, fat curls cover his head, and he's got the perfect amount of scruff when he skips the razor for at least a day. Two different-looking guys, two different personalities.

Which Ben will I see today?

I run a hand across the image of him on the sailboat as if I'm saying goodbye to the version I fell in love with all those years ago, before everything got so complicated.

And then I'm back to the attic. We splurged on the foam insulation during the remodel so it's only a few degrees warmer than the interior of the house. I pull out a folded beach chair and set it up next to the storage box. Remaining inside are a couple of bottles of water, a box of granola bars, a roll of toilet paper, and a bucket. I'm praying with everything in me that I won't need the bucket, but I'm prepared for the worst. After he gets here, I'm not sure when I'll have a chance to leave.

Once I'm as comfortable as I can be in the chair, I switch to the grid view on the tablet that shows all the camera angles at once, then I plug the headphones in. The conference he and Hank were attending ended almost an hour ago. If he comes straight home he could be here soon, but it's impossible to know for sure since he turned his location services off.

A text from him comes through just as I settle in to wait:

Of all the places I thought you'd be shopping I sure didn't guess the feed and seed store

What.

What is he talking about?

Before answering him, I pull up the app that shows my phone's location. He's right: The little blue dot is steadily blinking exactly where he said. I check the time and notice it's just before one. Aubrey should be at the festival next to the inn.

But she's not. She's at a feed and seed store.

"What are you doing, Aubrey?" I mumble as I switch back to the screen with Ben's text: haha they have some gorgeous mums here! Couldn't resist when I passed by!

It's a good thing I bought one yesterday when I got to town so he won't catch me in a lie.

He doesn't respond, which pisses me off because part of me thinks he texted me just so I know he's checking in on me. It's moments like this that reinforce I'm doing the right thing.

I settle in to wait.

And wait.

After almost an hour in the attic I've almost talked myself into the possibility that I've misunderstood everything and he's not coming, then I hear the rumble of the garage door opening. A minute or so after that, Ben enters the kitchen. I watch from the camera as he puts some mail on the counter. He's still dressed as Lawyer Ben, but he's barely through the door before he starts shedding that persona, transforming right before my eyes. He loses the coat and tie. His hands run through his perfectly styled hair until it begins to hang loose around his face. It won't curl until he washes all that product out, though. The shirtsleeves get rolled up. Relaxed Ben is here.

Even though I know it's not possible, it feels like the temperature in the attic increases by ten degrees when I see him. Sweat breaks out across my upper lip and my face feels flushed.

I have no idea what he would do if he discovered me up here. Found out I had hidden cameras around our home to spy on him.

This is one of those plans that sounded great and easy in theory, but sitting in this plastic chair surrounded by boxed-up Christmas decorations and remnant pieces of tile and wood from the remodel, it feels a bit insane.

It feels like something only a desperate person would do, which is what I am.

Carrying that briefcase, Ben walks directly through the house to his home office just off the foyer. I scan the little squares on the screen, watching his progress as he passes from room to room. Each image is small, and there's not much detail since six different angles are vying for screen space, but I know I can look back through each feed and zoom in if necessary since there is a backup video on the memory card in each camera.

He's behind his desk and seemingly jumps right into work.

I know he's gone to all the trouble to be here so he can meet with someone, but I also know that if Ben is anything, he's efficient.

I click on the little box, and the view of his office fills the screen.

Ben puts his briefcase on his desk then opens it up. From the camera angle, I can't see what's inside. He spends a few minutes digging around until he pulls out a large manila envelope, then begins taking items out one by one. There are a few papers, a few pictures, and one of those small media storage drives.

He studies the papers and pictures first. If it were me, I would have turned on some music or the TV, anything for a little background noise, but not Ben. He loves the silence. Says he thinks better when nothing is competing with his thoughts.

I've been with Ben for years but it's surprising what I'm learning by watching him when he doesn't know he's being watched.

I didn't know Ben talked to himself. Nothing earth shattering but a sort of running commentary as he works. Then there's the odd movements. Popping joints, clearing his throat loudly enough that I jump the first time he does it, and a head swivel/neck stretch that looks a bit painful. I'm almost in a trance observing him so unguarded.

Finally, he seems to be finished reading whatever's there and he picks up the drive. His laptop sits on the credenza behind him but just as he starts to swivel around to face it, something catches his attention.

I check the camera on the front porch since he's staring out of his window that faces the road.

There's a car coming down the driveway.

Ben gets up to get a better look.

"What the fuck . . ." His hands are on his hips as his head shakes slowly back and forth. Guessing this visit isn't the one he had planned today.

I switch the screen so I can watch what's happening outside. It's a bright red Mustang. But not a new one. It's an older model but shiny enough to assume it's been recently restored. It's still too far away for me to make out the driver.

Ben heads to the front door just as the Mustang stops in front of the house. The driver gets out and approaches Ben. He's Black, about the same height as Ben but a stockier build. He's dressed in jeans and a button-down.

Ben's frustration is long gone and he's nothing but smiles as he slaps the guy on the back and acts happy to see him.

"Eddie, good to see you," Ben says. You wouldn't know he wasn't being genuine unless you'd witnessed his reaction at the man's arrival.

They shake hands.

"Wasn't sure if I'd catch you at home but took the chance on surprising you," Eddie says.

"Oh, you surprised him, Eddie," I whisper to the screen.

They walk to the Mustang and spend several minutes looking it over, even going so far as popping the hood. They're clearly talking about the car, but they're too far away for the camera's mic to pick up their conversation.

I study them, trying to figure out what is going on. Is Ben considering buying this car? Hank is the one who loves old cars and fixing them up, not Ben. Ben is a "brand-new, straight off the lot" kind of guy, so I'm completely stumped.

After a few minutes, Ben gets in the driver's seat while Eddie takes the passenger side and they drive away.

What the heck? Where are they going?

I stare at the screen for several minutes while I debate what to do. Surely they're coming right back after a spin in that car.

Not long after Ben left in the Mustang, another vehicle comes down the driveway. It's an old brown work truck with a huge toolbox mounted on the bed.

Who is this?

The truck stops almost exactly where the Mustang was parked. The driver gets out and I don't recognize him either. He's a tall white guy.

Lanky. Dressed in jeans and a T-shirt, but it's hard to make out too many details since he's wearing a ball cap and it's pulled low over his face.

This guy takes out his phone and walks across the front yard toward the side of the house where the garage sits. Then he disappears from view.

"Where'd he go?"

A moment later I hear the familiar rattle of the garage door opening.

Oh my God! How did he get the garage open? Is he breaking into our house?

I stand up quickly, iPad gripped in my hands, and pace around in a tight circle. I pull up the camera in the kitchen that will show the door that leads to the garage, waiting to see if he comes inside.

Almost two minutes pass and there's no sign of him. And then I hear the garage door lower.

My heart is racing.

I try to sit back down but I'm too nervous, so I continue my pacing while I wait for him to appear on the front porch camera again.

And there he is, casually walking across the lawn back to his truck, where he leans against the lowered tailgate.

Before I can even think about what any of this means, the Mustang pulls back into the driveway.

The white guy waves as the car inches closer.

Does Ben know him? Did he give him a remote to the garage?

Ben parks the Mustang in the overflow spot near the garage and the white guy joins them as they get out of the car. He shakes hands with Ben and it's clear that yes, he knows this man too.

Ben leads them toward the house and then into his office, gesturing to the chairs in front of his desk. "Shane, Eddie, have a seat."

Okay, so new guy must be Shane.

I zoom in to see if I recognize them now that I've got a clearer view, but I don't. Ben quickly flips the pages he was reading earlier on top of the pictures, then leans back in his chair like he doesn't have a care in the world. I increase the volume in my headphones so I don't miss a single word.

"I didn't think the car would be ready for another week."

Shane shrugs. "You know how Eddie is, he's already got another one coming in so we needed to get it finished."

"Well, wasn't expecting this today but it's all good," Ben says. "Glad you've got some more business. And hey, I'm happy to recommend y'all to anyone looking to restore a car, because I wasn't really sure you were going to be able to pull it off. That car looked like it should've been in a scrap yard when I brought it to you. It's incredible what you managed to do."

Eddie laughs but it sounds forced. They chat for a few minutes about the car and what work was done to it.

Shane leans forward and pulls a piece of paper from his back pocket then hands it to Ben. "Here's the final bill and she's all yours."

I can't believe Ben bought a muscle car. This is not like him at all—something strange is going on, especially given the Shane guy poked around in the garage when he first got here.

"Oh, sure." Ben takes the bill and studies it for a long moment. While he's distracted with the invoice, both men take in everything around them. Eyes scan the room. But it's not just a cursory glance. They're studying the room like there's going to be a test later. Then Shane looks right at me. Or rather, right at the camera.

I jump back slightly. Does he see it hidden in the bookshelf?

Then he smiles.

Startled, I drop the iPad in my lap.

It's like he knows someone is watching.

That I'm watching.

Finally, he looks away when Ben stands up from the desk, check in hand. The guys stand too, and Ben comes around the side of the desk.

"Thanks again," Ben says as he hands Eddie the check. There's another round of handshakes between them, then he's escorting the guys out of his office.

Shane pulls open the front door but doesn't leave. Instead, he turns to Ben. "We appreciate your business. Still not sure how you found us but hey, we're glad you did."

Ben pauses a moment, watching Shane. Finally, he says, "My partner, Hank, gave me your name."

"Well, cool. Not sure who he is but tell him thanks."

Then they're gone. Ben stands in the open doorway then raises his hand in one final wave before the old truck pulls away from the house. He doesn't move until they have turned out of the driveway.

Then he slams the door shut.

Ben returns to his office, the frustration back and clearer than ever. I take in every detail, from the frown lines digging into his forehead to the cruel twist of his mouth to the balled-up fists that support him as he leans over the desk. Studying whatever is there in front of him.

He doesn't move for a long time.

Ben finally turns around to his computer and plugs in the drive he took from the envelope before Shane and Eddie arrived.

After a few clicks, Aubrey's face fills the screen.

CHAPTER 11

Hank

AFTER THE ALIBI
MONDAY, OCTOBER 12

My assistant, Lila, riffles through the mountain of paper on my desk while I rub my hands across my face. I ended up sleeping on the couch last night instead of going home, and by the way my body feels this morning, I'm going to regret that decision all day.

"I picked up your dry cleaning on my way in so at least you'll have a clean suit to put on."

When any new intern starts, they think Lila's a pushover because she's little, barely over five feet tall, and looks about ten years younger than she really is. Hell, when she applied for this job I thought there was a typo on her résumé because I would have sworn she was still in high school. But she's a force to be reckoned with, and they find out quickly they don't want to get on her bad side. "I'm guessing we need to clear your schedule as well as look at Ben's calendar."

"Yeah, cancel anything you can for me this week. Maybe next week too. Ben's stuff gets priority. Also, I need you to make a few calls for me. First, reach out to the company who monitors our alarm system and see if they can send a security guard over. If they don't offer that service, see if they can recommend someone who does."

Lila spins around. "You think we need that?" She's worked here long enough to read between the lines. I didn't have to tell her how Ben died for her to guess it was foul play. The news coverage showed the police response, which is only typical for a crime scene.

I shrug. "I'd rather be overly cautious." Until we find out who killed Ben and why, I'm not taking any chances with the safety of those who work here.

She nods and picks up her notebook. "You want them here just during working hours?"

"Yes. And tell everyone for now, no one is to be on the premises after hours. If they need to, take the work home, but I don't want anyone here without a security guard present."

"Okay, what else?"

"Call that psychologist we used as an expert on the Henderson case and see if he's available to speak with anyone who is struggling with this. And let me know if anyone needs time off." The firm employs twelve people, and from the receptionist to the paralegals to our own personal assistants, all of them saw Ben on a daily basis. This office is like a family, so it's expected we'd struggle with the loss of one of our own.

She stops what she's doing and looks up at me. "You can take off a few days too. No one says you have to jump into work less than twenty-four hours after you find out your partner's gone."

Partner. If she only knew. I have not shown her his request yet, since I was hoping to talk him out of his decision to part ways, but Ben's assistant, Tricia, knows since she was the one who typed up the proposed dissolution agreement. It's probably only a matter of time before that news spreads through the entire office.

"The idea of me being home alone for the next few days is ludicrous and we both know it. I'd lose my mind."

"It was just a suggestion."

"Did you tell Tricia she can have some time off if she needs it?"

"I did, but she's coming in anyway. Said she may take a few days once she knows the time-sensitive stuff is taken care of."

"Did you hear Ben wanted me out?" I debated bringing it up but then decided if the staff is talking about it, I need to be aware of it.

Lila gives me a sad smile. "Yeah, Tricia mentioned it last week. I think she was trying to give me a heads-up in case I needed to be looking for a new job."

I nod. "It's good y'all look out for each other. It feels strange that last week I was thinking the same thing. If anyone is worried or concerned about the change in leadership . . ."

She watches me struggle to get off the couch then silently moves to the closet in the corner of my office and pulls out the brace. "No arguments. Put it on. You'll thank me later when you can actually walk to your truck instead of limp."

I take it from her begrudgingly, even though I know she's right. I sit back down and pull up my pants leg, exposing the deep scars that crisscross my knee, then wrap the neoprene tightly around it.

She drops down on the couch next to me. "Whatever you're thinking—stop. Ben was a great guy and a good boss, but he insisted on keeping a professional distance from the staff. You went out of your way to get to know everyone here. If he would have forced you out, half of the office would have left with you, including me."

Her words give me some relief but they don't change the tragic circumstances that made this problem go away.

She gets up once she's delivered her pep talk and takes command of the mess on my desk in a way I never can. Once she seems satisfied with the piles she's made, she looks back at me still on the couch. "Let's get your calendar cleared first, then Tricia and I will tackle Ben's desk. We'll triage so we know what can wait and what can't. She mentioned he had a trial that was starting on Wednesday, but she'll alert the judge this morning and start the paperwork for a postponement."

Lila is trying to be all business, but there are mascara-stained tears rolling down her face.

I limp my way to her and pull her in for a hug, knowing we both could use it. "Thank you for coming in."

She nods against my shirt. "We all know you don't like to be here by yourself."

Laughing for the first time since I got the call from Camille, I give her one final squeeze before letting go. "You're getting a big-ass bonus as soon as this all gets sorted."

Lila glances at her watch. "Everyone should be here by now so let's get this part over with."

After an extremely emotional staff meeting where there were more questions than answers, I send Lila to help Tricia with Ben's desk and his files so we can get a grasp of the width and breadth of his work and financial life.

The sound of my door opening draws my attention away from the file I was working on. Assuming it's Lila, since she's the only one allowed to walk into my office when the door is shut, I'm surprised when I see Camille's dad, Randall Everett.

I stand from behind my desk when he enters the room. It's presumptuous of him to let himself in this way, but I give him the benefit of the doubt that the shock and grief we're all feeling are driving his actions.

"Mr. Everett, come in." I gesture to the chair in front of my desk.

We shake hands before he takes a seat.

"What can I do for you?" I ask.

His mouth turns down and his expression is pinched. "Wanted to come in and check on you. See if I can offer any assistance. Ben's death has been a huge blow to our family and I imagine to you as well."

I nod and swallow hard. I'm not good at talking about my feelings with anyone, much less a man I barely know.

"It's been devastating to us as well. We all thought the world of Ben. The fact that everyone came in first thing this morning and jumped in to make sure his clients get taken care of shows just how much they loved him."

He gives me a sad smile. "That's good. I'm glad to hear that. I know how difficult times like this can be on a business, especially since Ben was the captain of this ship, so to speak. It's easy for things to fall apart when there's not a strong leader to take up the slack."

Even though I get what he's trying to say, I can't help but bristle at his description. Ben may have started this firm, but I more than carry my own weight and contribute just as much to the success of this firm.

I don't respond to his jab, mainly because I can't think of anything that wouldn't make me sound like an asshole.

"Can I get you something to drink? Coffee?"

"Yes. Coffee sounds good. Black."

"My assistant is busy helping in Ben's office so give me one second to grab it."

I could text Lila and get her to bring him a cup but I decide to get it myself if only to give me a few minutes to get in the right headspace for this visit.

Randall Everett is not to be taken lightly.

Even though the Everetts don't live in Baton Rouge, most people here have heard of them. There have been whispered stories about their family for years. Freak tragedies that go unsolved, disgruntled former employees who conveniently disappear when they get a little too loud, and wealth that has not grown from legal means. All the good gossip involves the Everett family in some way.

Randall pretty much owns the entire town and surrounding area of Corbeau, just south of here, and his son, Silas, is being groomed to take over the reins when it's time. The bulk of their income comes from the endless sugarcane fields that surround the small town and stretch across the parish, and the pockets of natural gas underneath those fields. The rumor of how the Everett family obtained that land years ago is a much more interesting story.

It's said that Otto Everett, Randall's great-grandfather, won a small farm in Corbeau during a poker game in New Orleans when he was in his early twenties. He packed up and decided to give the life of a gentleman farmer a try, but the work was hard and it wasn't long until Otto was looking for other ways to monetize his newfound property. Then Prohibition started and Otto Everett had an idea.

He made a deal with some moonshiners, and using the waterways and rail systems that would normally take his meager crop to the sugar exchange, he cornered the bootlegging market instead.

As his coffers grew, he bought up tract after tract of land, with little care whether the farmer actually wanted to sell. The elder Everett put family and friends in important positions in the small town, ensuring he was the one really running things. The law officers looked the other way. The bankers helped hide the money. Once liquor became legal again, the business changed but not his hold on the town.

A hundred years later, an Everett still rules Corbeau. They are as corrupt as they are wealthy.

I worked with Ben for almost a year before I discovered Camille was Randall's daughter. She never talks about her family and quickly brushes off any comments when someone else does.

I return to my office with a cup of coffee in each hand, setting one down on the desk in front of Randall.

He takes a sip then settles in his chair like he's in no rush. The silence should be awkward, but we both seem content to sit and watch each other. Finally, he says, "Ben told me when he brought you on that you became the executors of each other's wills. Is that still the case?"

I nod. "It is."

Randall shrugs. "I wasn't sure if he had changed that after he decided to ask you to leave the firm."

Direct hit.

And again, I decide there's no appropriate answer to his question.

But he's not finished. "Do you feel it's right that you remain in that role? As well as taking his cases as your own?"

It's a series of aggressive questions I wasn't prepared for.

"I'm sure you understand my position," I say. "Ben handed me a *draft* for the dissolution of our partnership but it was far from settled. In fact, I believed there was a possibility we could figure out a way to stay in business together. And as far as the rest, I am the executor on record as well as the only living member of our firm, so I'm legally bound to handle both his estate and the clients who are represented by Bayliss and Landry."

We stare at each other another long moment.

"Seems like Ben dying before he could remove you from either of these positions has worked out really well for you. Has anyone asked you where you were on Saturday night?"

It takes everything in me to match Randall's cool and calm demeanor, because I refuse to give him the satisfaction of seeing how much his comments have pissed me off. "I suggest if you plan to throw insinuations around then you need to be prepared for me to protect my name and my reputation. What you are suggesting is abhorrent."

Randall smirks. "According to your original partnership agreement, Camille is entitled to compensation, a percentage of the income made from the firm for the next ten years. Between that and handling his estate, you have your fingers in every aspect of her financial well-being. Ben believed he had cause to have you removed from his practice, but his death prevented him from seeing that through. If I feel that you do not have my daughter's best interests at heart with regard to either of the roles you are currently fulfilling, I will make sure a suitable replacement is found."

I sit there, stunned, and watch Randall Everett exit my office. A few seconds later, my phone buzzes in my pocket.

It's a text from Camille.

> **Mom just told me Dad is on his way to see you. I have no idea why and I'm sure he's going to be an asshole. I'm apologizing in advance.**

I read her message then put my phone back on my desk. Camille had always made it sound like she and Ben didn't spend much time with her family, but it's clear her dad was still in close contact with Ben. That's the only way he would be that up to date with the inner workings of this office.

No matter how hard I try, I can't focus on the work in front of me. Randall Everett's flippant comment regarding my whereabouts on Saturday night has me rattled. Sullivan didn't ask me where I was when Ben was murdered, but he will.

And while Camille was able to show a clear digital trail of her time spent in St. Francisville, I don't have anything as ironclad.

I went home after I dropped Ben off. Changed into some old clothes, stained by oil and grease, and spent the rest of the day buried underneath the hood of the 1970 Pontiac GTO I've been restoring. And while it's normal for me to lose hours in my garage, there's not a single person who can verify where I was or what I was doing.

As far as alibis go, I've got an extremely weak one.

Once it's known Ben wanted me out, it will only take a few whispers in the right ears to catapult me into the top spot of suspects. Especially given how I am financially benefiting from his death.

If Randall Everett decides he wants everyone to believe I killed Ben, that's exactly what will happen.

CHAPTER 12

Aubrey

THE ALIBI
SATURDAY, OCTOBER 10

I've got a little time to kill so I figure I'll do what Camille requested while I wait. St. Francisville is small and I only have to drive about a mile before I'm in front of one of the multitude of boutiques here.

It takes a little while to find a parking spot, and the sidewalks are packed with tourists and shoppers enjoying this gorgeous fall day. The store I picked has everything from clothes to dishes to art. I make a lap while I try to decide what I'm going to buy and hope the sticker shock I have when I check the price isn't too obvious.

Camille and I had an awkward conversation about what it would be like shopping in a store like this. I kind of blew her off at the time, but now I understand what she was trying to tell me. She said I might feel uncomfortable in some of these stores. Out of place. And she's right. She said it would show in the way I touched things, because I'd be more afraid

I'd break something than excited about purchasing it. And she was right about that too.

It's why she decided I should look the part, because she felt it was highly probable someone would ask for her ID when I presented her credit card if I looked guilty using it. The last thing either of us wants is for me to be arrested for theft.

I agreed there was a chance that could happen, but I went along with the disguise for a more personal reason. If Ben somehow gets wind of what we're doing, I don't want to make it easy for him to turn this on me for the part I played. If he pulls any of these stores' security footage for proof of who was using her credit card, hopefully he won't be able to identify me.

Salespeople who work in high-end places like that pick up on body language in a second, so I try to relax and act like it's completely normal a plain white bowl costs $475.

Finally, I settle on a small glass rosebud vase because it's something my mom would have loved. I don't even check the tag before I bring it to the counter. I must put on a pretty good act because she doesn't ask me to confirm my identity.

With my package secured, I get in the car and head right back to the feed store. Luckily, the same space I was in earlier is still vacant.

Is Ben watching my movements right now and wondering why Camille is coming back here? No idea. Do I care if she'll have to explain this away if he asks her about it? No, I don't.

It's only a few more minutes before I see Deacon's black SUV pull into the lot. He cruises up and down each row until he spots Camille's car. There's an empty space four down from where I'm parked so he takes it.

I'm next to his car just as he's getting out. His eyes are hidden behind dark sunglasses, and between them and the heavy tint on the windows of his vehicle, I've always wondered how he can see where he's going.

Serenity hops out of the passenger side. She comes around the front of his vehicle and scrunches up her nose when she gets a good look at me.

"That wig is horrid."

I roll my eyes. "I thought I asked you to dress in something plain."

Serenity is dressed in wide-leg jeans and a white crocheted top that doesn't cover much more than her bra, and decked out in jewelry with a ring on every finger and several necklaces of various lengths. Her long blond hair is separated into thick braids that hang over each shoulder. She's in her early forties but could easily pass for ten years younger.

"This is as plain as I get."

"I guess it's fine for what I need you to do." I motion for them to follow me back to Camille's car, opening the driver's side door for Serenity. "Get in and we'll go through everything."

Serenity climbs in, running her hands along the steering wheel. "Oh, I could have a lot of fun in this car." She shuts the door then rolls down the window.

Deacon and I step closer to the car. "Not today," Deacon says. "Today we're sticking to the plan in every way."

"Serenity, please. I'm nervous enough. Don't make me worry you're going to go rogue on me."

She reaches her hand out of the open window and cups my cheek. "Sweetie, we're all in for you today. You know that. We're not going to do anything that jeopardizes what you're doing."

Smiling, I squeeze her arm. "Thank you." Then I pull out Camille's phone from my back pocket. There's a notification telling me Ben texted her a little while ago, but because of her privacy settings, I can't read the message.

I hand the phone to Serenity. "When you get out, stick this in your pocket and ignore all the notifications. It's locked, so all you need to do is keep it on you wherever you go. If anyone calls, especially Ben, just let it ring. Camille says he always texts if she doesn't answer and she will deal with it on her end from her iPad."

Serenity nods then puts the phone in the cup holder. "Just to clarify, I'm going to that little park near downtown and just walking around there. Right?"

"Yes. Camille wanted me to buy a few things there but we're not doing that. Don't want to take the risk of someone questioning you about her credit card."

Even with the wig, I would barely pass as Camille if someone was comparing me to her driver's license picture, but there's no way Serenity would hold up under scrutiny. She's barely five feet tall while Camille is five seven, and they look nothing alike.

"Just keep walking around. If that gets old, drive around and browse some stores. We just need movement. I'll spend more of her money when we switch back."

Camille isn't the only one who needs a few hours to be a ghost.

She nods. "Got it!"

Deacon and I step back and she raises the window while she pulls out of the spot. She gives us a final wave as she drives away.

"Is this a mistake?"

Deacon laughs. "This whole thing is either going to be the best idea any of us have ever had or it will blow up in our faces. Either way, we're on our path now and there's no turning back."

I follow him to his car and climb in the passenger seat. I pull off the wig and cap just as he turns onto the highway. I lower the visor to get a peek at my hair, only to discover it's sticking up in every direction. "Oh wow." I spend a couple of minutes trying to get it under control.

"I may have a brush in the glove box if you want to check."

Deacon is the one I'm closest to in the house. His full name is Francis Deacon, which I learned from a random piece of mail he received after he moved in. When I teased him about it, he rolled his eyes and said, "My mom is the only person allowed to call me Francis." Although I think if he gave anyone else an exception, it would be me. Over the years, I've witnessed a softer side of him that I don't believe many people get a chance to see.

"You think Ben was surprised to see Eddie pull up in the Mustang?"

Deacon nods. "I'd bet so. They're supposed to call me after they leave there."

The morning after Camille fled Doug's Tavern in the middle of a rainstorm, Shane and Eddie told us Ben had hired them to fix up an old Mustang. I was hoping it was some weird coincidence, but Deacon pointed out it was my name on the napkin with our address, not Shane's and Eddie's. And after talking to the guys, we realized there was more going on than Ben's desire to restore an old muscle car.

When Ben would drop by to "check on things," he showed very little interest in the car. He did, however, have lots of questions about who lived in our house. At the time, the guys just thought he was being nosy, but Camille's visit to the bar puts a different spin on things.

We decided that morning that Eddie and Shane would keep playing it cool with Ben until I could track Camille down for another conversation about her husband and Deacon had time to do a little digging of his own.

"She's probably freaking out watching that go down." Camille doesn't know Shane and Eddie are my housemates. And since Camille has never mentioned the Mustang anytime we've talked since that first night, I'm pretty sure he kept that purchase from her too.

Deacon laughs. "Yeah, I'm sure she is. Honestly, I'm going to be shocked if she's able to stick to her part of the plan and sit in that attic all day. My money's on her being the one who screws this all up."

Shifting in my seat, I pull one leg underneath me so I can turn toward him. For this part of the day, Camille has me wearing some designer jeans and a flowy silk top that probably cost more than the old Honda I drove here. It's surprisingly comfortable.

"How long before we get there?" My nerves seem to be getting worse with each mile.

"Not long. Another ten minutes."

I check the time and it's just before two. We're right on schedule.

Deacon is leaning back in his seat, one hand on the steering wheel. I find myself staring at that hand. Then at him. He really is so good-looking. He glances at me, one eyebrow raised, and I twist back around in my seat until I'm facing forward, slightly embarrassed at being caught watching him.

"How are you so calm?" I ask.

Thankfully, his attention goes back to the road. "Because this isn't the first time I'm doing something I'm not supposed to." While almost everyone else in our house has had brushes with the law, Deacon is firmly on the wrong side of it and makes no apologies for it.

I let out a deep sigh as I lean back against the seat. "I'm really nervous."

"I know you are. But we're all here for you, and I'm not going to let this go sideways." All playfulness is gone, and I'd love nothing more than to believe it's as easy as that. I trust this group—my friends—more than anything, but that doesn't mean something can't go spectacularly wrong.

"I really appreciate everything y'all are doing because there's no way I could have pulled any of this off on my own."

He glances at me, concern on his face for the first time today. "No, not having that right now. I can hear it in your voice. In your head, we've already screwed this up somehow. And if that's what you're thinking, that's exactly what will happen."

"Okay, you're right. We're just getting started."

He slows his car down and flips on his blinker. "We're almost there."

I glance up and see the sign.

LOUISIANA STATE PENITENTIARY

It's time to talk to Paul Granger, the man who was convicted of killing my parents.

CHAPTER 13

Camille

BEFORE THE ALIBI
SATURDAY, SEPTEMBER 12

"Are you sure you're okay?" Ben asks me for the third time tonight.

I nod and smile and try to relax even though I've been on edge since my conversation with Aubrey Price a few days ago at that bar. I've half expected her to show up at our house, demanding to speak with Ben, but so far she hasn't reached out to him... that I know of.

It feels like she's a ticking time bomb ready to explode.

That's my own fault, though. The easiest assumption was that Ben was having an affair. Once I saw that napkin, I never considered another option. It was my mistake going into that bar, thinking I understood what was going on.

Ben slides his arm around my waist, pulling me in close as we make our way through the crowded room. My lemon chiffon gown blends in with all the other shades of yellow the women are wearing to this fundraising gala for the Tarver Braddock Foundation. Of all the charity events Ben drags me to, this is one I actually look forward to supporting. Their main goal is to spread happiness to strangers with random acts of kindness in memory of the young man the foundation is named after, who passed away in an accidental fire several years ago. In the videos they post on social media, the pure joy when they surprise kids with scholarships or pay for groceries for unsuspecting shoppers right before a holiday is contagious.

"Camille! Ben!"

We both turn when we hear our names. It's our friends Phoebe and Wesley Heights. Phoebe hugs me when she gets close while Ben and Wesley shake hands.

"You look gorgeous!" Phoebe says as she pulls away from me.

"So do you! I love this dress!"

Phoebe hooks her arm through mine, leaning close. "Save me from my table. It's all of Wesley's work friends and two of the wives apparently hate each other. It's so awkward!"

"Ours may not be much better! I told Riley to sit with us, promising I'd introduce her to Hank. You know how much he loves me setting him up!"

She laughs because Hank has made it clear he doesn't like it at all.

I like Phoebe. I haven't known her long, but every time we're together we have a good time.

Over the years, I've drifted away from my high school and college friends, and now my inner circle are women I met because their husbands are friends with Ben. Part of that is because Ben is way more social than I am and always making plans for us. But the other part is that Ben didn't really love my old friends and they weren't exactly crazy about him, so it just seemed easier not to force them to be around one another.

We talk for a few more minutes before Wesley drags her off to introduce her to another couple.

Ben is back at my side, steering me toward our table, but then pauses in the middle of the room. "We need to speak to your family, so let's go ahead and get it over with." He pulls me in a new direction and we head toward where my parents are sitting with my brother, Silas, and sister-in-law, Margaret.

Ben's mask slips perfectly into place as we approach their table. My feelings are a bit harder to hide. Ben will spend most of the night trying to impress my dad, while Dad throws well-aimed barbs in my direction, dismissing my social media account as a waste of time and demanding we finally make them grandparents.

I take the open seat next to Margaret, letting Ben have the one closest to my parents.

"Oh, I love that color on you. Yellow can be so hard to pull off. Did you see the monstrosity Mrs. Weston's wearing? She looks like an ear of corn."

"I haven't run across her yet," I say, laughing at her description.

Margaret is blond and thin and naturally tan. The Southern Belle trifecta. And her forehead hasn't moved since high school. She's constantly getting work done to improve upon her natural beauty, even though most people would give their big toe to look half as good as she does without all the improvements. She takes another sip of her wine as she gives me a rundown on what everyone else is wearing. By the way she's giggling, I know she's on at least her third glass. Margaret likes to have a good time, and it's likely she'll be wobbling out of here tonight.

Silas leans forward, nodding to where Ben and Dad are deep in conversation on the other side of me. "Warning, Dad's going to push for you to come home for a church thing. It's all he talked about on the drive over." Silas is younger than me but with his deeply tanned skin from spending so much time working on the farm, he could easily be confused as my older brother.

"Okay, thanks for the heads-up."

It's only a few minutes later that Dad looks at me past Ben. "Camille, your mother wants to know if you're coming to the fall festival at church that's coming up in a few weeks."

My mother is sitting next to him, talking to an older woman I recognize from our hometown. She sent me one text about this a couple of weeks ago and nothing else since then. Dad only wants me there because he thinks it reflects poorly on him when I'm not present.

And honestly, it should, since he's the main reason I won't be there.

"I'll talk to her about it in a bit."

He throws me a look but doesn't say anything else. Thankfully, Ben distracts him by asking about the upcoming election.

I turn back to Margaret and Silas. Their heads are bent while they talk quietly, but the body language tells me they're arguing about something, which is not unusual. Silas would never say it but I think he's as unhappy in his marriage as I am in mine. While I've managed to keep a healthy distance from my parents, Silas and I are still close. We may not see each other very often, but he calls and checks in on me regularly and we grab lunch whenever he's in Baton Rouge. I'm worried about him, though. I was hoping he'd get out of Corbeau and not get sucked into working with Dad, but he seems to get deeper and deeper into the family business every year.

It's no secret Dad is shady as hell and gets away with things he shouldn't. The cops in Corbeau are on the payroll and the mayor is in his pocket. And Silas is following in his footsteps.

"Camille! It's so good to see you!"

Several friends of my mom's stop at the table and exchange pleasantries, all of them telling me how long it's been since they've seen me and asking when I'm coming to visit.

Silas escapes by going to speak with a judge who's running for one of the open state legislature seats. I'm sure my family is backing his campaign since our motto is "Can't have too many friends in power!"

As soon as the ladies move on to another table, Dad stands up. "Walk with me to get a drink."

I glance at Ben. He and Margaret are talking to one of Margaret's friends, whom I recognize as a bridesmaid at her wedding. "Okay, sure."

The line is long even though there are several bartenders working behind the counter. I'm already regretting this.

"Your mother is hurt you don't come visit more often."

Ugh. There it is—the guilt trip. I know better than to get cornered by him like this, especially after Silas's warning. "I see Mom when she comes to Baton Rouge to get her hair done or meet with the Garden Club."

"It's not the same as coming home for a visit. I don't know the last time you've stayed at the house. And you know she's ready for grandkids."

Nope. Not doing this with him. "Then maybe she needs to talk to Margaret. She'd see Silas's kids way more often than she would mine since they're practically next door."

Before he can say anything else, I decide to turn this on him and maybe even get a few answers of my own. "Hey, remember that guy from Corbeau who got arrested for that hit-and-run and went to prison?"

He leans a little closer. "Who?"

The music is loud and he's getting hard of hearing, so I step a little closer and repeat my question.

Dad gives me a confused look. "What guy?"

It's hard to resist rolling my eyes. Even though it happened a decade ago, he was the only person I've ever heard of from our town who ended up in prison. It's all anyone talked about for months after it happened. "That guy who killed that couple in that hit-and-run. Paul Granger."

His forehead creases as he considers my question. "Paul Granger. Why on earth are you asking about him?"

Obviously, I'm not about to get into the real reason. "I had forgotten all about it until someone brought his name up."

"Why would anyone be talking about that lowlife?" He says this loud enough that the people in front of us turn around and stare at Dad.

I shrug a shoulder. "Someone said he's trying to get his case reopened and I was just curious. I was out of the country when it happened so I didn't keep up with it in real time like everyone in town did."

I'm exaggerating a bit. It didn't take much digging to find a handful of posts Paul's mom made on social media over the last several months, saying he had been framed that summer a decade ago and that "the truth that had been buried would be brought to light." That Paul would soon be free. The way she said it, with such certainty, made his release feel imminent.

"I would think you'd have something more productive to do than gossip. Aren't you still taking pictures of cheeseburgers?"

And there's the dig.

"Randall!" The man behind Dad taps him on the shoulder so we turn around.

"Gus! Marie!" Dad says in greeting.

Dad introduces me to the couple even though I've known them for years. And just like that, all conversation about Paul is over.

The moment Aubrey said Paul Granger's name, a chill raced down my spine, and I've been searching for every piece of information I can get my hands on.

Aubrey was right when she said I recognized Paul Granger's name.

He was born and raised in my hometown and was several years older than me. When I was in college, Paul was a thirty-year-old drug dealer who was still hanging out with high school kids. The kind of drug dealer who would only be a big fish in an extremely small pond, where options are severely limited. The kind of drug dealer every small town has.

Ten years ago, Paul Granger drove his truck drunk and high and ran through a stop sign, plowing into the side of another car and killing both passengers inside.

I took Aubrey's advice and did a little research to see how she was connected to Paul.

The couple Paul Granger killed that night were Aubrey Price's parents and it's all I can think about now.

Dad and I finally get our drinks and make our way back to the table. Mom has moved to the next one over to speak with the group of women there, while Silas and Margaret are across the room. Ben is waiting for me, though, and stands as we approach. "Ready to head to our table? They'll be serving dinner soon."

"Sure."

Ben shakes Dad's hand, telling him we'll catch up with them later, while I walk away without saying anything else to him.

My friend Riley catches me just before we get to our table. "I didn't think y'all were ever coming over here. Does Hank know I'm sitting with y'all?"

Ben snorts when I answer, "Yes! He's excited to meet you!" "Excited" may be a bit of an exaggeration.

When we get to our table, I stop next to where he's already seated. "Hey, Hank. This is my friend I was telling you about! Riley Murphy."

He stands, shooting me a look before plastering on a smile, then turns to her. "Hey, Riley. Nice to meet you."

She beams as she takes the empty seat next to him. I can almost hear his internal groan.

Ben and I sit across from them just as the lights dim. A video presentation begins, showcasing all the amazing things the foundation has accomplished this year.

I watch Ben as he watches the screen and try to make sense of my jumbled thoughts. It feels like my mind hasn't stopped spinning in days.

After I found Aubrey's name on that napkin, I checked the travel history on Ben's Range Rover and discovered he'd not only been to the bar where she works but her home as well, infidelity seemed like the only logical answer.

Aubrey's reaction to that accusation made it clear I jumped to the wrong conclusion, but it didn't change the fact that Ben was keeping tabs on her. And thanks to me, Aubrey suspects Paul Granger and her connection to his case as the possible reason why.

Ben must feel my stare because he leans close. "What's going on with you?" he asks in a frustrated tone. "You've been pouty all night."

Pouty.

"Nothing. I'm fine."

He turns away and I close my eyes, wishing I knew what I should do.

Wishing I was brave enough to have an honest conversation with him.

But I'm honestly scared to tell him where my thoughts are taking me. How events from ten years ago are colliding in my mind with recent ones, sending me to a very dark place.

Scared of what he would do if my suspicions are right, because Ben's got a lot to lose if I am. And the financial hit if I can trigger that prenup clause wouldn't be the only threat he'd face.

Once Aubrey mentioned Paul Granger's name and I discovered that wreck had left her an orphan, my mind started making connections that I would never have considered before.

The summer of the accident ten years ago, Ben and I had just finished our sophomore year in college. He had to go back to Corbeau to work, but I was studying abroad in Spain. In a town as small as Corbeau, there's very little for teens to do, so inevitably people ended up hanging out at places like Paul Granger's, which is why Dad always made sure Silas and I were gone for those couple of restless months.

I remember asking Ben what happened when I got home and heard the news. He didn't want to talk about it at all. It was a touchy subject since there were times Ben hung out there as well, and everyone was trying to distance themselves from Paul.

It was the same summer things changed between Ben and me. Before, Ben and I were joined in our frustration with how Dad tried to run my life. We talked all the time about how we were going to distance ourselves from my father and the power he held over me. We promised each other we were going to run off together, leave Corbeau, and never come back, in the dumb way nineteen-year-olds do when it's all talk and neither of you has any money to follow through.

But things were different when I got back home at the end of that summer. My dad and Ben were different, not only to each other but about each other. Ben had found a new and nauseating admiration for my dad that had not been present before. That change in their dynamic stumped me for years.

Then Aubrey Price muttered Paul Granger's name and things started clicking.

Paul has always said he wasn't the one driving his truck that night. At the time, he threw out over a dozen names of people who had been partying at his house that night. Half the people I had gone to high school with were questioned since most of them were home for the summer. Just like Ben was.

I know Ben well enough to know he'd never take Paul's case, no matter what cryptic truth his mother was alluding to in her posts.

So why is he checking up on Aubrey Price? Does she know something that would help Paul get his conviction overturned? It would be just as important to Aubrey that the right person was behind bars as it would be to Paul.

If Ben isn't helping the truth come to light, is he trying to stop it from happening?

The video ends and the lights come back up, shaking me out of my thoughts.

Ben leans close, the frustration gone. "You know what I was thinking?"

I shake my head. "No idea what goes through that head of yours."

He laughs and reaches forward, sliding his fingers through mine. I hate that my first thought is this affectionate gesture is all for show. "I know how much you don't want to go back home for that church festival, but we both know your dad isn't going to let it go. I've got to be in New Orleans with Hank that weekend for a continuing ed seminar, but why don't I book you a weekend away somewhere close to Corbeau? Maybe St. Francisville. They always have cool stuff going on there. You can get some content for your account and be close enough to make an appearance for your dad but not have to stay with them."

This isn't the first time he's done this. Made plans for me while he was busy. But for some reason this time feels different. My first impulse is to agree but I decide to take a different approach.

"I don't know. I may just stay at home. There are a few things I've been wanting to do around the house."

He smiles but it doesn't reach his eyes. He may fool a lot of people with his charm and easy demeanor, but I've known Ben a long time and it's easy to see the tells that most people miss.

"I know what will happen if you stay at home. You'll get bored and then get mad at me that I'm not there. Plus, your dad isn't going to give up. He's going to insist you're there. I'll book you a room at the inn in St. Francisville. Close to your parents while still feeling a world away."

A ready solution to a problem I only just learned about. It feels like that rock in my belly just doubled in size. I may not understand why, but it's clear he wants me out of the house that weekend.

Is it connected to the napkin in his briefcase with Aubrey Price's name? Or is it something else?

Either way, I know he's scheming something.

And now there's another feeling coursing through me. A teeny, tiny glimmer of hope. If I can get proof of whatever it is he's up to, I may have a way out.

CHAPTER 14

Hank

AFTER THE ALIBI
MONDAY, OCTOBER 12

Lila knocks on my open door to get my attention. "There's a Detective Sullivan here to speak to you."

I rub my hands across my face. My eyes are tired and there's a headache that's been building ever since Randall Everett showed up here this morning that feels like it may level me when it hits full strength. I glance at the clock and groan. This has been the longest day of my life and it's only four p.m.

"Okay, send him back."

She nods, then adds, "Security guard is here. He's parked out front and will do random patrols on foot around the exterior of the building throughout the day. There's also a panic button at the front desk in case someone comes in while he's making his rounds."

"Okay, good. Thanks for getting on that so quickly."

In a few minutes she's back with the detective.

I start to stand but he motions for me to keep my seat. "Don't get up for me. You look like you're about to pass out as it is."

"Thanks, Sully. Obviously, didn't get much sleep last night."

"I bet." He takes the seat in front of my desk. "We're finished at the Bayliss house."

"Any leads you can share?"

He gives me a pained look. "Hank, it wasn't that long ago you were on my side of this. You know I can't share anything like that right now."

"Hell, never hurts to ask. Figured you might throw me a little something for old times' sake."

He watches me, as if debating what he can say. "I can tell you we're exploring all leads and will be offering a reward for any information."

I sink back in my chair. When I was in the DA's office, that statement always meant they didn't get anything solid from the scene, so no real suspect. Everyone connected to Ben will be looked at very closely.

Nodding to let him know I understand what he's telling me, I change the subject. "I'll get a cleaning crew over to the house." I don't want Camille to have to deal with the mess forensics left behind or have to clean up after Ben's injuries.

I know there's more to this visit since he could have called with this info, so I patiently wait for him to get to it.

Finally, he says, "I'm going to need to do a formal interview with Mrs. Bayliss as soon as possible."

"Of course. Camille and I both want nothing more than to do whatever we can to help. She's at her parents' house, about half an hour from here. I know they're meeting with the funeral home people today and I just got word there is a Rosary at Ben's church being said for him tomorrow. Can we do the day after that? Wednesday?"

"Was really hoping to talk to her sooner than that." His expression tells me he doesn't like me putting him off.

"I get it. But she's not eating. Barely talking. It's going to be a struggle to get her through the funeral planning not to mention that Rosary, since you know everyone is going to show up there, asking her questions. Let me get her past all that and then she's all yours."

We both know he can force her to speak with him sooner, but he wants her willing. He wants her talking freely. Not quietly combative. Because of who Ben was, Sullivan knows she's not your typical witness who he can easily bully into thinking she has no rights. And because of who I am, he knows if he pushes too hard, I'll advise her to say next to nothing, which won't help his case. There are real benefits to being connected. He got enough initial information yesterday at the scene that he can't say Camille hasn't been helpful. So as much as Sullivan hates it, he'll let me get away with postponing their interview for a couple of days.

I need some uninterrupted time with Camille to find out as much as I can before walking into a meeting with him.

"Wednesday. I'm assuming you'll tell me why she can't come into the station to speak with me next."

"Sully, you know me too well. She'll be more relaxed here."

Even though being questioned is standard procedure, the media would have a field day getting pictures of the two of us walking into the station. The local coverage on this story has been nonstop, which is not surprising.

He pulls out his notebook and pen. "Since I'm here, got a few minutes for me to ask you some questions?"

"Of course." It's no surprise he'd want a formal interview with me as much as he'd want one with Camille.

Sullivan pulls out his recorder, hits the button, then sets it on the edge of my desk. "Detective Sullivan questioning Hank Landry, partner at Bayliss and Landry, regarding the events of the weekend of October ninth through eleventh." He gives me a nod to check that I'm ready, then launches into his first question. "Yesterday at the scene you stated that you returned with Mr. Bayliss from New Orleans earlier than originally planned and that the two of you arrived at his home just after one p.m. on Saturday, October tenth, since your personal vehicle was parked there, correct?"

I nod. "Correct."

"Did Mr. Bayliss tell you his plans for the rest of the day? Did he mention meeting anyone?"

"No, all he said was he had some stuff to do. I didn't think anything of it."

"Did you know he would be taking possession of a 1970 Ford Mustang that he had restored from a group named FP Restorations?"

My first impulse is to show my surprise but then I remember the advice I give my clients and work to remain still and calm. But I do make a mental note of the business name for later.

Shaking my head, I answer, "No, I did not."

"Any pissed-off client I need to know about? Someone looking for revenge after Ben got a client acquitted for killing their family member?"

"Not off the top of my head, but we're pulling all his case files and I'll be going through them over the next few days. You'll be my first call if something stands out."

Sullivan makes a few notes then asks, "What about a scorned lover?"

Even though I should have expected that question, it still takes me aback.

"No. Not at all. Ben's not that kind of guy."

Sullivan smirks. "But he's the kind of guy who comes home from out of town early but doesn't tell his wife."

There're so many ways this line of questioning can go, and I'm not crazy about the insinuations. "I know Ben and I know Camille, and I'm telling you theirs was a happy marriage."

Sullivan turns back a few pages in his notebook as if searching for something specific. "Here it is," he mumbles. "There was an open FedEx package on his desk in his home office. It was originally delivered to Mr. Bayliss here at this office on Thursday. He signed for it personally at one fifty-five p.m. The only item inside was a document listing the contents as a replacement key for a Defense Force 24 gun safe. We didn't find any evidence of a safe like that in his home. Do you have any idea why he would request a replacement key to a safe he doesn't own?"

"No, I'm sorry I don't have an answer to that."

Finally, he asks the question I've been dreading. "Did you and Ben have any problems? Any issues in your professional partnership?"

There's no easy way to say it. "Ben approached me recently about dissolving our partnership."

This news lands the way I expected it to. Based on the surprised reaction from Sullivan, he hadn't gotten wind of this yet, but it would look worse for me if he heard it later from anyone else.

"Why did he want to dissolve your partnership? If I'm remembering correctly, you only joined him here . . . what . . . three years ago?"

"Two. His reasoning was he thought he wanted a partner and then decided he didn't."

Sullivan's head cocks to the side. "That's it? No fight, no argument preceded this?"

Shaking my head, I answer, "No. I was actually shocked when he mentioned it. I didn't realize he was unhappy with our current arrangement." This is mostly true. Ben and I were having some issues when it came to the future direction of the firm.

"What was your response to this?"

I let out an uncomfortable chuckle. "Well, it caught me off guard. And then I was a bit frustrated since he's the one who talked me into leaving the DA's office. Honestly, he only presented me a draft of the proposed dissolution last week so I was still processing it."

"But the two of you still went to New Orleans together?"

"Of course. Like I said, I was surprised but there wasn't an issue between us. No reason not to keep the plans we had made."

I lean back in my chair, making sure to show Sullivan I'm relaxed and not bothered by this questioning.

Sullivan makes a few notes, then looks back at me. "Can you give me a rundown of your time on Saturday after leaving Mr. Bayliss's home until the moment Mrs. Bayliss called you on Sunday morning?"

"Yes. After I left, I drove to my house, which is only a few minutes from his. As you're aware from my days in the DA's office, I've been fixing up a 1970 GTO in my garage for the last several years and nowhere near done," I say with a laugh, hoping to cut a little of the tension. "Spent the rest of the day under the hood. Since I had thought I'd be in New Orleans all weekend, I didn't have any plans made that night. Went inside after dark, showered, and went to bed. Was still at home the next morning when I got the call from Camille."

Sullivan leans back in his chair. "Can anyone corroborate that?"

"No."

There's a heavy silence that I try not to read into.

Then Sullivan closes his notebook and shuts off the recorder.

"I appreciate your time, Hank. I'll reach out if I have any other questions. Otherwise, I'll see you and Mrs. Bayliss here on Wednesday."

I don't get up to show him out. Instead I replay our entire conversation, looking for anything I said that could backfire on me.

Even though there's a mountain of work in front of me, Sullivan's visit has left me unsettled. Thanks to that dissolution document and my weak-ass alibi, it wouldn't be a stretch pinning Ben's murder on me.

Getting up from my chair, I move to the other side of my office to the table I use when I like to spread out. Ben's briefcase and files from his home office are still sitting exactly where I put them last night.

Normally, I'd sit back and let the police do their job, but I'm afraid the pressure on them to close this case quickly could blow up in my face if they decide I'm an easy target. So maybe it wouldn't hurt to do a little digging of my own. See what Ben was up to right before he died.

Give the police someone else to focus on.

Remembering the way Sullivan stacked these folders, the one on top now would have been on the bottom of the pile when it was on Ben's desk.

Opening the folder, I skim the first page. This is the case file for the trial that was supposed to start on Wednesday. It makes sense he would have been reviewing it this past weekend.

Putting it to the side, I move to the next one. It takes me a few pages to get the gist of what it's about. It must be a new case since it's not familiar. We have . . . or had . . . a standing Monday morning meeting every week where we go over new business, so there's a chance this was one he planned to take on.

I move through the pile, going through every folder.

And then I get to the last one. The one on the bottom. The one that was open on Ben's desk.

Even though we handle our own cases in our own way, we both have a system. And after reviewing the previous case files, it's immediately clear this one is different. There's no cover page with client info, including address, phone numbers, emails, etc., which had been present in every other file.

This one contains a report on a woman named Aubrey Price, seemingly from a private investigator, but I don't see any business name across the top. There are a few pictures of her printed on the back pages.

I flip the report over and unease seeps in. Underneath the information on Aubrey is a document on a prisoner named Paul Granger, who is currently housed at Louisiana State Penitentiary.

What the hell?

Why does Ben have this?

Paul Granger's case was sent to *me* several months ago. A friend from law school is big in one of those pro bono programs created so that inmates at Angola can ask for their case to be reevaluated either because they maintain they are innocent, or because they feel their sentence was unjust. I mentioned over drinks that I was interested in potentially being involved. Since we deal with some pretty shady clients, it wouldn't kill us to have a little positive PR where we right a few wrongs. My friend sent me several cases to review, and Paul Granger's struck me as one that I would have a good shot at getting overturned. The DA's case was weak and the police work sloppy, not to mention the court-appointed defense attorney didn't put up much of a fight.

I went to the prison and met with Paul, mainly to get a feel for him and what kind of client he would be. I left even more sure his case had potential. I brought it up to Ben at the weekly meeting after my visit and he shot me down. Was adamant that I not take it, actually. At the time, I brushed it off because Ben and Paul were from the same small town and maybe there were some hometown politics he wanted to avoid, but seeing this here and knowing it was on Ben's desk the day he was killed has all those little hairs on the back of my neck sticking up.

I'm not sure how Paul is connected to Ben, but now I'm convinced his case demands a closer look.

I move back to my desk and start a new to-do list, adding Paul Granger's and Aubrey Price's names to the top of it. Then I remember what Sullivan said about the Mustang in Ben's driveway. It was delivered just after I dropped him off, but Ben never mentioned he was having a car restored even though he knew this was a passion of mine.

The third item I add to the list is FP Restorations.

Even though I'm exhausted and ready to call it a day, it feels like this can't wait.

CHAPTER 15

Aubrey

BEFORE THE ALIBI
TUESDAY, SEPTEMBER 15

A soft knock on my door startles me. I relax when I realize it's one of my housemates since it's coming from the door that leads to the interior part of the house.

"Come in," I call out, since I rarely lock that door.

Deacon's head pokes in. "Hey, did I wake you?"

I sit up in bed, pulling the covers close since I'm in a thin tee that doesn't hide much. "No, I'm still up. What's going on?"

It's not uncommon for Deacon to pop into my room, but given it's close to midnight, it feels like this visit is because something is wrong.

I gesture at the end of the bed since it's the only place to sit in my tiny room.

"Chris checked into that lawyer, Ben Bayliss. Dude is about as crooked as they come."

This wakes me up. I've been debating what to do about Camille Bayliss and the news she dropped on me at the bar last week. I wanted to show up at their house and demand some answers but Deacon cautioned me to wait. To let him do some digging first. I have no doubt if Ben Bayliss was doing anything dirty in this town, Deacon's cousin, Chris, would know about it.

"What did you find out?"

"He's got a couple of judges in his pocket. A state senator too. Some credible rumors that he intimidates and blackmails witnesses to recant their testimony against his clients before trial."

"Ugh. So do you think his interest in me has to do with Paul?" Paul has been sending me letters for the last couple of months, telling me he's trying to get his case reopened because there's new evidence that will prove someone else was driving the truck that killed my parents. I have no idea if that's true, but just the idea that my parents' murderer is roaming free has been incredibly upsetting. So when Camille told me her big-shot defense lawyer husband had my personal information, my first thought was he had taken on Paul's case.

Deacon nods. "Yeah. Asked around and found the PI Ben uses. Guy named Vic. He's a shady piece of shit too. And also has a massive gambling addiction. Until recently, Vic owed his bookie a substantial amount of money."

I'm confused. "Owed? Did he pay it off?"

"He didn't. But we did."

I lean forward. "Wait. What does that mean?"

"Chris basically took over Vic's debt from the other book so now he's got to deal with us. We made him an offer. He tells us what Ben's up to and why he's interested in you, and in return he's free and clear."

This was not what I was expecting. "Why would Chris agree to this?"

Deacon shrugs. "He can be a tough son of a bitch but we're family. And I told him how important this was to me."

His words settle over me like a warm blanket. It's been a really long time since anyone has cared enough about me to go out of their way like this.

"Did the PI agree?" This is huge. We can stop guessing and get real answers.

"He couldn't start talking fast enough."

My mouth gapes open. "Oh God, what did he say?"

Deacon leans closer. "Paul reached out to one of those groups that helps inmates appeal their cases. Somehow, his case landed on Ben's partner's desk. A guy named Hank Landry."

"So Ben's partner is taking his case?"

He shakes his head. "No. Vic said Ben lost his shit when Hank brought it up. Made it clear that no one in his office would be taking that case."

I hold my hand up. "But wait, I'm not following. Why does Ben care if Paul appeals his case?"

Deacon shrugs. "Vic said Ben only tells him what he wants, not why he wants it. Ben hired him to find out what new evidence Paul is claiming to have and where it is. Said he wanted it 'no matter the cost.'"

I twist the comforter in my hands. "I'm guessing he hasn't found it yet."

"No. But something changed a couple of weeks ago. Vic thinks Ben may have found out some details on his own, but he's not sharing. He promised me he's going to try to get me more info out of Ben."

Shaking my head, I reach for Deacon's arm. "No. What if that guy tells Ben we know what he's doing and he comes after you?"

Deacon laughs. "He's more scared of Chris than he is of Ben. As he should be. And the amount of money he owes Chris is significantly more than what Ben is paying him. Guys like him are only loyal to the dollar."

I drag my hand back and run it through my hair. "But I don't understand what I have to do with any of this."

His shoulders slump just a bit. "Didn't get a clear answer on that either. Ben wanted a profile on you but didn't say why. Probably how Ben learned Shane and Eddie lived here and knew hiring them to restore that Mustang would get him access to the house, just don't know why he'd want it. It's another answer I told him to go back and get."

I hug my arms around my waist. "What do you think is going on? What does all this mean?"

Deacon chews on his lip while he considers my question. "Hell, I'd be guessing, but breaking it down—Ben wants to get his hands on evidence that would prove Paul Granger was innocent *no matter the cost*. But it doesn't seem like he'd use it to help Paul. So the only logical reason was if the evidence getting out could be used against Ben in some way. Honestly, I don't know, but most men act desperate, which is what this sounds like, because they're scared or have something big to lose."

He makes a very sound argument. "I hate dragging you into this."

Even though he looks the part of the tough enforcer, I've seen a side of him that wouldn't be good for business. Not only does he show up at Doug's most nights to offer me a ride but I've also found extra laundry detergent pods in my almost-empty container that are the same brand he uses, and my food has been replenished on multiple occasions. Even now he doesn't hesitate to help me.

"Stop. You're not dragging me into anything. In fact, Ben Bayliss is the one who dragged all of us into this. By stalking you, buying that Mustang, and hiring Shane and Eddie to restore it."

I wilt against my headboard and can't stop the tears that flood my eyes.

I was sixteen when my parents were killed. Everyone thought it was best to shield me from the details at that time. All I was told was the bad man who had crashed into my parents' car had been arrested and was going to jail for the rest of his life. It wasn't until I graduated high school that I started looking into what happened that night. Searched for details. What I found left me with more questions than answers.

Two years later, I went to talk to the detective who handled the case, and he was nice enough as he walked me through everything, but the case against Paul looked thin, even to my uneducated eyes. I went back a few weeks later armed with questions, and he blew me off. Told me I was too young to understand and to trust they got the right guy and be glad he'll never hurt anyone ever again.

Around the same time, my aunt and uncle decided it was time for me to move out of their house. They had taken me in after my parents died, but the moment I graduated high school and turned eighteen, their obligation to me was done.

Getting to the bottom of what happened on that dark road took a back seat to surviving. The little bit of money my parents had left me was gone. My aunt and uncle made sure to use all of it to "raise me," although I'm sure it went to other things, like my uncle's new fishing boat and the cosmetic procedures my aunt routinely got.

While most of my friends started college, I went to work. It was hard enough trying to figure out how to make enough money to live that I didn't consider school an option. And it's so easy to get settled into the rut of a routine, especially when you make *just* enough to get by.

Then Paul started sending me letters and Camille walked into the bar.

"You think Ben was involved that night with Paul and that's why he's going to all the trouble to get his hands on this evidence?"

Deacon shrugs. "That's my best guess. Ten years ago he was twenty with not much to lose. He's in a much different position now."

"If he does get it and it implicates him in some way, it will disappear forever." It kills me to think that someone who played a part in the deaths of my parents won't be held accountable for their actions.

Deacon squeezes my foot through the comforter. "Hey. We're going to figure this out. Let's give Vic a chance to get us some more info and we'll make a plan. Just may need to get creative."

CHAPTER 16

Camille

THE ALIBI
SATURDAY, OCTOBER 10

Ben leans back in his chair once the video on the drive begins to play. I can just make out the screen over his right shoulder. It's Aubrey Price, the woman currently in St. Francisville posing as me.

It's my fault Aubrey was tipped off that Ben was watching her, and my only choices were to sit back and let Aubrey make a big stink with Ben or to promise to work with her to find out the truth of what happened that night ten years ago.

Obviously, I chose the second option, especially since the first option wouldn't further my own goal of leaving my marriage with some financial stability.

And now I'm sitting in my attic, spying on my husband.

The video opens with Aubrey sitting at a table in a nondescript room.

"Detective Walton, thank you for agreeing to meet with me. I know how busy you are, and this isn't considered a high priority case . . . anymore." She's nervous. And fidgety. Keeps pushing her hair behind her ear even though it never stays where she tucks it.

I can't see the person she's talking to, but his voice comes across the recording loud and clear, as if he's sitting right next to the camera's mic. "My apologies it took this long for me to get back to you. The detective who handled this case originally recently retired. What is it that you wanted to discuss with us?"

Aubrey takes a deep breath and sits up a bit straighter. "I wanted to see if it was possible for you to review the case against Paul Granger."

"We are not in the habit of reviewing cases of those who were rightly found guilty by a court of law." There's no missing the censure in his voice. "But more importantly, why would you want that?"

"I got a letter from Paul. He told me some things that are making me question everything."

"He's not supposed to be contacting you. Ever. I'll call the warden . . ." His voice booms so loudly that Ben and I both flinch.

"No! Wait, please. Just listen before you call and get him in trouble." Her hands are out in front of her, and she looks on the verge of tears. "Just hear me out. Please."

She seems desperate. Her words, her mannerisms are a far cry from the woman I met at the bar, hell-bent on getting answers.

A very different Aubrey than the one I've gotten to know.

"He shouldn't be contacting you," he says, the judgment in his voice coming over loud and clear. "And you should have contacted Angola immediately."

She shrugs. "I didn't come in here to talk about how I heard from him but what I learned when I did. He makes a compelling argument."

"They always say they didn't do it." The frustration in his voice is clear. "He was convicted of killing your parents. It is highly inappropriate for him to contact you."

Aubrey pushes her hair back again. "He says there is new evidence."

"Is this what you wanted to talk to me about? Delusions from a convicted felon?"

She bristles at his response. "I may have been young when it happened and didn't know everything back then, but I've been looking into it now. There's always been something that felt off. Stuff that didn't add up. Paul has always said he didn't do it, even after all these years. Someone connected with the case came to see him. Told him he was framed."

"Did he say who the person 'connected with the case' was? Did you get a name?"

"No, he didn't tell me that part."

The man scoffs. "Of course he didn't. But you believe the word of a convicted murderer over the police officers and prosecutors who worked to get justice for your parents."

She stands up so quickly her chair nearly tips over. It wobbles a few seconds before settling back in place. The top of her head moves just out of the camera's frame. "Looking into what he says doesn't mean I'm believing him over y'all. I'm not asking anyone to let him out of prison. I'm not even asking for anyone to reopen his case. All I asked is if you would review it with fresh eyes. If you won't even consider the possibility that maybe there was more to what happened that night, then why did you agree to see me?"

"You were insistent that you speak to us about your parents' case—"

She interrupts him. "So, what, you're humoring me." She has a wild look about her, almost hissing at him.

Ben is glued to the screen as he takes in every word.

Everything she's saying now she has said to me, but there's something visceral about seeing her grief surface. She's always so calm and in control with me.

"Look, Paul Granger was a known drug dealer. Arrested for selling and possessing more than once. He hit your parents' car then fled the scene, but he couldn't even do that right since he left his truck behind. Maybe I'm not inclined to take a lying, stealing drug dealer's word on what he says happened that night. I'm trying to be considerate, but you're coming in here and telling me our department got it wrong, the prosecutor got it wrong, the judge got it wrong, all because a murderer in prison said so."

His words knock her back into her chair. Her voice is softer when she says, "I'm coming in here asking you to follow up on every lead. You're the one taking it personally."

"Your mother died instantly but it took longer for your father to succumb to his injuries. It was an hour before anyone stumbled across your parents' car, and by then it was too late to do anything for him. If I were you, I'd take it personally that Paul was a coward who fled the scene instead of making sure your dad received timely medical attention that could have saved his life."

Ben and I both flinch at the brutal way he's talking to her, and I can't help but wonder what is going through Ben's mind. Hearing this would certainly bring up memories of that night if Ben was somehow involved.

In the video, Aubrey wraps her arms tightly around her waist. It's clear his words slice right through her.

When it doesn't seem like she's going to say anything, he adds, "There are ways for Paul Granger to introduce new evidence, but getting the victims' kid to come down to the station isn't one of them."

Victims' kid.

It's hard to watch this asshole talk to her like that.

"You're a dick, Walton," Ben mutters.

Well, at least Ben and I agree on one thing.

Aubrey slumps in her chair and her tears are falling freely now, with no attempt to wipe them away. Then she gets up and disappears from view. Seconds later, the video ends.

It's impossible not to feel sorry for her. For what she's been through.

Ben doesn't move for several minutes, just seems to stare at the frozen screen. Finally, he spins around in his chair, and I can see his face. His head leans against the back of the chair and his eyes are closed. There is tension in his features that wasn't there before watching the video.

After several minutes, he straightens and focuses on the desk in front of him, shuffling the pile of papers while muttering to himself every few minutes.

"Fuck!"

He screams so loud I swear it reaches the attic. Ben stands up abruptly, his right hand sweeping across the desk, causing papers to fly off the surface before floating gently to the floor.

Oh, he's pissed.

Deep, heaving breaths rush in and out as he stares at the mess. It takes a few minutes for him to get himself back together, then he takes his time picking up each individual piece of paper like he didn't just lose it. One by one, he stacks them neatly on the corner of his desk. Finally, he turns back to the laptop on the credenza behind him, ejects the drive, then drops it on his desk.

Once everything is back in order, he goes to the bar cabinet in the bookcase that lines the side wall. He pours a healthy amount of whiskey in one of the cut crystal tumblers I gave him the first Christmas we were married. The same pattern that matches the wineglasses from our registry. He throws the drink back in one swallow, letting out a quick cough after it goes down.

I thought the drunken night at the DU banquet was odd, but it's definitely out of the norm for him to hit the hard liquor midafternoon. Honestly, though, I'm going to need several drinks myself when I get out of this attic.

Ben refills his glass and takes his time with round two, pacing in front of his desk while he sips his drink. When his glass is empty again, he seems to contemplate a third drink but instead turns away and heads back to his chair behind his desk.

He pulls out some of the papers from the same envelope that held the drive. "Aubrey, you just couldn't leave well enough alone, could you?" he mutters to himself.

Okay, here we go. While the delivery of the Mustang threw me off, it seems we're back on track. Aubrey believes he wanted me out of the house today because Ben was finally getting his hands on the evidence Paul says will set him free. Knowing that if that evidence implicates him in some way, Ben won't hesitate destroying it. It's why I'm here, armed with cameras to try to get what we can. While Paul would need something that would be admissible in court to change his fate, I won't. I just need enough evidence of his illegal activities to trigger that clause in my prenup.

After he reads through the document in front of him, Ben picks up his phone and places a call. Thankfully, it's on speaker.

The call is answered on the second ring. "Yeah."

Ben doesn't bother with hello, just goes straight into the reason for the call. "When did she visit the cops in Corbeau?"

"Couple of months ago. My contact didn't hear about it until a few days ago. The whole department is chaotic right now ever since Walton took over."

I know Ben keeps a couple of PIs on the payroll and I'm guessing this is one of them.

"I'm not paying you for old information." Ben gets up from his chair and paces behind his desk. "You assured me Aubrey didn't know anything significant. That Paul hadn't told her anything specific. She told Walton someone connected to Paul's case went to see him! That's pretty fucking specific! How hard do you think it would be to get a list of Paul Granger's visitors?"

It takes a moment for the man to reply. "Not much slips past my guy, but this did."

"Now we have to give Aubrey something or she's going to become a problem. I don't relish making that girl's life any harder but I need her to stop questioning this."

Whatever small part of me thought we could have gotten whatever this is all wrong just vanished.

"I hear you and I'll take care of it. When are you going for the safe?" the PI asks.

Ben glances at his watch then gets up and heads to the kitchen, taking his phone with him to continue his conversation. He grabs a bottle of water from the fridge and twists open the top, taking a long drink. "Got a couple of meetings here first, then I'll head over there around six."

He's leaving? And what safe is he talking about?

He can't leave. I have the cameras set up here.

"Foster's place will be empty, right?" Ben asks. "I'm going to be pissed if I drive all the way to Corbeau and someone's there."

What.

He's going to Corbeau?

Foster? Does he mean Kevin Foster?

"The house will be empty. Mrs. Foster's nephew, Nathan, has been in and out of there for the last week, helping out. He dropped her off at her sister's house last night."

Ben picks up a FedEx envelope that was on the corner of the kitchen counter with all the mail he brought in earlier. The envelope is already open so he just turns it upside down, shaking the contents out. A single sheet of paper and something long and narrow falls out. He picks it up and examines it. "This fucking key better work."

The PI says, "It will. What are you gonna do if it's not in the gun safe?"

Oh shit. I slump in my chair while my mind tries to keep up with what I'm learning. No one is bringing the evidence here to Ben. He's going to get it, and for some reason he believes it's in a gun safe at Kevin Foster's house.

Foster is my dad's go-to guy and his hands are as dirty as Dad's, but I'm still not sure how this is connected to him.

Maybe Foster helped Ben cover up his involvement in that accident in some way?

Ben paces around the kitchen while spinning that odd-shaped key in his hand. "If it's not there it doesn't exist, because I have looked everywhere else."

I'm so distracted by this new information that I don't realize anyone has pulled up to the house until I hear the doorbell. This must be one of the meetings he just mentioned. I take a quick peek at the camera I placed on the front porch, but whoever is there has already passed by it.

Ben looks out of the window. "I'll call you back," he says, ending the call. He starts to move to the front door, then remembers the key in his hand. Glancing around as if trying to decide what to do with it, he moves to my small desk next to the fridge, where I keep my calendar and pay the household bills. He drops the key in the glass jar I use to hold pens, markers, and scissors.

The second he swings the door open, I get a clear view of who is on the other side.

My mouth drops open. "What the hell . . ." Standing on my front porch is my sister-in-law, Margaret.

CHAPTER 17

Aubrey

BEFORE THE ALIBI
MONDAY, SEPTEMBER 28

Deacon and I pull into the parking lot, one row over from where Camille's car is parked.

"Don't be nervous. You're holding all the cards," Deacon says as he puts his hand on my knee to stop its bouncing.

"I know. You're right. But what if she's surrounded by a bunch of people when she comes out?"

"Then we'll catch her somewhere else."

This will be the first time I've spoken to Camille since she showed up at the bar to confront me about sleeping with her husband. I've been preparing myself for this conversation with her for the last few days, mainly to make sure I wouldn't be blindsided like I was last time.

The PI who Ben hired has fully flipped on him and is feeding Deacon info as he gets it. Deacon was right—his loyalty lies where he financially gains the most.

Ben broke down and had to bring Vic in on his plans when he was faced with a task he couldn't handle on his own. When you believe the information you're seeking is locked away in a home gun safe that is five feet tall and weighs more than four hundred pounds, you're going to need a little help getting inside it.

To break into a safe like that, you'd either need a knowledgeable locksmith, which would be hard to find considering you're asking them to open a safe you don't own, or you'd have to drill through the lock, which would alert the owners that their safe was breached.

But the funny thing about a gun safe is there's always a backup way to get inside that's honestly not that hard to get . . . as long as you don't mind waiting about a week. In the model they are trying to break into, there's a keyhole hidden behind the electronic lock face. All you need is the serial number of the safe, which can easily be found if you have a dolly and enough manpower to tip the safe on its side so you can look underneath it. Then you request a replacement from the manufacturer, which is also surprisingly easy since they don't keep ownership records on their safes.

And that extra manpower was Ben's PI, Vic.

Ben will receive the key sometime next week and plans to get into the safe when he knows the house will be empty.

"There she is." Deacon points to the group of women exiting the building, leaving their Junior League meeting. Thankfully, Camille says her goodbyes and breaks away from the group, walking in a different direction to her car.

Just as I'm about to get out of Deacon's car, he stops me. "Remember, keep it simple. We need her to think Ben has someone bringing it to him, not that he's going to get it."

I nod. "Okay. Simple. I can keep it simple."

My nerves are at an all-time high. Ben is going to a lot of trouble to make sure Camille is out of the house, so we need Camille to be there to see what he's doing. We also know a big part of Ben's plan is getting into a safe at Foster's, which is why we'll also need to get a tracker on Ben's car so we know when he's headed that way. But we decided to keep that part to ourselves. Camille has to believe she's in control of any information uncovered, because I'm not sure she'll willingly share it with us. When Deacon said we may have to get creative, he wasn't joking. I feel like if I screw this up, our whole plan falls apart.

Deacon gets out with me but stays by his car while I start walking toward her.

"I'll be right here if you need me," he assures me.

Camille stops abruptly when she sees me. "I was wondering when you were going to turn up." She opens the driver's door, dropping her purse inside, before turning to face me.

I cross my arms in front of me, hopeful I look tough instead of terrified. "You must have looked me up by now. Know who my parents were."

My words are meant to hit, and from the slight flinch, I see they do.

"Yes. And I'm very sorry for your loss."

"I looked you up too. Both you and Ben. You're from Corbeau. Where they died."

Camille nods then glances around the parking lot to see if anyone is near enough to hear this conversation, but thankfully, we are alone.

I take one small step toward her. "Ben would have been what, twenty, twenty-one when that happened? Funny what you can find on the internet. His mom still lives a few houses down from where Paul Granger lived. What are the chances they knew each other? Hung out together?"

Her mouth tightens as if she's stopping herself from saying something she might regret.

Remembering the lines I've practiced with Deacon, I go in for the kill. "Your husband is dirty. Your family is dirty. Crooked. Corrupt," I say, then pause for effect. "And I don't believe my parents got the justice they deserved."

My words hang in the air between us.

Camille straightens, as if finally finding a little backbone. "What is the purpose of this visit?"

This is the moment where this works or it backfires on us. She'll either be scared enough to help or she'll run straight to her husband and tell him everything. Deacon and I went over the pros and cons of approaching her like this for days but it finally came down to the fact that we really didn't have a choice. For there to be any chance to get my hands on what Ben is searching for, I need Camille. And I've got to sell this in such a way that she believes her only choice is to work *with me*, not against me.

I let out a deep breath. "I need your help. And honestly, you need mine too. There's something you should know. Ben played a part in the accident that killed my parents and that information is coming out. There's nothing he can do to stop it. And Ben knows it. I'm on to him. I know what he did. That's why he's been watching me." It's a bluff, but I can see it in her face—she's buying it.

She takes a step back. "I don't understand . . ."

"There is evidence to show Paul Granger is innocent. The same evidence that will show Ben's guilt." An exaggeration, yes, but the fact that Ben is so obsessed with getting his hands on whatever is floating around out there tells me our hunch isn't far off.

The color drains from Camille's face.

Now I need to soften my approach.

"Camille, if I'm being completely honest with you, I know the chances of holding Ben accountable for what he did all those years ago are so slim. He's connected in ways I can't even fathom. And if this whole experience has taught me anything, it's that if people want to bend and break the law to protect themselves, that's exactly what will happen."

She's shaking her head. "What are you saying?"

"No matter what, your husband will find a way to stay free and Paul will still be in prison."

"So what are you doing all this for?"

"I want to finally know for sure what happened to my parents. I want to stop wondering and have real answers. The not knowing is killing me. Ben will get his hands on it before me, that is something I'm very sure of. I just want to know what it is before he destroys it. And then I can move on with my life."

Tears are trailing down my cheeks even though I didn't want to show her this much emotion. While some of what I'm telling her isn't true, the last sentiment is. I need to be able to move past this in any way I can.

"Aubrey, I understand what you're saying and my heart is breaking for you. It really is. But I don't know what you want from me. How you think I can somehow help you."

I wipe away my tears and pull myself together. "I can't tell you how I know this, but Ben will be meeting someone at your home next Saturday and they will give him what he's been searching for then."

She deflates at my words.

And I jump on it. "I'm taking a wild guess, but will you be out of town that weekend? I know you travel a lot for your food blog."

She nods but doesn't say anything else.

I think back to her demeanor when she showed up at the bar. She was a mess. She'd gone out in a thunderstorm just to ask me if I was sleeping with her husband. A woman doesn't do that unless her marriage is in a pretty rough place.

So I add, "I feel like I'm not the only one who wants to know who Ben really is and what he's done."

She tenses at my words. "If I refuse to help you, what will you do?"

It's a question I expected. Hoped for. "I've been thinking about my options. The police aren't much help since they don't like looking into closed cases. But there's the media. I could find one of those podcast groups that love to dig through old cases."

I don't have to know Camille to know she would hate to be dragged into the public spotlight like this.

"How do you intend for us to see what evidence you think Ben is getting?"

I try not to look shocked by her question. Honestly, I felt like it was a very slim chance she would consider helping me.

"We need to figure out how to make sure you're home too, but without him knowing. You can set some cameras up." I motion to Deacon behind me. "We can teach you how to prepare so you see what he's seeing. That you're recording it."

She's shaking her head. "Ben tracks me. My phone, my car, credit cards. There's no sneaking up on Ben. He watches my every move."

My head tilts to the side as I consider her words. Being tracked is nothing new. Before my parents died, my mom followed my every move using Life360, but my friends and I worked hard to make sure she only saw what we wanted her to. "What if he watches my every move instead, thinking it's you?"

CHAPTER 18

Hank

AFTER THE ALIBI
TUESDAY, OCTOBER 13

"Hey, Hank." Camille's voice is scratchy.

"Hey, just calling to check on you and to let you know Detective Sullivan came by yesterday. They're finished at your house."

"Oh! So soon?"

"Yeah, it's doesn't take too long, especially since they would have focused on Ben's office. I have a service going over there to clean up behind them. Dusting for prints makes a huge mess. Hopefully they can start tomorrow, but at the latest on Thursday. Should be done either Friday or Saturday and then you'll be free to go home."

"I don't love being at my parents' house, but I don't think I can go back there, especially until they catch whoever did this. Did the detective tell you if they had any leads?"

I lean back in my chair, turning it so I can look out the window. "No.

And he won't be able to tell us much. He'll risk his investigation otherwise. So for now, we'll be in the dark until they're ready to make a public announcement."

It's a long few seconds before she responds. "Do you think they have a suspect?"

"I think they're looking at everyone associated with Ben."

She's quiet on the other end of the line so I change the subject. "There is one thing I wanted to ask you about. The 1970 Mustang parked near the garage. Is that Ben's?"

Another long pause. "Yes. He bought it not long ago."

Staring at the traffic going by outside my window, I consider this and find it doesn't match up in any way with what I know about Ben. But I'm not pushing it with Camille.

"I hate to pile anything else on you right now, but Detective Sullivan needs to interview you formally."

"What do you mean, 'formally'?"

"It just means it will be done by appointment, not like at the scene on Sunday. He'll have prepared questions. You're Ben's wife. You're the one who found him. It's expected they will want to speak with you, more than once probably. There is no reason for us not to be helpful."

"Of course," she mumbles. "Where will they interview me? Do I have to go to the station?"

"We'll do the interview in the conference room at the office tomorrow. Wanted you to be able to get through the Rosary this afternoon first."

"Ugh, the Rosary. I told my mother to just wait until we have the funeral and do it then but she and Dad had this planned an hour after I got to their house on Sunday night."

The funeral won't be happening until they release his body, which could take a while. "Yeah, I agree it's soon, but I think most people feel like they need to do *something*, you know. Even if it's just praying for him."

She moans pitifully. "It's going to be a nightmare. I know everyone means well, but I'm not sure how many more times I can hear 'Sorry for your loss,' and it's only been two days." She lets out a teary laugh. "God, what's wrong with me? Everyone is nothing but nice and I'm bitching about it."

The heaviness of this conversation has me leaning forward in my chair, resting my elbows on my knees. "I may not know the right thing to say, but what I can promise is that you can say anything you want to me without judgment or fear. I'm from a small town too, so I have a good idea of how many well-meaning people have shown up at your parents' house to pay their condolences within minutes of you getting there and how taxing that must be."

She lets out a heartbreaking sob. "It took me some time but I had finally come to terms with being seen only as *Ben's wife*, as if that were the only way to define me. Always expected to dress the part, everything about me defined by that position. Every effort made not to do anything to dim the light shining on him. And in the blink of an eye, I'm now the *murdered lawyer's wife*. I don't know what that wife is supposed to do or say."

The silence between us stretches as I take in her words. Weigh them against the Camille I thought I knew and the Camille I'm discovering today. I wonder for the first time if I'm not the only one who felt that twinge of relief upon hearing Ben had died.

"I feel like the murdered lawyer's wife gets to do whatever the fuck she wants. Or nothing at all. I also believe she can tell everyone to go to hell if the mood strikes. You don't owe anyone anything."

A breath shudders out of her. She's sobbing and I feel like an ass for taking that approach until she says, "Thank you for not tiptoeing around me. For giving me the space to say things most people would be horrified to hear." Then she changes the subject. "What will that detective expect of me? I don't know who . . . who did that to him. To Ben."

"The only expectation is that you answer his questions truthfully." I take a few seconds to think about how to phrase the next part. "You can tell me anything. You know that."

I can't shake the feeling she's hiding something from me. And I can't help her if she doesn't trust me.

She's quiet on the other end long enough that I have to check to see if she's still on the line.

"Thank you, Hank. I appreciate that."

"I'm always here for you. I'll see you at the Rosary."

She ends the call and I stare out the window at the busy street, giving myself a few minutes to digest everything she said, until the sound of my office door opening grabs my attention.

Lila has a blue file folder tucked under one arm, a brown paper bag in one hand, and a tall cup of coffee in the other. She places the bag and coffee on the corner of my desk with a pointed look. "I figured if I didn't bring you lunch, you'd gnaw off your own arm rather than go get something yourself."

I grab the coffee first. "I'm not sure what I would do without you."

"Me either." She holds the folder out to me rather than dropping it on the top of the pile in the corner of my desk. "One of Ben's clients is in the waiting room. He's adamant about seeing you today. Here's his file."

Groaning, I take the folder from her and flip it open, the name on the cover page surprising me—Pete Sanders, CEO of one of the biggest private contractor companies in Baton Rouge.

"Tell him I'm finishing up a meeting and I'll be with him shortly."

"Will do," she says, then shuts my door behind her.

For a case this big, there's very little information inside. Nothing more than contact information and bullet points about his business, not much about the crime he's been accused of other than a copy of the original indictment. As a firm, we typically don't take on too many white-collar crimes, but Ben made an exception for Pete since he's well connected in the social circles Ben runs in.

Pete's been charged with good ole bribery. He's been accused of offering cash to DOT officials in exchange for the contract to rebuild several bridges that were damaged during the last hurricane that tore through here. He's maintaining his innocence and blaming the losing bidders for spreading the false accusations.

I glance at the stack of files on the table that I got from Ben's home office. If memory serves me correctly, one of them is full of documents on this case. Once I retrieve it and bring it back to my desk, I open it up.

There is a wealth of information inside, including handwritten notes about the case.

And then it occurs to me. Ben was keeping one set of files here and a completely different set at home.

In the handwritten notes dated about six months ago, it's clear why. There is a list of names of those who have accused Pete Sanders of wrongdoing, as well as details of their personal lives, including family members and addresses as well as sensitive information none of them would want made public. And then a very cryptic note that says, "Chief will provide date and times."

Who the hell is Chief?

The more I read, the uneasier I feel. Ben was clearly either planning to intimidate witnesses or already had.

The absolute last thing I want to do is have a conversation with Pete Sanders, but it's better to rip this Band-Aid off now.

I message Lila to send him back.

The door opens and Lila extends an arm, motioning for him to enter my office.

Pete is in his late fifties. He's average height but heavyset in a way that makes him look stumpy. And instead of embracing his male-pattern baldness, he's trained the hair on the back of his head to swirl around to the front and settle on top.

I stand when he comes in the room but don't go around to greet him like I normally would.

We shake hands from across my desk, and I gesture to the chair next to him. "Have a seat and tell me what brings you in today."

He takes his time getting settled while watching me the whole time. I relax and give him the impression I have all day.

"Since Ben is dead, is this conversation protected by client–attorney privilege?" His question isn't completely unexpected but the abruptness is jarring, as is the lack of condolences on Ben's unexpected passing.

"Yes, of course."

"Okay, good. I need to know what's happening to my case now."

I rock back in my chair as I explain exactly what will be in a letter Lila is drafting that will go out to all of Ben's clients tomorrow. "When a member of a firm passes away, the remaining member or members, me, in this case, will review each open case and decide if the firm can continue representing the client or if the client needs to be referred to new counsel. Obviously, the client has a say in this process and can choose either to leave or to stay, depending on the firm's decision."

Pete doesn't know it yet but his is definitely one I will be passing off to someone else.

He leans forward, his hands resting on his knees. "No. You're not understanding me. What happens to *my* case. Ben had it all but handled, so what happens now?"

I tilt my head to the side, giving him the impression I'm confused by his question. "Handled?" I flip through the sparse pages in the office copy of this file. "Were you accepting a plea deal or . . ."

Pete leans forward to the point I fear he will face-plant on my desk. "Fucking handled! As in those pieces of shit at the DOT will recant or risk their own dirty little secrets coming out. Those bastards were all too happy to take my money, but the second they got questioned, they ratted me out."

I wasn't sure if he'd play dumb or come right out and say Ben was intimidating witnesses, but there it is.

I hold a hand up. "Mr. Sanders. Let me just say I'm unaware of what you're referring to, and I feel sure Ben would act in your defense to the best of his abilities while also obeying the laws we all are held to . . ."

He doesn't wait for me to finish. He stands and sweeps his hand across the top of my desk, and file folders go flying. I try to grab as many as I can before they tumble to the floor but all I get is air.

"What the hell are you doing?"

Pete is red in the face, pointing his finger at me. "Drop the moral high ground bullshit speech. This fucking firm was built on backdoor deals. Please tell me you don't believe a kid fresh out of law school won Representative Wells's case on his own, given the mountain of evidence they had on him, without someone making that evidence go away. Figure out how Ben was going to make my case go away and finish what he fucking started. You will not like what happens if this case goes to trial."

He storms out just as Lila pokes her head in.

She watches him go, then comes running to help me pick everything up. "What in the world was that about?"

"That son of a bitch thinks he's going to threaten me," I mumble as I gather everything off the floor and plop it all on top of my desk.

Now I'm wondering how many clients like Pete Sanders Ben has.

"Will you get me a printout of all of Ben's open cases. Just the clients' names." I'm going to cross-check them against the stack I took from his home office. "Also, Ben references the name 'Chief' in his notes. Ask Tricia if she knows who that is. Maybe it's a PI he uses . . . or something along those lines."

What the fuck, Ben.

CHAPTER 19

Aubrey

THE ALIBI
SATURDAY, OCTOBER 10

To say I'm nervous about going inside a maximum-security prison would be an understatement.

The land the prison sits on was once a plantation named Angola, so most people call it by that name rather than its official name—Louisiana State Penitentiary. Angola is the largest maximum-security prison in the United States and a brutal place to be incarcerated. It's got a long, ugly history. Really ugly. Advocacy groups have been campaigning for change there for decades and have had some small wins over the years, but there's a long way to go. My stomach turns every time I think about how awful it would be if Paul Granger was sent there for a crime he didn't commit.

Deacon stops close to the entrance then turns to face me once he puts the car in park. "Are you absolutely sure you want to do this?"

I nod and swallow down the lump in my throat. "I feel like I have to, especially after everything I've found out over the last few weeks."

"Okay. Take as long as you need. I'll be waiting out here."

I get out of the car before I can second-guess myself. The walk to the entrance of the vistors' center is daunting, knowing what's on the other side of the tall fence lined with razor wire.

There's a line of people waiting to sign in, and it takes about ten minutes before I can approach the counter. The guard watches me as I step up to the window. There is a thick piece of glass separating us with a small drawer at the bottom that is open on my side. "Identification and name of the inmate you are requesting to visit."

I pull my license out of my pocket and drop it in the metal bin. "I'm here to see Paul Granger."

He pulls the drawer so that it closes on my side and opens on his, then studies my license before typing my name in his computer. You have to be on an inmate's approved list of visitors to be allowed inside. Paul Granger has been writing me letters asking me to visit for some time, so I know I'm on the list but there's no way Deacon would be, which is why he has to wait for me outside.

We both read through the rules a dozen times. I made sure I'm not dressed in clothing similar in appearance to the inmates or the corrections officers. I'm not wearing anything too tight or revealing. I only have my ID on me, nothing else, so there shouldn't be any reason for them not to allow me entrance.

The drawer slides back open. My license is inside along with a laminated card.

"Please read the instructions and give me a verbal response that you understand the rules."

I read the card.

> The inmate you are approved to visit is allowed contact. Visitors may embrace (hug) and exchange a brief kiss, to indicate fondness, not a lingering kiss, with their visitor at the beginning and end of the visit. During the visit, the only contact permitted is holding hands. Excessive displays of affection or sexual misconduct between people in prison and visitors is strictly prohibited. Any improper contact between a person in prison and visitor shall be grounds for stopping the visit immediately.

I drop the card back into the drawer and look at the guard. "I understand the rules."

"Proceed to the screening area. You are allowed a maximum visit of two hours."

I get in another line. This one is similar to TSA at the airport. IDs are shown again and all belongings are put through an X-ray machine while we walk through a metal detector. What makes this different from the airport screenings are the large dogs being held on chains by more guards.

I can't imagine a scenario where you would risk sneaking in contraband past those dogs.

Once we clear the security area, we are loaded on an old school bus that's been painted white with the prison's official name down the side. It's a short ride to the building where we will finally be able to meet with the inmates. From my research, the moment I stated I was here to see Paul, guards would notify him that he had a visitor and start the process of bringing him to meet me.

We're ushered off the bus into a large rectangular building. It's a big open space with tables scattered through the room. By the time I make my way to an empty one, I can feel the sweat trickling down my back. I'm not sure I've ever been more nervous in my life.

A guard approaches me and asks, "Name of inmate you're visiting?"

"Paul Granger."

He nods and makes a note on his clipboard before walking away.

The room is full of people since visiting hours started at noon, and so loud I can hardly hear myself think, which may be a good thing. Guards patrol the room, enforcing the limited contact we all had to agree to before coming inside.

I spot Paul the second he enters the room. The guard points him in my direction, and it's not long before he's sitting down across from me. Even though it's only been ten years, he looks like he's aged twice that. He's forty, but he's almost completely gray and his face is wrinkled and leathery.

It feels like my throat is closing up. Like I can't swallow my saliva.

"I can't believe you're here. That you came to see me after all these years." He looks relieved. Happy in a way that makes me uncomfortable.

He waits for me to say something, anything, but I can't seem to make my mouth work.

"Aubrey, are you okay?"

This is my first time in the same room with him since he was sentenced to prison. I jerk my head in a nod, finally taking a deep breath, then clear my throat. "I have some questions to ask you."

He nods rapidly several times. "Ask me anything."

"In the letter you wrote me, you said there was evidence that would show you weren't driving your truck that night, but you wouldn't tell me what that evidence was. I'm here, sitting in front of you, telling you it's time you share that information. What is it?"

He seems taken aback by my question. I need his answer, though. And there's no reason he shouldn't give it to me. He's never mentioned Foster's name to me, so he wouldn't think I knew that's his source. We only learned who it was because Ben's PI flipped on him.

The risk we're taking today is huge, and we need as much information as possible. We need to know what we're looking for, whether it's something digital or physical photos or a voice recording. Or if it's just a stack of papers. We need to be able to narrow our search when we're given the opportunity.

When he doesn't answer me immediately, I remind him of what he just said. "What happened to 'ask me anything'?"

"Sorry. I'll answer you. But please, I'm trusting you with this. You don't know how easy it is for evidence to disappear. And I'm afraid if the wrong people know what's out there, that's what will happen."

"I wouldn't be here if I wasn't taking this seriously."

A few more seconds tick by.

"It's a video from a security camera at the gas station on the corner of the intersection where the accident happened."

I wait for him to say more but he just watches me.

"And this . . . person who came to you and told you this, did he say when he got it? Way back then or just recently?"

"He said he got it the morning after the accident."

"I'm guessing it was a cop who came to see you?" I'm pushing Paul to see if he'll trust me with Foster's name. "I mean, who else is checking surveillance cameras the morning after an accident."

Paul's eyes get big. "I . . . uh, please don't make me answer that."

So, the answer is no, he's not trusting me that much.

"Did you ask him why he didn't turn over the video that morning?"

Paul shrugs. "I did. All he said was, at the time, he was doing someone a favor."

"But it does show something? Something that would prove you weren't the driver?"

"Yeah, that's what he says."

This is so frustrating on so many levels. "Did he tell you who the driver was?"

Paul shakes his head. "No, he didn't tell me that. He didn't really want to tell me any of this. He only came here to apologize to me since it was his fault I'm stuck in here. Told me he found God and he had to make things right. He knew I didn't kill your parents, but he let me take the fall for it anyway. I told him the only way I would forgive him is if he got me out of here. That's the only reason he told me about the video. Then he said he'd try to figure out a way to get me free but that he's in a tough spot. There are some very connected people who are gonna be pissed off if he flips on them and he's worried about his wife and kids. He asked me not to say anything until he figured out how to get the video to the right people."

"But you did tell people. I saw your mom's posts on social media. She's telling everybody."

His eyes squeeze shut, a pained expression crossing his face. I'm guessing he's not allowed online so he probably didn't know. "She wasn't supposed to do that. Mama contacted that group that helps us get our case appealed after I told her there was new evidence. Figured a lawyer's gotta keep my secrets so that was fine. But I didn't know she was going to go public with it like that." He runs a hand across his face. "Shit, that's probably why . . . that guy . . . hasn't been back. He's probably pissed at me for telling Mama."

I sink back in my chair. Oh, God, Paul doesn't know. Kevin Foster died more than a month ago.

"I need to go. I'll be in touch if I discover anything." I can't be the one to tell Paul that Foster is dead.

Paul's face drops. "You're leaving already? I get up to two hours for a visit."

"Sorry, I can't stay any longer."

He pulls something out of his pocket and pushes it across the table. It's a leather bookmark. "Thank you for visiting me."

I don't touch it and instead look at the guards. One of the rules was very clear—there is no exchange of items between visitors and inmates.

Paul must see the concern on my face because he says, "It's okay. I got approved to bring this in and give it to you. Since I made it in the shop here, I can gift it to anyone I want."

It's not the only handmade leather item I've gotten from Paul. He always included something with the letters he sent me.

I pick up the bookmark and then get up from the table, walking quickly to the exit. There's a process to get out just like there was one to get in.

Finally, I'm on the bus heading back to the entrance. That was so much harder than I thought it would be. I may not have gotten all the answers I was looking for, but at least I know what's supposedly floating around out there. For ten years I believed he was responsible for my parents' deaths and now I'm not so sure.

Deacon is waiting for me right as I exit the visitors' entrance. He pulls me in for a hug as I blink my tears away.

"You okay?"

I nod against his chest.

"Okay, let's get out of here."

He leads me to his car, and then we're back on the road to St. Francisville. Lowering the visor, I start slicking my hair back in preparation for putting the wig and cap back on and fill him in on my visit. "It's a surveillance video from a gas station."

"With a clear shot of the driver?"

I shrug. "He made it sound like it was but I'm sure he hasn't actually seen it. Also, Foster didn't tell him who was driving. And Paul doesn't know Foster's dead."

Deacon turns the radio down then leans back in his seat. "The best thing we've got going for us is no one knows that we're aware of what Foster's got in his safe, so it's good Paul doesn't know he's dead. Fear of pissing Foster off is the only thing keeping Paul quiet right now."

"Yeah, I guess you're right."

"I got a text from Shane while you were in there. They were able to get the tracker on Ben's Range Rover. So if he takes either that car or the Mustang to Foster's, we'll know it."

I get the wig settled back in place and close the visor. "Okay, good."

But Ben won't be the only one who shows up to Foster's house. Deacon plans on being there too.

"What if he doesn't go there tonight like we think he will?" I ask, turning in my seat to face him.

"Plan B. We know he has the key and thanks to Shane and Eddie, we know we can get in his house. If he doesn't go tonight, then we go take the key from Ben and get in the safe ourselves."

I really hope it doesn't come to that.

The trip to Angola felt like it took forever, but the ride back to St. Francisville goes by in a blink. We're back at the feed store. Deacon pulls in the spot in the same corner of the lot where we all met up earlier and throws his car in park.

"I texted Serenity when we left Angola so she should be here any minute," Deacon says. "You going to be all right here for the rest of the day?"

"Yeah, it'll be easy. Just going to follow the rest of what she had planned for me to do today."

"Don't be afraid to bail if you need to. Don't get in a bind for her."

Reaching over, I squeeze his arm. "I'm worried about you. What if things don't go the way you think they will when Ben goes to Foster's?"

Deacon gives me a big smile. "Don't worry about me. This is just regular Saturday-night work."

"That doesn't make me feel any better."

He leans closer. "Seriously, don't worry. He won't be expecting me. We're going to surprise him, take whatever he's got, and be on our way."

Serenity pulls up, which ends this discussion. I hop out of the car and meet her in front of Deacon's vehicle.

"All good?" I ask her.

"Yeah, all good." She gives me a hug and whispers, "Be safe and we'll see you back at the house."

I sit in the driver's seat of Camille's car and watch them pull away. Glancing at the clock, I calculate how much time until I meet up with Camille. It's four p.m. so I only have eight hours to go. Nothing more than a shift at the bar.

I put her car in drive and stop at the first boutique I come to. Time to spend some money.

CHAPTER 20

Camille

THE ALIBI
SATURDAY, OCTOBER 10

Margaret Everett.

My brother's wife.

Even in this small, grainy image, she's stunning, just as she's been since she started dating Silas in high school.

Is this the *meeting* he has planned before going to Foster's house? Why would he need to plan a meeting with her?

Ben gestures for her to enter. "Come on in. Would you like something to drink?"

"Sure, water, please."

I move around the attic quietly while I watch them. I've been up here several hours now and am feeling very restless. I expected to watch as someone brought Ben information, but so far it's been nothing like that. It's hard not to feel like I've been set up in some way. That Aubrey knew more about what was happening today than she was telling me and I'm some pawn in her game.

Instead of taking her to his office, he brings her to the kitchen. Ben takes his time going to the fridge and pulling out a small bottle of water, setting it on the island countertop, then he gestures at the stool closest to the corner. She sits as directed and unscrews the top, taking a small sip, while Ben moves back to the other side of the island so he's across from her.

"Thanks for seeing me." She's batting those eyes at him in the same way she's done to my brother. Why is she here?

"Of course, you know I'm always here for you." Ben's posture is casual but the tilt of his head and the line of his mouth tell me he isn't pleased about this visit.

My mind floods with memories of moments between them that I had shoved aside. Small touches that weren't exactly inappropriate but felt a bit too intimate. A look between them that feels like they share the same secrets. Nothing overtly sexual but a familiarity that shouldn't be there.

But Ben's body language now confuses me. "Silas sent you, didn't he." It's not a question.

She shakes her head, squeezing the bottle tight enough that water spills out. "No, he doesn't know I'm here."

He stares at her for a long moment. "At the fundraiser you said you needed to speak to me. In private. So what's going on?"

"I think Silas is about to do something drastic. He's freaking out. He knows you've been keeping tabs on Aubrey and he's convinced Foster sent her what he had before he died, and it's only a matter of time before you get it from her."

What.

Why do Margaret and Silas know anything about Aubrey?

And Foster's dead? When did he die?

No, no, no.

I don't like this.

I don't like that I seem to be the only person in my family that doesn't know what's going on.

Before Ben can say anything, Margaret adds, "He's got someone watching her too. Got some pictures of you talking to those two guys that live there and work on cars in the garage." She gestures in the general direction of the driveway. "Working on that car that's outside your house."

What in the hell is going on?

Shane and Eddie live in that house with Aubrey? When I did a little research after finding that bar napkin, I concentrated on the other woman who lives there. I thought Ben was cheating so I paid little attention to the guys there.

My mind is spinning so quickly I almost feel dizzy. And then I get pissed. So freaking pissed.

Ben's laugh fills the room. "Are you fucking kidding me. You go to all this trouble to tell me Silas is watching me?" He looks up at the ceiling, slowly shaking his head from side to side. "This is unbelievable. You've underestimated me if you think I'm not aware of everything your husband is doing."

"No, that's not why! We all should be working together. But y'all aren't and it's going to blow up in our faces if you don't."

Ben looks incredulous as he stalks around the counter so he's closer to her. "I tried that. Randall and Silas are forgetting the only reason they even know about this shit with Foster is because I told them after his file landed on Hank's desk."

Margaret laughs loudly. "Well, excuse me. I'm just trying to make sure no one does anything crazy, because it seems like all of y'all are losing your minds over this. They think you're going to use the evidence against them. That's what's got them worried. You just need to tell them you aren't!"

He takes another step forward, causing Margaret to lean back on her stool. "They should be worried. I guarantee you the first thing I will do is use it to extricate myself from underneath Randall Everett's thumb, where he's kept me pinned all these years!"

"You know this won't end well for you if you get it first. Neither of them will ever let you have power over them in any way."

His face comes closer to hers. I can see a vein popping in his forehead. "I didn't agree to cover for Silas that night he killed those people just so Randall fucking Everett could control the rest of my life."

Wait.

Wait, wait, wait.

What is he saying?

Ben was involved that night, right?

Ben.

Not Silas.

Silas wasn't even in Corbeau that summer. I backpacked through Europe and Silas worked on a cattle ranch in Texas.

It's why I never even considered Silas could have been involved in this.

Ben steps away from her, his hands shoved in his pockets; a weird calmness settles over him. "I would have never agreed to be his alibi if I had known it meant I'd be Randall's puppet all these years, no better than every other person who does his dirty work for him."

I feel sick. And confused.

Silas was the one who was driving Paul's truck that night?

And everyone in my family seems to know about it but me.

Rage starts deep in my belly and spreads through every limb. I'm shaking I'm so mad. And sad. And sick.

This is a nightmare.

Ben gives her a pointed look. "Why are you really here? This conversation could have been a phone call."

She turns toward him. "I told you, I'm worried about Silas. And I think he wants to tell Camille everything. It bothers him she doesn't know what happened or how involved you are with Randall. And you know how pissed she'd be."

He crosses his arms. He can be very intimidating when he wants to be. "I don't give a shit what he tells her. She'll bury her head in the sand like she's done her whole life. She loves to pretend she doesn't know where the money comes from, walking the moral high ground, as long as her lifestyle doesn't change. This is no different."

Sinking down on the floor, I have to cover my mouth to muffle the scream begging to be released.

Margaret paces around my kitchen in a tight circle while he watches. "Randall won't just sit back and wait to see what happens."

Ben slams his hand down on the counter and she jumps. "I'm done with Randall. Done with taking the cases he wants me to, just to keep his scumbag friends out of prison. Done with helping him line his pockets. It's time I line my own. And I'm not even starting down this path with Silas. This bullshit ends tonight. And the last thing I need is your fucking help to do it."

I fall back against the chair and try to catch my breath. I had no idea Ben has been so wrapped up in my dad's bullshit all these years. This is exactly what I didn't want. I never wanted to live like this. It's why I've been so hesitant to start a family, because I never wanted to bring a child into this dirty way of life.

There's a nervous quiver to her voice when she says, "You have a plan. I can tell. What are you going to do?"

Ben moves closer so there's very little space between them. His jaw clenches. I know that look. He's trying hard not to lose his temper. His hands encircle her wrists, holding her in place. "Did Silas send you here? You switch sides on me?"

Her head shakes back and forth. "No, he's at the farm! I swear, he didn't send me!" I can tell from her expression that his grip must be tighter than what's comfortable.

"We've known each other a long time, Margaret. Don't forget, I'm the keeper of the secrets."

Margaret pulls free from him and steps back. "I better go. He'll be expecting me soon."

My gut twists and my head throbs.

Bile starts up my throat. I rush to the bucket and throw up everything in my stomach until I'm dry heaving. Sweat breaks out all over my body and I feel clammy. It takes a while before I can crawl back to my chair.

By the time I pick the tablet back up, Margaret is gone and Ben is back in his office, working as if he doesn't have a care in the world while I'm in the attic feeling like mine just blew apart.

I'm so dumb. So, so dumb. On the phone earlier he said he had a couple of meetings before going to Foster's and my stomach drops thinking about who will show up next. I'm not sure I can handle learning anything else about Ben or my family.

His phone rings. "Yeah." He leans back in his chair while he listens to the caller. "Take a picture and send it to me."

The call ends. I can't see the phone screen from this angle but it seems like he's waiting for the image he requested to come through. It's obvious when he finally gets whatever it is because he sits up in his chair.

He stares at his phone for a long moment then taps on his screen, his movements a bit frantic. A few minutes later, he lifts the phone back to his ear. "I'm leaving the house now," he says as soon as his call connects, then ends it just as abruptly.

I don't know what's calling him away but I'm grateful because I need out of this attic and out of this house before I lose my mind. Before I do something I'll regret.

He packs up quickly, shutting down his laptop and grabbing his keys. Within minutes, I hear the telltale sounds of the garage door rising.

As soon as I hear it close again, I'm on the move. I exit the attic and run down the stairs to the first floor, straight into the kitchen, grabbing the camera. Then I sprint to his office to get the one there. Pulling the chair close, I stand on it so I can reach where I've hidden it in the bookshelf. I don't know what I'm going to do with the footage I have but I'm not leaving it behind, because there's a good chance I'm never stepping foot in this house again.

"You're not supposed to be here."

I scream and fall, landing on the floor next to the overturned chair.

And there's Ben, leaning against the wall, staring at the cameras on the ground next to me.

CHAPTER 21

Ben

TEN YEARS AGO

It takes a few minutes before the knocking wakes me up. I stumble from the bed, headed to my bedroom door, only to realize there's no one there. Did I dream that?

Knock, knock, knock. "Ben! Open up!"

It's coming from the window. I cross the room, still not fully awake, and pull back the curtains to see Margaret's face.

I throw the window open. "Are you bleeding?"

Her hand goes to her forehead as she wipes the blood away. "I guess a little." She turns and yanks Silas closer, all but shoving him through the window. "We need your help."

It takes a few minutes of me pulling and her pushing before we get him inside. He groans when he lands on the floor, a hand going to the spot on his forehead where he's also bleeding.

"What the hell happened to y'all?"

The call about Mom this afternoon was a shitty ending to an already shitty week, and the last thing I need at midnight on a Friday night is whatever shit Camille's little brother and his girlfriend have gotten into.

Margaret doesn't answer until she's crawled through and closes the window then the curtain. "It's bad, Ben." She finally looks at me. "Your house was the closest place I could think to go."

If they got into some trouble in this part of town, it's definitely not good.

Silas is in rough shape. He barely looks conscious and there's a steady stream of blood pouring from his forehead. His right knee is twice the size of the left one.

Silas seems to come to, his glassy eyes slowly taking in my room. "Where the fuck are we?" His voice sounds scratchy. I'm not surprised he doesn't recognize my room since he's never been here. Hell, Camille has only been here a few times even though we've been dating since senior year.

Margaret drops down beside him. "We're at Ben's house."

Silas seems to focus on Margaret. "We were in that truck."

She nods.

He tries to sit up but falls back against her. "Shit, my head hurts."

God, what a fuckup.

I pick up a towel off the floor and toss it to Margaret. "I'd rather he not bleed all over the carpet." I watch as she mops up his face.

These two are a disaster. Silas is the definition of an entitled asshole who knows money solves all problems and consequences don't apply to him. Daddy has always fixed everything and always will. Margaret is from my part of town, lives a couple of streets away, and latched on to Silas their junior year of high school and hasn't let go.

There are a lot of similarities between Margaret and me, and it's not lost on me that most people in this town lump us together when discussing the Everett kids' dating choices. It's clear Randall would prefer both his kids spent time with people he considered socially equal, but there's no one that fits that description in this town. The Everetts are in a class all their own.

There was a big push for Camille to keep her options open once she started college at Tulane. And it would have been easy to do since I went to LSU, but somehow we've managed to stay together. Although I'm not sure our relationship will survive the summer while she bounces through Europe. Her calls and texts are growing more and more infrequent.

Randall likes to ship both of his kids off for the summer. Silas is supposed to be working on some cattle ranch in Texas but he keeps sneaking back to town to see Margaret any chance he gets.

"Somebody tell me what happened!"

Silas looks at me, his face washed in confusion, then turns to Margaret. "We got in that truck." His memory seems to stop at that moment.

I pinch the bridge of my nose and force myself not to lose my shit on these two dumbasses. "I'm guessing y'all were in an accident?"

His hands go to his head and he grips his hair, groaning in pain. "Why were we in that truck?"

"How much did he drink? And what did he take?" I ask Margaret. "And whose truck were you in?" Silas drives a jacked-up Jeep, not a truck. Margaret doesn't have a car.

She ignores me, focusing on Silas. "You wanted to get food. Remember?"

He jerks his head up. "If I fucking remembered, would I ask you why we were in it?"

This takes the air right out of her.

"Okay, let's settle down," I say. "She's trying to help you, Silas. Don't be an asshole."

Margaret throws her hands up, defending him even though he doesn't deserve it. "It's okay, Ben. He's confused. And hurt."

I can't keep watching this without knowing what's going on. "Margaret, you can either tell me what happened or y'all can crawl right back out of my window and find somewhere else to go."

Silas turns to her as if he's as curious about the answer as I am.

"We were at Paul Granger's—"

I interrupt her and turn to Silas. "Your dad will lose his shit if he finds out you're hanging out at Paul's."

"Let her finish." And now he's taking up for her.

She glances at me then gives her full attention to Silas. "Everyone was there—Grant and Emily, Jack, Nathan and Sam. Partying. You wanted to stay behind when the others left to go to the gin."

The cotton gin is right outside of town, where high school kids hang out since there's nothing else to do here.

"Silas, aren't you supposed to be in Texas right now?"

He lies back on my floor, covering his face with the towel.

Big, fat tears fill Margaret's eyes. "I talked him into coming home for the weekend."

Margaret and Silas just graduated in May and they're in that weird summer where nothing has really changed but you know that change is coming since college is only a handful of weeks away. There's an itch that you can't scratch. A want for something but not knowing what it is, which usually leads to stupid behavior. My friends and I used to hang out at

Paul's too, but we've moved on. Silas's group is just getting started over there, though.

"Why didn't y'all leave with everyone else?" I ask her.

"He got hungry but his Jeep wasn't there. Paul was passed out so we took his truck." Her voice is high and shrill.

Silas shuffles around on the floor, trying to find a comfortable position for that bum knee while still holding the towel to his forehead. "I remember being at Paul's. Remember talking about getting food. Everything's blurry after that." He's slurring his words and I'm not sure he'll remember this conversation in the morning, much less the wreck. "You shouldn't have let me drive."

Margaret lets out a huge sob.

"So y'all take his truck to get food and have a wreck."

Again, both of us look to her for confirmation. "Yeah. There was a car. It was just there all of a sudden."

"Where was this? Was anyone hurt?" I ask, terrified to hear the answer.

She shrugs and tears spill from her eyes. "On Maple. We got out of Paul's truck and just started running." That's only a few streets over from here.

Silas throws the towel down. "Fuck!" Then he slams one hand into the carpet over and over. "Fuck!"

"Keep it down, you're going to wake my mom." My mom is passed out in her room, and even though I don't think a bomb going off would wake her, Silas needs to lower his voice.

I pull my phone out of my back pocket. "Silas, I'm calling your dad."

His head pops up. "What? No! Why would you call him?" He genuinely looks scared.

"Because this is more than I can handle! You stole someone's truck and hit another car then left the scene. And he may be pissed when he finds out but we both know he's the only one who can fix this shit for you."

Silas slumps, but it's clear he knows I'm right. "Where's your bathroom?"

"Across the hall."

Margaret helps him up and tries to walk there but he shakes her off. "I don't need your help taking a piss."

She steps away and he nearly falls on his ass but catches himself on the end of my bed. If this wasn't so tragic, it would be comical.

Silas stumbles his way out of my room while Margaret sinks back down on the floor. "Don't tell Mr. Everett I'm here. That I was with him." Her voice is small. Broken. "He already hates me. He wants Silas to break up with me."

In that moment, I begrudgingly acknowledge a camaraderie with her. We're both fighting tooth and nail to remain in our relationships against the wishes of Randall Everett.

"Get out of here. Go home. I won't mention you were here but I can't promise Silas won't."

"He won't. He knows how his dad will react. Silas loves me."

It's hard not to roll my eyes. Pretty sure Silas only loves himself, and it will be a miracle if they're still together a month after fall semester starts.

Silas looks marginally better when he stumbles back in my room since he washed the blood off his face, although his shirt is still stained with it.

Margaret pops up from the floor and launches herself at him, almost knocking them both over. "Ben said I should leave before your dad gets here since we know how he'll be. Call me later when you can talk."

He nods and she steps away as if parting from him is painful. His expression does not mirror hers.

"You can use the front door," I tell her.

Once she's gone, Silas sinks down on my bed, then falls back. "Call him and let's get this over with."

This won't be swept away as easily as everything else has been. This is just the beginning.

I hesitate just a second or so before I tap on Mr. Everett's number. It's late but I know he'll answer.

"Ben, is there a problem?" His voice is gruff, like I've woken him up.

"Yes, sir. Silas is here at my house. There's been an accident."

"Put him on the phone."

I hold the phone to him. "Hey, Dad. I fucked up."

His head hangs low as he speaks quietly into the phone, repeating everything we both just learned from Margaret. And just as she predicted, he doesn't mention her involvement. Then he listens to whatever his dad is saying.

When he ends the call, we sit in silence for a long moment.

"He's on his way over," Silas finally says. "Can I get some coffee?"

The adrenaline from the accident and running here probably cleared his head some, but it's obvious he's not sober and I'm assuming he wants to be before his dad gets here.

"Sure, give me a minute."

I head to the kitchen. Our coffeepot is old, but it still manages to make a decent cup. I bring back two, one for me and one for him since it feels like this is going to be a long night. I pass him his along with a couple of painkillers. "Here, take these too."

He gets up and limps around the room, sipping from his mug, as if even in his drunken state he knows he needs to be prepared for what's coming.

"Are you injured anywhere other than your forehead and knee?" The last thing I need is Randall Everett's only son dying in my room from some internal bleeding I can't see.

"Hell, I don't know. I hurt everywhere."

It will take at least twenty minutes for Mr. Everett to get here and that's only if he doesn't take time to get dressed.

Silas puts his empty mug on my bedside table and lies back down on my bed. "I'm never getting out of Corbeau now."

I'm in my desk chair so I swivel around when he says this. "What do you mean?"

"I fucked up. Dad's gonna fix it. And then he'll hold it over me forever." His words are so quiet I almost don't hear them. And then he passes out.

While he sleeps it off, I pace my room. The longer it takes for Mr. Everett to get here, the more nervous I get.

Finally, my phone beeps with a text, alerting me he's outside. I walk to the bed, and it takes me forcing Silas into a sitting position to wake him up.

"Your dad's here."

Silas follows me into the hall, steadier than he was when he got here but still not clearheaded.

Randall is waiting for us on my small front porch. The lights are off but there's enough moonlight to just make out his features. He stares at us both, and for some reason it feels like I'm in trouble too.

Mr. Everett scans the front of my house, and I try to picture it through his eyes. He's known where I've lived since I started dating Camille, but he's never been here before. It's a far cry from their house right outside of town. The first time I saw their place was on a field trip in eighth grade, when our social studies class was studying Louisiana history. The Everetts gave our class a tour of their farm and explained how sugarcane grows and is harvested. Their house was the biggest one I'd ever seen.

I know he hates that I'm witnessing this, knowing he'll fix it. Because if there's one thing I'm a hundred percent sure of, it's that he will fix this.

He steps closer to Silas and grabs his chin, tilting his head back to get a better look at him. "Do you need stitches?"

"No, sir." The sharp tone and attitude he had with Margaret are long gone.

"His knee may need to be looked at."

Mr. Everett doesn't spare me a glance as he inspects Silas further.

"What a fucking mess," he mutters. He steps back, the disgust on his face clear. "Who else is aware of what happened tonight other than you and Ben?"

I wait for Silas to say Margaret's name. He hesitates long enough to make me think he won't tell him about her involvement but he eventually comes clean. "Margaret was with me. Helped me get here. Honestly, without her, I'd still be sitting in that truck."

"If it wasn't for Margaret, you would be in Texas working and not hanging out with low-life drug dealers."

Silas doesn't say anything else, just stares at the ground.

"Is Paul Granger aware you took his truck out for a joyride?"

"I don't think so. He passed out before we left."

When he realizes he isn't getting anything else out of Silas, Mr. Everett turns to me. "I'm sure you're smart enough to figure out what we need from you but I'll explain it so we're clear. This is going to be a fucking disaster to clean up. So this is what happened tonight. Silas chose not to go with everyone else to the gin because he had already made plans with you. You came and picked Silas and Margaret up from Paul's shortly after everyone else left. Once they were in your car, you dropped Margaret off at her house." He pauses a second, looking at Silas. "I'm assuming that's where she ran off to once she heard I was on the way here."

"Yes, sir." I barely recognize this meek version of Silas.

Mr. Everett turns his attention back to me. "After you dropped Margaret off, you and Silas went to our condo in Baton Rouge, where you both stayed the rest of the weekend. As you had originally planned. And if anyone comes asking, that's exactly what you'll say."

I'm not sure what I was expecting but it wasn't this. "You want me to be his alibi."

"Do you love my daughter?"

His question is so surprising, I take a step back. "You know I do."

"That makes you family." By the way he flinches at his own words, I'm assuming they were painful to say. "Family helps each other out. Family protects family. Family makes sure family succeeds in life." He pauses for effect. "If there was ever a moment where the ball is in your court, it's this moment right now. You'll never get an offer like the one I'm giving you again."

He knows how enticing this is. If I cover for Silas, he won't stand in the way of our relationship.

But he's not finished. "And there's the matter of what happened this afternoon."

My mom.

She hasn't been the same since my dad died last year. I got a call from her earlier this afternoon while I was at work. She was drunk and crying and rambling on about how we were about to lose everything. The house, her job, her car. I knew she was struggling emotionally and financially, but I didn't know it had gotten that bad. And there isn't much I can do for her until I graduate, since I'm barely getting by on my own. Scholarships, student loans, and a summer job are the only way I'll able to go back to school this fall.

The second call I got this afternoon was from the president of the local bank. Apparently Mom had gone up there to beg them to give her more time to pay the mortgage and car note. From what it sounded like, she made a scene. I told him I would come and look into it, which I planned to do on my lunch break on Monday. I shouldn't have been surprised he called Mr. Everett after getting off the phone with me. He wouldn't have missed this opportunity to tell him about my family's situation, since I'm dating his daughter.

"How is your mother now? I heard she had a rough afternoon."

This shouldn't feel as humiliating as it does. She's a grieving woman. I have to clear the emotion from my throat to answer. "She's resting."

She actually passed out before I got home. Slumped over on the couch with an empty vodka bottle next to her. I got her in bed without her waking up.

"Another benefit of being a part of a family . . . my family . . . is we make sure everyone we care about is taken care of. And since you obviously care about your mother, so do I, which is why I'll make sure she gets the help she needs and ensure the bank understands a little leniency and forgiveness are called for in tough times like these."

Shit. He knows he's got me now. Because agreeing not to stand between Camille and me doesn't mean Camille and I are guaranteed to stay together. But offering to help Mom is a game changer. She needs help with the depression plaguing her, driving her to drink. She needs financial help. All the things I can't give her.

"Ben, am I right to consider you a part of our family?"

I hesitate only a second before saying, "Yes, sir, I would be honored to be a part of your family."

Mr. Everett's face relaxes for the first time since he got here. Silas is staring at me, though, seemingly shocked I've agreed to his dad's plan.

Mr. Everett extends his hand and we shake. I can't help but feel I just made a deal with the devil.

"I expect the two of you on the road to Baton Rouge within the next ten minutes. Do not stop on the way. Not anywhere. I will call to check in tomorrow."

"What about Margaret?" Silas asks.

"I will speak with her personally."

I can tell there's more Silas wants to say but doesn't.

"And none of us will mention this to anyone." His gaze focuses on me. "Even Camille. Do you understand? We cherish the women in our family. Make sure they never have to worry about the things we do to protect one another."

"Yes, sir," we both mumble.

Mr. Everett turns to walk away but he stops when Silas asks, "Do you know if anyone else was hurt in the accident?"

The look Mr. Everett gives him sends chills down my spine. "What accident?" And then he's walking away.

Just before I turn to go back inside to get my things so we can get on the road, Silas says softly, "You have no idea what you've just agreed to."

CHAPTER 22

Hank

AFTER THE ALIBI
TUESDAY, OCTOBER 13

Pete Sanders's visit has left me with a simmering rage that is threatening to boil over. It's been three days since Ben's body was discovered and it feels like everything I've worked so hard for is crumbling around me.

One of our paralegals, Scott, is by far the best researcher I've ever come across. He can find a needle in a haystack in record time. So I've pulled him from his cubicle and set him up at the table in my office.

I'm done with playing catch-up.

We've been working for a couple of hours and he's already pulled all the information on Paul Granger's case, including the transcript from his trial, as well as information on Aubrey Price and the two guys who own the business that restored the Mustang, Shane Phillips and Eddie Reynolds.

Shane and Eddie have worked as mechanics in various repair shops throughout town over the last decade. They started a restoration business for old muscle cars not long after moving to the house they share with Aubrey Price. A recent social media post showed them celebrating an anniversary, so they are a couple as well as business partners. Shane was popped for auto theft when he was twenty and served a six-month sentence. Eddie has either never broken the law or never gotten caught.

At this point I'm not even surprised at the way they are all connected.

Now we're getting into the weeds of Paul's case. When I looked at it the first time, I read through the summary the pro bono group made and that was all I needed to see to believe I had a good chance of winning an appeal on his case. There was a lack of forensic evidence and no eyewitnesses who saw Paul drive his truck that night. The prosecutor argued the kids who had been partying at Paul's had left an hour before the accident, which also meant none of them were there to see Paul leave his house behind the wheel. It seems like the moment the police identified the owner of the truck as Paul Granger, there was no reason to assume he wasn't the driver. It's half-assed and lazy work but also sort of expected from a department that has little to no experience with processing scenes like this.

But now we're digging in.

"Scott, pull up the arrest records and give me a rundown."

Scott taps away. "Paul Joseph Granger. White male, age thirty. Arrested at his home at 742 Oak Street, Corbeau, Louisiana, on July eighth, 2016, at seven twelve a.m. Arrest made by Kevin Foster." A few more clicks. "Foster was also first at the scene of the accident on Maple. Report says he arrived at one thirty a.m. He's also the one who collected all the witness statements."

I flip through the pages in the files Ben had in his home office. "There were over two dozen people at his house that night. One cop took all those statements?"

Tap, tap, tap. "Huh."

Scott's confusion has me turning to him. "What?"

"Kevin Foster was the chief of police for Corbeau for the last thirty years."

I get out of my chair and come stand behind him so I can see what he's seeing. "You're telling me the chief of police was the first on the scene in the middle of the night."

Scott shrugs. "That's what the report says."

There's a niggling feeling in my brain that I can't quite pinpoint. "Did someone call 911 about the accident? How was the accident discovered?"

"No mention of a 911 call coming in. Doesn't mean there wasn't one. All it says is what time Foster arrived there."

Looking at this as if I were Paul Granger's defense attorney, Kevin Foster would be the first person I tried to discredit. I would pull apart every witness statement he collected, looking to see if he potentially influenced the memories of the witnesses or collected the information incorrectly. Since he was also one of the first responders, I would try to determine if he mishandled any evidence or didn't follow the correct procedure in collecting it.

"You said he was the chief of police? Is he not anymore?"

"No. Retired a few months ago."

Scott is switching screens too fast for me to read what's popping up before it's gone again. "Oh, wait. He's dead."

This has me straightening up. "Dead? When?"

Within a few seconds, Scott has his obituary pulled up. "September first. Pancreatic cancer. Hold on. His Facebook account is still up and wide open."

I watch as Scott pulls up an old post. "Diagnosed in December last year."

We both read the entry where he details how he found out and what his prognosis is. We scroll down and see pictures of him in the hospital getting treatments, as well as links to a GoFundMe drive and a MealTrain sign-up.

Scott pulls up a picture of him from May in a fishing boat. He's almost not recognizable as the person in the earlier images.

"Man, he looks like he's aged ten years," Scott says, and I have to agree.

There's a long post with the image sharing that his cancer had spread. He had made the decision not to seek further treatment and instead enjoy his last days as much as he could. This must have been right before he decided to retire.

Scott continues to scroll through his feed, then stops on a graphic Foster posted in late May. It's an image of Jesus in front of the pearly gates. "And here it is. He found God. Knew that was coming."

"Sure you did," I say as I read some of the comments.

"Seriously, my grandpa did this too. They found he had like eighty percent blockage in one of his arteries, and next thing I know he's at daily Mass with my grandma even though he hadn't attended in years. The docs put some stents in and told him he was going to live and he hasn't been back to church since."

After that first image of Jesus, Foster starts reposting nothing but religious content about salvation and Heaven and repenting for your sins and begging for forgiveness.

"Yeah, he's freaking out about dying and going to hell. Wonder how many skeletons were hiding in his closet?" Scott asks.

"Yeah, it's a bit dark," I say, reading a long, rambling post that he was going to "leave this world with a clean slate and pure heart."

"Okay, let's move on since we're not going to get anywhere with Foster. Who was the public defender assigned to Paul?"

Foster's social media page disappears and we're back to the court documents. After a few minutes, Scott says, "A guy named Mike Knox, but he's not practicing anymore. Moved to New Orleans about five years ago."

"And the judge on the case?"

Click, click, click.

"Judge Landis. Retired."

I straighten up and move back to the other end of the table. "Will you go through the witness statements and make me a list of everyone the police talked to and a list of everyone who was partying at Paul's that night?"

Scott nods. "On it."

I dig through the file Ben had on Aubrey Price and Paul Granger again. I can't help but feel like I'm missing something.

Rereading one of Ben's notes stops me cold: *Chief—Angola June 6th.*

Chief.

Kevin Foster was the chief of police in Corbeau.

Every single file that Ben kept at home or in his briefcase makes some sort of reference to this name. The same files that detail the type of behavior that would cost him his license. I've been trying to figure out who was helping Ben, and Kevin Foster has jumped to the top of my list.

But why would Ben make note in Paul's file about Foster going to Angola?

I think back to Foster's social media posts and Scott's comment about Foster "freaking out about dying and going to hell." Did Foster's visit have anything to do with repenting for his sins and asking for forgiveness? Asking Paul for forgiveness?

When I look at the rest of the notes in the file on Aubrey, I do it through the lens that "Chief" is Foster, and they take on a whole different meaning.

And then I glance at the dozen other files Ben kept at home, duplicates that show he had help tampering with evidence and intimidating witnesses. All of that help referred back to "Chief."

Foster was in Corbeau, so it makes sense he could have covered up a crime there, but he wouldn't have that kind of pull in Baton Rouge. So how was he helping Ben with his cases here?

I pull Pete Sanders's file back open, skimming until I find the list of names Ben had started down the edge of one page next to a particularly graphic entry about one of the people who came forward as a witness against Pete. "Chief" is at the top and then an arrow to a dozen other names, some I recognize and some I don't. All of them have been scratched out.

The names I know are all locals in a variety of positions—other lawyers, a judge, a couple of PIs, and a handful of guys the DA's office has been trying to take down for years for various criminal offenses.

I read back through the list three times before it hits me.

Once Foster retired and found religion, I'm guessing he wouldn't have been the help he once was. So Ben was trying to figure out who Foster turned to when he needed something done outside of Corbeau.

I go back to the file on Aubrey. *Chief—Angola June 6th.*

What if Paul Granger wasn't the only person Foster felt like he needed to ask for forgiveness?

How many people scattered throughout these files would be scrambling to save their own asses if Foster was repenting for his sins and the truth came out?

How big a problem would it have been for Ben?

Huge.

Career ending.

But would it be life ending? Could this be the reason Ben was killed?

There's a piece I'm still missing, but now my internal list of who could have killed Ben and why narrows to the group of files on this table.

"Scott, any way you can see who Foster's biggest campaign donor was?" I'm pretty sure I know the answer to this but I'm not making any assumptions.

"Sure, give me a minute."

I read back through some of the other files, making note of every time "Chief" is mentioned while I wait for Scott to get that info.

"Okay, so Foster ran unopposed for his last three elections but he still took in campaign donations." He leans close to the screen. "Oh, wow. For a police chief seat in a town the size of Corbeau, he had some pretty big donations."

Oh, I bet he did.

Scott sits back and looks at me, a concerned look on his face.

"Whatever you found, it's okay. Just tell me."

He nods and looks back at the screen. "Biggest donor is Randall Everett. And the next below him was Mr. Bayliss."

CHAPTER 23

Camille

THE ALIBI
SATURDAY, OCTOBER 10

"You're not supposed to be here."

Ben pushes away from the wall he was leaning against and moves closer. I'm still on the ground so I scramble back until I bump into the bookcase. The overturned chair is still on the floor between us.

He stops suddenly. "Obviously, we have a problem."

It's not a question so I don't answer him.

"Get off the floor." He offers me his hand and I hesitate taking it. He doesn't move, just stands there with it outstretched, waiting for me to allow him to help me up. I'm back on my feet within seconds and pulling my hand from his just as quickly.

"I was going to call and tell you I was coming home. I just started feeling sick and wanted my own bed." My mind is spinning.

He cocks his head to the side and arches one brow. He pulls out his phone and turns the screen toward me. "Then who is shopping in St. Francisville using your credit card and driving your car while in possession of your phone?"

It's Aubrey in the wig. She's standing in front of a register, holding a framed print of pressed fern leaves. The image is mostly from behind but you get a bit of profile in the picture. Someone who didn't know me so well might believe it was me, but it would be obvious to Ben that it's not. I'm not telling him anything. He would lose his shit if he knew it was Aubrey.

"Honestly, I was a little stumped when I got this picture. If your phone and car were in St. Francisville, where the hell were you? Then I checked the location of your other devices," he says, nodding to the iPad clutched under my arm. "Imagine my surprise when that little blue dot popped up here."

I don't say anything. Just stand there, frozen. I didn't think he could track that.

I'm dumb. So, so dumb.

Ben bends down and picks up the cameras I dropped when I fell off the chair. "What are these?"

I start shaking. Ben has never been physically abusive but I'm terrified about what he's going to do to me when he finds out what I've gotten on record today.

His expression changes when he realizes what they are. "How many more are in the house right now?"

"A . . . a couple more."

His brow creases. "Show me each and every one."

Ben follows closely behind me while I move to the front door. I don't dare look at him when I pull the small camera out of the potted plant on the front porch, giving me a clear view of the driveway.

"What the fuck, Camille!"

I turn around and hold the camera out to him. He snatches it out of my palm. "Did these upload to the cloud?"

Shaking my head, I say, "No. Just an internal memory card."

He moves to the kitchen and grabs one of those cooler bags he uses for drinks when he plays golf, shoving all three cameras inside. "Where are the rest?"

It's deathly quiet as we go from room to room collecting cameras. I don't know why I'm giving myself up like this other than the fear of what would happen if he found them on his own.

"This it?" He shakes the now full bag in front of me, making the cameras rattle as they bounce off one another.

He throws the bag on the counter and points to the stool where Margaret was sitting just half an hour ago. "I'm not sitting there." I move to the small kitchen table and drop down in the nearest chair.

He opens the back of each camera and pulls out the memory cards. They're tiny, smaller than my thumbnail, and I watch as he moves to the kitchen sink and turns on the faucet, throwing the cards in so they'll wash down the drain. Then he turns on the garbage disposal for good measure. The sound of grinding metal fills the room.

He finally joins me, sitting in the chair next to me. He looks calm, but it's deceiving. Under that facade, he's boiling right now. "You've gone to great effort to make sure I wasn't aware you were in the house. That I wouldn't know you were filming me. Why?"

I'm not going to let him turn this on me. I may be terrified but I'm also pissed, so I dig into that feeling. Let that emotion rise to the surface. "You've gone to great effort to make sure I thought you were still in New Orleans. Why?"

He leans closer, leaving only a few inches between us. His mouth twists into a smile. "I like seeing you mad at me right now. Better than the pouty brat you've been lately."

What the hell? Does he think this is some game?

"I have no idea what you're talking about."

He gets up and leans over me. His hands are on the arms of my chair, caging me in. "Sure you do. You've been extremely difficult to live with the last few months. Moody. Lashing out at me then giving me the silent treatment. So tell me. What could you possibly have to be pissed off about? Say what you want to say. I know it's been killing you."

I shove his chest, causing him to rock back slightly, but he stays in place. He's goading me, putting me on the defensive, pushing all my buttons. He wants to know what I know. What I heard. What I learned today and what I came in knowing. And for some reason I can't stop myself from reacting the exact way he wants me to. "Was I included in the deal you made with Dad to cover for Silas? In exchange for an alibi, were you guaranteed a wife?"

His face drops and he takes a step back. "You have no idea what I've done for your family. For your brother. I've done everything they've wanted me to for years." He holds his hands out wide. "I've made sure you've had a charmed life and you repay me by creeping around the house, spying on me."

I stand up from the chair, sending it sliding backward until it hits the wall. "It seems more like my father is the one who has made sure *you've* led a charmed life. It's clear you would never have been this successful without his help."

We stare at each other. He presses his lips together as if he's trying to hold his words in. Finally, he asks, "Why are you here, spying on me? You've been blissfully unaware for fucking years. Happy to take what is given to you and keep your head buried in the sand. So what changed?"

It's the second time he's said that about me. "Keep my head buried in the sand?" A ragged cry escapes me before I can stop it. "I knew you were up to something. I just didn't know what it was." I'm not ready for him to know Aubrey is involved because I'm not sure how he will react to that. I'm just praying he doesn't recognize her in that picture he just showed me.

He lets out a shocked bark of laughter. "Holy shit. All this because you thought I was 'up to something.' How fucking ridiculous. And what were you going to do? Divorce me? Because that's not happening."

"You can't stop me from divorcing you! I don't care what dirty work you've done for my dad or Silas! I've learned enough to know I don't want to be married to you anymore."

He shakes his head and softens his features. "What do you think you learned today? You heard Margaret and me talk about something that happened a decade ago. That I did what your father asked to protect your brother. And will you tell someone what I did? Will you tell them what Silas did?" I flinch at his words. "You can leave me but you'll be leaving with a lot less than you came to this marriage with, thanks to the prenup you signed. And I can guarantee you, your dad will be on my side of this instead of yours, since I'm one of the only people who could send his prodigal son to prison."

I'm shaking when he takes a step forward. His right hand takes my left. "And where are you going to go, Camille? Back home to Corbeau? All I'm trying to do is to get out from under your dad. Same thing I've been trying to do for years. Just like we talked about. You assumed the worst of me so everything you saw and heard was twisted in a way to make it true. We still want the same things. For your dad to be out of our lives. That's all I'm trying to do."

I'm starting to doubt myself, but I try to remember he's a master at this. "No, you're twisting this around."

"I'm not twisting anything. You assigned your own thoughts and feelings to my actions. You made it about you, not me."

What is happening? He's trying to make me feel guilty and it's seriously working.

I don't know what to believe, and that's the worst part.

He moves another step closer. "I've already put plans in place that will change everything. Free us both from the noose your dad put around my neck all those years ago. We can figure this out. Find a way to make things work again. I know how much you don't want people talking about you. About us. About your family. You just need to trust me like you used to. Trust me like I trust you. It kills me your faith in me has fallen so low. All I've ever wanted was to take care of you. To give you the life you deserve."

He's turning this on me, making me the bad guy.

Am I the bad guy?

I realize I'm letting him control this conversation like I always do. He's good at working people . . . his clients, the jury, anyone he encounters.

"I'm leaving." I start moving to the kitchen door.

He's one step behind me. "Who is helping you? Who is this woman?"

I spin around and see that he's got that picture back up on his phone. "Who sent you that picture? What were you trying to catch me doing?"

His face turns red. He absolutely hates that I spied on him. That I know everything he did here today but he doesn't know what I did, who I've got helping me. I'm sure his mind is racing as it goes through the day minute by minute so he can determine just how much I know.

Ben stares at the picture then glances back in the direction of his office then to me. I start for the door again but he grabs my arm. He's pulling me out of the kitchen and across the foyer until we're back in his office. We're beside his desk, where I see a picture of Aubrey Price in the open file. He lets go of me so he can pick up the image of her. When he's got both pictures side by side, it's clear who is helping me today.

"You've got to be fucking kidding me." His eyes bore into me. "Of all people, why is Aubrey Price pretending to be you?"

Oh shit. The vein in his forehead is bulging.

I don't answer. I don't open my mouth.

"You have no idea what you've done." He flings both the printed picture and his phone on his desk. "This shit is on you now." Ben takes a step away. He's backing away from me. "You can answer to your dad about why you pulled her into this."

And this scares me more than anything else.

I don't waste time trying to figure out what he means, I bolt for the door and run back to where the Honda is parked.

Once I'm inside the car, I let out a scream. My hands are shaking and I feel like I'm going to throw up again. Tears are streaming down my face.

What have I done?

I grab the plastic bag from the back seat and pull out the prepaid phone

I bought from Target, powering it on. I figured there might be a time I'd need a phone and wouldn't have one since Aubrey would have mine. I make a call I don't really want to make, but I don't feel like I have any other choice. My brother answers on the second ring.

"Hello."

"Si, it's me. Cam."

He hesitates a moment then says, "Whose number is this?"

"It's one of those prepaid phones." My voice cracks. "I'm in trouble and I don't know what to do."

"You did the right thing. You called your family. What's going on?"

A sob escapes me and it takes a few seconds before I can find my voice. "It's Ben. He caught me spying on him and he freaked out."

"Tell me everything."

So I do.

CHAPTER 24

Hank

AFTER THE ALIBI
TUESDAY, OCTOBER 13

I make it to the church for the Rosary for Ben with a few minutes to spare.

It would be easier to just slide into one of the pews in the back, but I know I need to be up front, close to the family. There are more people here than I expected, and my steps echo as I make the long walk down the center aisle. It wouldn't surprise me if half the people attending this are here for the gossip and to get a close-up look at the recently widowed Camille Bayliss.

I spot her in the first row, flanked by Ben's family on one side and hers on the other.

A hand flies up from the third row and I see Lila there, waving me down. "Saved you a seat," she says to me. I slide in past a few guys I know Ben played golf with so I can sit next to her. Tricia and the rest of our employees are scattered throughout the pews behind us.

"You're almost late," she says in my ear.

"Almost doesn't count," I reply back.

She hands me her phone with the Notes app open. "Here's what you've got going on tomorrow."

I skim the list, prepared for any other bombs that are ready to explode. There's the formal interview with Camille and Detective Sullivan, then an appointment with Judge Whittaker. He wants to talk about Ben's trial that was supposed to start tomorrow. Apparently it had already been postponed three times and the judge wants a new date set immediately.

I finish reading the rest of it then give Lila her phone back. "Can you send that to me?"

"I already shared it with you in a text. Just open it up and accept it. I'll update it as needed and you can add notes back to me. Figured this may be easier since your phone hasn't stopped."

She's right. I'm buried in notifications.

When Lila first started working for me, I was a little worried about the dynamics. She was young and attractive, and it didn't take long before I was depending on her for just about everything since she did such a damn good job of keeping me on task. We're a good team, but thankfully there was absolutely no spark or chemistry between us. In fact, most days I feel like she could have outdone my mother with the mothering.

"Thanks, Lila," I whisper. "For everything."

She nudges me with her elbow. "Don't make me cry. I just redid my makeup."

The priest enters from the sacristy and walks to the pulpit. The murmurs die down as he adjusts the mic.

"Good evening, everyone. I know I speak for the entire Bayliss family when I say it means so much that you all are here to pray for Benjamin." His words echo through the sanctuary. "His wife, Camille, and his mom, Suzanne, as well as the rest of the family, are comforted by the outpouring of love and support they have received. Before we get started, I just want to say that Benjamin was a special person. No matter how busy he was, I always knew I could count on him if we, here at the cathedral, needed anything. Whether it was serving on the church board or providing members of the congregation legal help when they needed it but didn't have the funds to pay him. He will be missed by many, and I, for one, am close to the top of that list."

He makes the sign of the cross and begins praying the Rosary. Even though his voice is projected through the space by the speakers set in the rafters, he's almost drowned out by the swell of the crowd praying aloud with him.

I'm Catholic, but not a particularly good one. My mom is probably rolling over in her grave knowing Mass on Christmas and Easter are about the only two I manage to make. But no matter how long it's been, I know all the prayers without having to think about it. I sit back and let the words being spoken swirl around me, adding my voice to the others. By the time they hit the third Hail Mary, the cadence of the prayers becomes almost hypnotic, the same words being repeated over and over in a somber rhythm.

The setting sun bathes the room in red and green and yellow as it filters through the stained glass windows. The tall stone walls manage to keep the interior of the church cool. Refreshing. It feels like an oasis from the heat and humidity still plaguing the city this deep into fall.

The priest's words replay in my mind against the backdrop of the murmured prayers. It's obvious when a person doesn't really know the deceased, just relies on the information passed along by the family, but that's not the case here. This priest knew Ben well since he was a much better Catholic than I ever thought of being. What Father said about him was true but also exaggerated. We found half a dozen active cases that were flagged with a reference back to this very church, but Ben wasn't handling them for free. In all of them, there's a trade. In exchange for legal services, Ben received things like a full year of lawn-care service, two new sets of tires, and free haircuts. That poor woman would have had to cut his hair for a decade for them to be even.

Ben rarely did anything for free.

Being this close, it's easy to watch Ben's family sitting just two rows ahead of me. Suzanne, Ben's mother, started sobbing the moment the priest said his name and shows no signs of stopping. Ben's dad died when he was in college, and his mom remarried a man named William Lynch just after Ben graduated law school. I think Ben liked William although he never really spoke about his family.

It's hard to get a good look at Camille. Her head is tilted forward, her face mostly hidden behind her long hair. She's also wearing big black sunglasses. I don't have to see her face to know she's tense, though. It's obvious with the set of her shoulders and the effort to make herself as small as possible. There's a good six inches of empty space on either side of her despite how overcrowded the pew is. The crushed tissue in her fist is used to wipe the fresh tears away at the beginning of each new prayer.

Camille.

I've had my share of guilty clients, and if I'm really honest with myself, I've suspected they did what they were accused of within minutes of meeting them. I think back to the second I saw her sitting on the front steps, and I would have bet every dollar in my bank account that her utter shock at finding Ben dead inside that huge house she shared with him was genuine.

The most honest reaction you can get from someone is in the first couple of seconds of them hearing new information, good or bad. No time to digest it, no time to school their reaction. It's either shocking or it's not. It's why most detectives break the news of a death to a potential suspect in person.

If only I could have seen *her* initial reaction when she discovered Ben's body, but all I have to go off is what she shows me now.

We say our last prayer, then the priest tucks his rosary back into the hidden pocket in his robes before clearing his throat as if he's trying to find his normal voice after speaking so long in that monotonous tone.

"Again, thank you for gathering here today to pray for Benjamin. The family and I invite you to the parish hall for a light refreshment."

Father steps down from the pulpit and genuflects in front of the altar before moving to the front row where the family sits. He leans closer, speaking to them quietly, then the front row stands and follows Father into the aisle and toward the back of the church.

As soon as they pass, everyone makes their way to the parish hall. By the time I get there, the receiving line to speak with the family stretches through the room and out the door, probably weaving through the parking lot.

I debate leaving and heading back to work, but the entire office is here and it would look shitty if I bailed.

Suzanne and William are the first to greet people as they come through the door, then Camille, with Ben's older sister and brother-in-law on her other side.

And then there's Camille's family. Her parents, Randall and Marie, and Silas and Margaret. Camille steps away when she sees me, giving me a quick hug, then her mom is pulling her back to introduce her to someone in the line. Randall gives me a firm nod, which I return. I've got no desire to speak with him again.

I drag a chair behind the receiving line, where I'm mostly hidden, and wait for this to end.

Even though Ben and Camille are from the same small town, their families couldn't be more different.

Ben's mom works as an aide in the small hospital there and his stepdad sells insurance. They live modestly in the same house Ben and his sister grew up in. A far cry from the behemoth of the house Ben and Camille restored. While William and Suzanne live a simple life, Ben seemed to strive to emulate the lifestyle Camille grew up with.

Most people here are friends and acquaintances of Ben's and Camille's from Baton Rouge, but there are a fair number from Corbeau. Based on the snippets of conversation I hear as people pass along the line, the people here from their hometown are in two very distinct categories—those who are connected to Ben's side and those who are connected to Camille's.

It's interesting to see the differences and hard to ignore the lack of crossover between the two groups.

And then there's the group of past and current clients, who have to introduce themselves to everyone. I've been studying Ben's calendar and files for the past two days, making it easy to recognize their names. They are quickly passed from family member to family member since no one really wants to talk to a bunch of alleged criminals.

But the most fascinating thing to watch is Margaret Everett try again and again to tend to Camille, while Camille actively rebuffs her every time. Margaret has offered to get Camille something to drink, something to eat, suggested she take a break, and even tried to stand next to her at one point, until Camille moved nearer to Ben's sister, making her the buffer between them.

There is obviously a problem between the two of them. Camille's parents seem oblivious to this, but Silas is dialed in and watching every interaction. It's also interesting that Margaret is matching Camille tear for tear.

My ass has gone numb in this metal chair, but there are enough of our clients still here helping themselves to free punch and cake that I'm staying in my hiding spot. Add *What about my case?* conversations to the list of those I'm trying to avoid. Hopefully, we're almost at the end of this line and I can get out of here.

About thirty minutes in, Camille turns and looks at me. I wasn't sure she was aware I was back here but it's clear she was. She's throwing me what I assume is a pleading look before turning back to the woman in front of her. I take it as a cry for help since the line still stretches out of the door. I think back on our phone call yesterday; it looks like she's had all the condolences she can take.

I stand and come up behind her, making sure to speak loud enough that the other family members hear me. "Hey, I'm sorry to pull you away, but a few of our employees wanted to talk with you a moment and let you know how sorry they are."

Ben's mom squeezes her arm. "Oh, Camille, how nice of them to be here for this. You must go speak with them."

That's all the permission she needs as she jumps out of the line and attaches herself to my side. With my hand on her lower back, I steer her to the far side of the room, where I had already scoped out an easy exit to the parking lot.

"Thank you," she mumbles as I push the door open.

The sun has almost set, leaving the sky washed in shades of orange and pink and yellow. Even though she doesn't need them, the sunglasses stay in place.

"You should have signaled me earlier. There's no reason you had to greet every single person who came through that door."

She lets out a frustrated laugh. "My mother would disagree with you."

We're leaning against the side of the building. The lot is full of cars but clear of people.

"Seems like you're not a fan of your brother's wife." I'm not sure why I'm bringing this up other than that my curiosity is getting the better of me.

Camille cocks her head to the side. "It's that obvious, huh?"

I give her a small smile. "Probably just to me since I had a front-row seat."

She turns away, her head falling back against the wall in a defeated sort of way. "Margaret loves any attention she can get, and the role of the grieving sister-in-law is giving it to her. But honestly, my whole family is screwed up. It's why I made Ben promise after he proposed that we would distance ourselves from them."

We've had a lot of conversations over the years, but her family has never been a topic we discussed. And from what I've uncovered, I know that not only was there no distance between Ben and Randall but it seems Randall was the one responsible for much of Ben's success.

"I'm guessing he didn't do what you asked?"

"When Ben and I first got married, we did keep some separation. Or I thought we did. My dad has a way of sinking his claws into you. Finding your weakness and exploiting it. Dad found Ben's weakness years ago."

We stand silently for several long moments.

"Do you know why Ben wanted out of our partnership?" I finally ask her.

She doesn't look at me when she answers. "I don't presume to know anything about Ben. Not anymore."

The door opens, startling us both. It's her mom. "Camille, your father has someone he wants you to meet."

There is a moment where I think Camille's going to tell her mother she's done and not going back in, but she caves. I follow her back inside if only to take the first opportunity to drag her away again.

Camille is put firmly back in her place, her mom on one side and her dad on the other. And I drop back down in the same chair as before.

I spend a few minutes checking my emails and updating the shared note with Lila while keeping one eye on everyone in the line.

Camille suddenly takes a step back, as if something has startled her. I glance around but nothing sticks out to me. Her action was jarring enough that not only does it get my attention, her mom turns to ask her if she's okay.

"Yes, yes, I'm fine. Haven't eaten anything and I just got a little dizzy. I think I'm going to splash some water on my face. Be right back."

And then she's out of the line and moving toward the ladies' room. I stand up to watch her progress and maybe even grab her something to eat when I catch sight of another woman who looks familiar. It takes a moment for me to place her.

Then I realize it's Aubrey Price, whom I recognize from the photos in Ben's file.

She came in through one of the side doors, and she's watching Camille cross the room too.

Before Camille pushes through the bathroom door, she glances in Aubrey's direction. Aubrey heads that way.

Just as I decide to cut her off and find out what she's doing here, someone calls my name. I turn and let out a groan when I see it's one of Ben's clients.

"Mr. Landry, glad I could catch you. Can I ask you about my case?"

"Yes, of course, but can you give me one minute to check on something first?"

"Oh, yeah, sure. I'll wait right here."

And in that short time, Camille and Aubrey have both disappeared through the bathroom door.

What the hell is that about?

CHAPTER 25

Aubrey

AFTER THE ALIBI
TUESDAY, OCTOBER 13

To say Camille is pissed I'm here is an understatement.

But there was no way I was missing out on this opportunity to talk to her. The last four days have been a nightmare. Sunday, everyone in the house was glued to the local news coverage of Ben's death. And then hours later the police show up asking Shane and Eddie about the Mustang.

That was a terrifying moment.

And the fact that there hasn't been an arrest made has us all on edge. Ben's killer is still out there, and it's easy to assume his murder is connected to his plans on Saturday. Plans that we knew about.

If I had any idea Ben was going to wind up dead that night, I never would have involved my friends.

It's time to have a very frank conversation with Camille. And I'm betting she's not coming back to the bar anytime soon. I knew if I showed up here, she would have to talk to me.

Camille is standing near the row of sinks with her arms crossed in front of her when I push through the bathroom door. "You shouldn't be here." She's angry but nervous too.

I glance at the two stalls and see the doors are open so we're alone. For now. Someone else could walk in any minute.

"Well, obviously we need to talk!" I mirror her pose and expression so she knows I'm pissed too. "I'm freaking out!" And then I ask the one question that was important enough to risk coming here. "Was Ben killed while I was pretending to be you?"

Her face pales. "I . . . I don't know. The police haven't told us what time he died." Then she seems to gather herself. "You really can't be here."

"What in the hell did you expect me to do? I haven't heard from you."

Camille steps closer. "I haven't been alone long enough to take a deep breath much less drop by your bar. Do you have any idea what the last couple of days have been like for me?"

She looks wrecked, but I try to ignore that. That could all be for show. The waves of grief rolling off her right now could be fake. "Did you kill him?"

Her jaw drops slightly and she takes a step back, as if my question physically assaulted her. "No, I didn't kill him! Is that what you think?"

"What *else* am I supposed to think? The news keeps saying he was dead awhile before you found him Sunday morning, and you were hiding in your house until almost midnight on Saturday!"

She's shaking her head. "No I wasn't. He caught me right after some

PI he uses sent him a picture of you dressed like me shopping in St. Francisville."

This takes the fight out of me. "What?"

Camille won't look at me.

"Did Ben know it was me instead of you in the picture?"

She nods.

And then my anger spikes. "Why didn't you tell me when we switched cars at the gas station!" I start pacing around the small room. "Wait! Why did you let me finish out the day as you if we were busted?"

"Both of us were keeping things from each other. Or did you not have anything to do with your housemates bringing that Mustang over?"

Oh shit. I wasn't expecting her to put that together.

My face must give me away, because her eyes narrow when she scolds me. "Then don't sit here and yell at me for not telling you everything. We may not have trusted each other before but we are going to have to trust each other now. You and I did enough questionable shit on Saturday that it would be easy for the DA to pin this on one or both of us. Ben's death is huge news, and there's only so much my family can do."

It feels like she's leaving out a big part at the end of that sentence . . . there's only so much her family can do to protect *her*. If I don't keep my mouth shut about what we did, I have no doubt that I would become the sacrificial lamb, same as Paul.

"It won't take much for someone to discover you weren't in St. Francisville. We were just trying to make sure I'd pass an inspection if someone compared me to your driver's license, not stand up to the scrutiny of a full investigation."

She stares at me a long moment. "Then it seems we are very much in this together. We just need to make sure there's no reason anyone wants to dig too deep." She turns around to the sink and flips the water on, wetting her fingers then pressing them against her face. She really doesn't look good.

She takes a paper towel and dries her hands then turns back to me. "If we don't panic, this will be over soon and we never have to see each other again. Ben is dead. I know you wanted answers, but whatever chance we had at getting them died with him."

My shoulders jerk at her words. "So that's it? What about Paul? Did you know there's a video that shows the crash?"

Camille flinches, but I can't read her well enough to know if this is new information or not.

I push on. "I still want to see it. See the moment my parents were killed even if the man who did it is dead!"

She steps forward. "I don't know anything about a video! And we don't know for sure if he had anything to do with that accident. My husband is dead. My life is a fucking disaster right now. I'm sorry if I can't think past that!"

Our raised voices cease immediately when the door opens. We turn away from each other, taking a few steps in opposite directions. An elderly woman walks in and zeroes in on Camille.

"How are you holding up, sweetie?"

Camille pulls herself together. "Hanging in there." Her features are strained and she looks shaky.

I walk to the sink and start washing my hands so I have something to do as the woman shares a story about Ben when he was a little boy. By the time I'm drying my hands, the woman has entered one of the stalls.

Camille steps close enough to whisper in my ear. "I will call you at the bar in a few days to check in but I need to get back out there and you need to leave."

She spins on her high heels and exits the bathroom. I'm only a few steps behind her. I watch as she takes her place back in line as I make my way toward the exit.

But I stop cold when I see him.

The guy standing next to her, dressed in a suit, in the line greeting people like he's family. A blond woman is on his other side, her hand clutching his arm as she dries her tears with a tissue.

He must feel me watching him because his eyes meet mine from across the room.

It's him.

The guy I sat next to at Chantilly's on Saturday night.

The guy who flirted with me and asked me to dance.

The guy who is clearly related in some way to Camille Bayliss.

I send a text to the house group chat the second I'm on the bus headed home.

911 meeting. Will be home in 20 mins

Deacon calls as soon as he sees it. "What's going on?"

"Okay, I know you told me not to go to that Rosary but I did. I had to talk to her. And you're never going to believe this! That guy I talked to at Chantilly's . . . he was there! Standing right next to her in the receiving line." Several other passengers have turned around and are staring at me so I drop my voice to a whisper. "Do you think she set me up somehow?"

"Shit. I don't know. Where are you right now?"

"On the bus."

"Aub, I would have taken you."

"No, you wouldn't have, because you told me not to go. I'll be home in a few minutes."

"Okay, I'll see you there."

We end the call and I'm shaking by the time I get off at my stop. Luckily, it's only a two-block walk to our house.

When I come through the kitchen door, everyone is here. Deacon pulls out the chair next to him, indicating I sit there.

"I talked to Camille in the bathroom at the Rosary for Ben. He found out she was hiding in the house Saturday afternoon. Someone sent Ben a picture of me dressed up like Camille, shopping." I look at Deacon. "I think it was that PI who was helping us." I'm gripping the edge of the table so hard my knuckles turn white.

"That son of a bitch," Deacon says, his fist pounding the table. "Tell me what she said."

I fill him in and he gets up from the table, pulling his phone out of his pocket. He walks in the other room to make a call. Pretty sure he's about to have words with Vic.

Eddie drops down in the chair Deacon just vacated. "Look at some pictures I pulled up. See if you recognize the guy."

Once I'm seated, he turns the phone to face me. The first image is a match. "That's him."

"Shit," he mutters. "That's her brother, Silas."

"What!"

Shane is pacing next to the table. "What does that mean? That can't be a coincidence."

Serenity lets out an exasperated sigh. "Of course it's not a coincidence. Don't be an idiot. Camille Bayliss offed her husband while Aubrey gave her a perfect alibi. I bet the brother was there to solidify it." My mouth hangs open and she looks at me, confused. "What? That's what I would've done. That's freaking rock solid."

I'm shaking my head. "I just talked to her. She's a wreck. And she said she didn't do it."

Serenity laughs. "And you believed her? She wanted out of her marriage and boom, now she is."

"Shit, you may be right," Eddie says.

I sit up. "I didn't cover for her so she could murder him!"

He points to his chest. "I know that's not why." Then he points at me. "You know that's not why." He gives me a look like the next sentence will be painful to say. "There's a real good chance that's why, though."

Deacon walks back in, catching the end of our conversation. "It's not the time for half-assed theories."

"What did Vic say? Was he the one who sent the picture to Ben?" I ask Deacon as soon as he sits down on my other side.

He nods. "Yeah. Ben had him go check on Camille to make sure she was where she was supposed to be. Said she had been acting weird and he felt like she was up to something. Vic had no idea that wasn't her. And since we didn't share our plans with him, he wouldn't have known he was screwing them up."

I drop my head in my hands.

"He's also freaking out," Deacon adds. "He knows it's only a matter of time before the cops come talk to him."

Popping up, I ask, "Will he turn on us? Tell them what we were doing?" Because it will just make me look more guilty than I already do.

He shakes his head. "I just reminded him what will happen to him if he does."

I twist my hands in the hem of my shirt while I take in everything he said. "The thing is, I feel like Camille is way more exposed than I am. I had her phone. Her car. Her credit cards. That's a lot of trust to put into someone. Into me. Would she really do that if she planned on killing her husband? And if she did, y'all know I screwed something up. Got caught on surveillance video or something. And then it will just look like I was helping her!"

Shane tilts his head to the side. "Gotta agree with Aubrey. That's a big risk to take."

Deacon's worry for me is clear on his face. "The problem is Ben's dead and both of you went to great lengths to hide your actions that day. If it comes down to her word against yours, who is everyone going to believe?"

My stomach flips so quick I put my hand over my mouth because it feels like I'm about to puke. Of course they'll believe her. And she has connections I don't.

Deacon gets up and runs the dish towel under the faucet, then brings it back to me. "Put that on your throat."

The coolness helps more than I thought it would.

"What do I do now?"

"Nothing," Deacon says, and everyone nods in agreement. "You don't say anything. You don't talk to anyone. You said it yourself; his wife is more exposed than you are. We wait and see what happens."

"She said she was going to reach out to me in a few days. Do I talk to her?"

Shane stops next to my chair. "Hell, no. In fact, run the other way if she tries to talk to you."

The back door opens and we all turn toward it. It's Serenity's boyfriend, Frank. He seems surprised to see us all sitting here. "Shit, sorry." Then he nods at Serenity. "I'll wait for you in the truck." Then he ducks out, shutting the door behind him.

She hops up from the table. "Gotta go. Someone fill me in on what I miss when I get back."

I stare at her as she flounces out of the kitchen without a care in the world and wonder how she can be so calm. But I guess it's not her neck on the line, it's mine.

Shane and Eddie also take their leave, but they're only going as far as the garage. Then it's just Deacon and me at the table.

Deacon fumbles with his set of keys until he frees one from the ring. "I gotta get back to work too. Go up to my room, soak in my tub. I've heard you talk about it enough that I know you want to. I won't be back for a couple of hours so it'll just sit empty."

"Are you serious? I can use it?"

Deacon moved in about six months after me into what would once have been considered the primary bedroom. He saw the FOR RENT sign when he came to "chat" with one of the neighbors. It's one of the units I would have loved to upgrade to . . . the claw-foot bathtub alone made me think long and hard about the higher rent. It worked out for the best, because otherwise Deacon wouldn't have moved in, although that tub is completely wasted on him since there's no way he can stretch out comfortably in it.

Deacon gives me a lopsided grin. "Of course you can use it. I'll get you a key made so you can use it whenever you want."

"This is so nice, thank you." He's close enough that I can lean forward and give him a quick hug.

He gets up and moves to the door but stops before he leaves. "I'll be back in a bit. Call me if you need me."

"I will." I feel calmer now than I did when I first got home, but I know this respite will be short-lived.

Do I believe Camille killed her husband?

No, I really don't.

But that doesn't mean the police won't set their sights on her . . . or me, if they find out what we did on Saturday.

CHAPTER 26

Ben

TEN YEARS AGO

The Everetts' condo in Baton Rouge is nicer than my house back in Corbeau.

It was almost two a.m. when Silas and I got to Baton Rouge. He had passed out in the car on the way here and I struggled getting him inside. He came to long enough to jump in the shower and only fell once trying to get out since he was still drunk.

He's on the couch, choosing to sleep there rather than one of the three bedrooms. The cut on his forehead finally stopped bleeding but it probably needs a stitch or two. Gonna leave an ugly scar. His knee is still swollen but it looks like it's just bruised.

Mr. Everett wants us to stay here until Sunday. He also wants us "out and about" to further cement this alibi. But having people see him all banged up the day after the accident seems dumb to me.

I've been up for a couple of hours when my phone rings and I see Camille's name flash across the screen. I wait until I'm back in the room I slept in before I answer.

"Hey, I've been trying to get you." It's hard to keep the frustration out of my voice. I feel like things are shaky between us right now, and with the distance, I'm trying not to give her any reason to break things off. Especially after last night.

"Sorry, the time difference here makes it hard to connect. When I think about calling you, it's in the middle of the night there."

"Where are you now?"

"Seville. Spain. It's one of my favorite places so far! And the food is so good. I'm going to have so much content for my site when I get back."

Camille took a marketing class last semester where she had to make an account for a project. The class is over but the account still lives on.

"That's cool! I can't wait to see it."

I lie on my bed and listen as she recounts everything she's done since I spoke to her last. I'd be lying if I said I wasn't worried about what she was doing or who she was meeting over there. People who run in the same crowd as her and have the financial means to hop around Europe all summer like she's currently doing.

And as much as she hates the power her father wields, she sure doesn't hate what that money affords her. Tuition paid in full at Tulane, the little BMW she drives, credit cards with no limits . . . and an all-expenses-paid trip to Europe. It's a bit hypocritical in my opinion.

But then again, I'm just jealous.

I'm determined to be as rich and powerful as Mr. Everett one day, if not more so. And helping cover for Silas last night just made that path a little bit easier.

"So what have you been up to?" Camille finally asks.

"Not much. Work. It's not nearly as exciting here."

"I'll be home in a couple of weeks."

"I can't wait to see you." And then I float something out there to see how she takes it. "Ran into your dad the other day. He was surprisingly nice to me. I think I'm slowly but surely winning him over."

Camille is quiet.

"You still there?"

"Yeah. He probably just wants something from you. You know how he is. And you know how I feel about us getting wrapped up with him."

"Oh, yeah, I agree. Just thought it was kinda crazy."

It's clear Camille isn't going to be on board if I accept the help her dad is willing to give me, so I'll just have to keep that to myself.

"I've got to go. We're heading to some cooking class we signed up for. But I'll call you later. Love you."

"Love you too."

We end the call just as I hear Silas stirring out in the living room.

"What the hell," he says, when I walk back into the room.

Rolling my eyes, I drop down in the chair next to the couch. "Please tell me you remember everything so I don't have to relive what happened last night."

His dazed expression hardens as the details come back to him. He falls back against the couch, his eyes shutting. "Shit, this is so fucked."

"Yep."

Silas cracks his eyes open. "Was anyone hurt in the accident?"

"No idea."

He groans and lies back down. At least he cared enough to ask.

"Where's Margaret?" His voice is muffled.

"Ran home after she heard your dad was coming to my house. But I think he planned to talk to her himself after you told him she was with you."

"Shit. This is so bad. God, I'm sure Dad is super pissed. And I'm scared to find out if anyone was hurt. Or died. Not sure how I can live with that."

This has me sitting up. "If someone died, there's nothing you can do to bring them back. You find some way to make things right later, when you can, but be grateful right now you're not sitting in a jail cell."

Silas turns away to hide the tears flooding his eyes, burrowing under a throw blanket. I have to push down my frustration. He acts like a fuckup then gets all emotional when things go to shit, while I would give anything to have the kind of support he does. Have a parent willing not only to bend but to break the law for me.

My phone rings again and it's Mr. Everett. I sit up straight in my chair even though he can't see me. "Hello?"

"How's Silas?"

"Just woke up. He was a little foggy at first but he's clearer now. Do you want to talk to him?"

"No. I'll deal with him later. Bring him home tomorrow night. Kevin Foster will be here when y'all arrive. Silas's name is already in the group of people who were seen at Paul Granger's house last night so we will have to address this. Make sure your story is straight. Make sure he can tell it with little emotion, if any. This will be the moment that counts. Do not disappoint me."

Before I can reply, he ends the call. With the shape Silas is in right now, I've got my work cut out for me.

Kevin Foster is the chief of police in Corbeau and a good friend of the Everetts'. Not surprised he'll be the one there to meet us and take our statements. Mr. Everett made a big deal about having our story straight, but honestly we could tell him anything and he'd take Silas off the list of suspects.

Silas is going to owe me forever for this.

"That was your dad."

Nothing. He doesn't move.

"He wants you back home tomorrow night. Foster will be there to take our statement."

And again, nothing.

Just as I'm about to pull the blanket away and make him acknowledge me, there's a knock on the door. This gets both of our attention.

Silas sits up, eyes wide. "Do you think it's the cops?"

I shrug and head to the door, peeking through the peephole. "No, it's your girlfriend."

He groans behind me as I pull the door open.

"What are you doing here?" She looks like shit. Eyes red, nose raw.

"I need to see him."

"Let her in," Silas says behind me.

Margaret slips past me and all but runs to the couch. He holds the blanket up, allowing her to slip underneath it with him. They're covered from head to toe, but it's thin enough I can hear them as easily as if it weren't there.

"How are you feeling?" she asks him.

"Like shit. What about you?"

"I'm okay. Just worried about you. Worried about everything." I can tell from the hitch in her voice that she's crying.

"Did my dad come talk to you last night?"

"Early this morning. He scares the shit out of me."

Yeah, same.

"What did he say?"

"He asked me what happened and I told him. He said a bunch of stuff about how friends are like family and family sticks by each other. He was trying not to make it sound like a threat but I know that's what it was."

They're quiet for a few minutes, and I feel a little bit sleazy sitting here, listening to their conversation, although they don't seem worried about talking in front of me. There are three bedrooms if they want privacy.

When Silas doesn't say anything, Margaret adds, "You know he doesn't have to threaten me. Your secret is safe with me always."

One thing I know for sure is I'm not wasting this opportunity, and it seems like Margaret isn't either.

CHAPTER 27

Camille

THE ALIBI
SATURDAY, OCTOBER 10

I got back to St. Francisville hours before I was supposed to. I confessed *almost* everything to Silas, telling him what led up to me meeting Aubrey Price and how she convinced me to spy on Ben. And then I walked him through everything I had learned.

Silas listened quietly, then told me what happened that night ten years ago.

It was the most honest and raw conversation we've ever shared. Silas sounded so broken. A darkness has hung over him for years, and I've finally learned why. There is no excuse for what he did. He was a dumb kid who made a really horrible decision getting behind the wheel that night.

I had asked him how long it took before he found out that couple had died and he said, "Too late to own up to it. Once Dad got involved, I could have screamed it from the steps of the courthouse and no one would have listened to me."

Anyone not directly related to Randall Everett would have called bullshit on that answer, saying it's never too late, but I knew what he meant. Our father had fixed it before Silas was even sober. He had Ben on board as an alibi and basically threatened Margaret within an inch of her life if she ever spoke of it. He had the chief of police willing to look the other way. All within hours of that accident.

He is a force that we have never been able to withstand.

In that long-overdue phone call, I realized I've never had the distance with my family that I believed. Ben has been connected to Dad and Silas in ways I never understood. By covering for Silas, he secured his place in one of the most powerful families in south Louisiana.

And he wasn't the only one. Margaret secured her place that night too.

Silas told me to go back and wait in St. Francisville until it was time to meet Aubrey. He was insistent that I let her finish the day out as me, not to alert her to what happened with Ben. Aubrey is the unknown in this scenario, and neither of us wants her to know Ben busted me and discovered she's here, pretending to be me.

I thought about going back to my room at the inn but I felt claustrophobic just thinking about it. I would climb those walls while I waited for the clock to count down to midnight.

So I've been following Aubrey at a distance from stop to stop. She's just finished dinner and was supposed to go to a nice bar where she would have a cocktail until it was time to meet me back at the gas station but somehow she's found herself at some run-down honky-tonk.

"Why are you stopping here?" I ask aloud, and park at the edge of the lot, near the road, and watch her hobble into the bar. She definitely should have practiced walking in the heels. I think I put too much emphasis on the wrong "be me" part. I should have been more worried about her unsteadiness in those heels than about her ordering my drink of choice.

Aubrey disappears inside and I throw the Honda in park. My stomach is in knots while I wait for this night to be over. Silas was going to go to my house and talk to Ben but I haven't heard from him yet and that's got me really nervous. I can't imagine that conversation went well at all. And I don't want to think about what the days ahead will be like when I have to deal with Ben.

But that's an issue for tomorrow. There's a little more than an hour before I change cars with Aubrey and so I'm not thinking about anything other than that until then.

This bar has a steady flow of traffic. I'm watching everyone come and go when someone familiar catches my eye.

"What in the hell!"

My hand slides around the passenger seat until I feel the burner phone. I tap the last number I called, watching Silas's reaction when he feels his phone vibrate in his pocket. He pulls it out while scanning the lot.

"Please tell me you're not here right now," he says.

"Me! You're the one who shouldn't be here!"

I can tell the minute he spots me. When I spoke to him earlier, I spared no detail, telling him everything from the old beater of a car I bought to Aubrey's full schedule. Silas ends the call as he walks toward me. He slides into the passenger seat and we stare at each other. It's only been a few weeks since we've seen each other but so much has changed since then.

So many secrets between us. So many lies. But down deep, we know we're the only ones who will truly know what it's like to have Randall Everett as a parent.

"What are you doing here?" he asks.

"I couldn't go back to the inn. I'm a nervous wreck. Aubrey hasn't spotted me." I may be two years older than him but I am forever the little girl who will always try to follow orders, afraid to let anyone down. "What did Ben say?"

His jaw clenches. "I didn't get a chance to talk to him. I knocked but he never answered." Silas just shrugs. "He was either gone or he was avoiding me. But he can't hide from me forever."

The one thing I left out when I spoke to Silas earlier is Ben's plan to go to Foster's, mainly because I was scared about what Silas would do if he followed Ben there.

"Then why are you here?" I ask.

He nods toward the bar. "Got to the restaurant you said she'd be at right as she was leaving. Followed her here. Was giving her a minute to get settled before I went in."

"But why?"

"I'm worried that whoever sent Ben that pic of her shopping earlier is still around. I thought I'd come by and make sure everything was okay. She shouldn't be involved in this. Not after everything she's gone through." He ducks his head like he's embarrassed.

"She wanted to do this. It was her idea actually. She's a lot tougher than you think."

He gives me a sad smile. "I'm sure she is."

Twisting around in my seat so I can look at him more closely, I ask, "Did you know Margaret was going to see Ben today?"

"No. She shouldn't have done that. I told her I was going to handle this."

"She told Ben you have someone watching Aubrey? Why?"

"Hank was sent Paul's case in late June, then went to see him soon after. He told Ben about his conversation with Paul at Angola. Paul said 'the guy' who had evidence from that night was trying to get it to the 'right person.' Dad put a tail on Foster, since we all knew he's the only person it could have been. He went to that bar where Aubrey works a couple of times, but Foster never talked to her. We think he was trying to decide whether or not to pass it along to her. Ben bought that old car so he could get close to her." He adds quietly, "If Dad knew you had her parading around this town as you, he would lose his shit."

"I don't want anything bad to happen to her." I'm proud of the firmness in my voice.

Silas is still leaning back but his head turns toward me. "I don't either, Camille. And I've been working to save her ass while also saving my own. I knew Ben was lurking around her house. That's why I've got someone watching her. You have no idea what it's been like having this hanging over my head all these years. That she's an orphan because of me."

"It's my fault Aubrey's been drug into this mess. I should never have gone to confront her that night."

Silas shakes his head. "If anyone is to blame for pulling Aubrey in, it's Kevin Foster. He had one foot in the grave and felt the flames of hell licking up his leg and stirred all this shit up. He could have turned what he had over to the Feds. Or sent it to the local news stations. But he didn't. He went crying to Paul and dangled it over his head like a carrot on the end of a stick."

My stomach twists at his words. "Do you feel bad Paul is serving time at Angola?"

His face falls. "Do I feel bad Paul is serving a sentence for a crime he didn't commit? Yes. Do I know for a fact that Paul has done a dozen things that would have landed him in the same prison for the same amount of time, also yes. So honestly, my feelings toward Paul are a bit more complicated."

"What do you think Ben is going to do? I don't want him to turn on you and say he was forced to give you that alibi or something."

He lets out a soft laugh. "Ben's no Boy Scout. He may not like getting his hands dirty but all his success hasn't just come from that big brain of his and pure fucking luck. Very few of his clients are innocent. And who does he call when he needs evidence to disappear or witnesses to have a sudden bout of amnesia? He calls Dad. Dad calls Foster . . . or used to. Ben gets what he wants in the end."

"Ben made it sound like Dad makes him take those cases. Like he didn't really want to do it."

"And Ben is lying his ass off. Every case he took on his own, he asked for help." Silas rests his head against the back of his seat. "And don't worry about him going to the cops if he gets what Foster has. He'll just try to find some other way to use it against me, but that won't be as easy to do as he thinks."

"You wanted to get away from Corbeau and Dad as much as I did," I say, changing the subject, since Ben may be getting that evidence right now.

He gives me a grim smile. "Well, I lost the right to choose after I took Paul Granger's truck. My position was set after that."

"I'm afraid you're going to turn into Dad," I whisper. "More than you already have."

Silas lets out a ragged breath. "Lord knows, I've made mistakes I wish I could take back and done things I'm not proud of, but ever since I graduated and came back home, all I've done is try to rein him in where I can and mitigate the damage if I can't. I may not have gone to jail for what I did to Aubrey Price's parents, but I'm behind a different set of bars, serving a different kind of time."

"You could have told me all this years ago. You could have trusted me."

"I don't trust anyone."

I'm about to say something else but he holds a hand up. "Don't go back to Baton Rouge. Promise me you'll come to my house tomorrow after the thing at church Mom wants us at. We'll get it figured out."

I nod and then he's out of the car. He walks across the parking lot and into the bar, while I think about my options. I could be a coward and avoid Ben, go hide out at Silas's and let him fight my battles for me.

But if I don't stand up for myself now, I never will. I'll be the same ole Camille who does what she's told and lets the men in her life control things.

Everything's changed now.

I know enough that neither Ben nor Dad will be able to hold that prenup clause against me. I'm going back to Baton Rouge first thing in the morning and telling Ben I want a divorce.

CHAPTER 28

Hank

AFTER THE ALIBI
WEDNESDAY, OCTOBER 14

The phone on my desk buzzes and Lila picks it up since she's closer. "Hey." She starts to straighten my desk while listening to Julie, the receptionist. "Okay, thanks." She hangs the phone up and looks at me. "Camille is here. I'll go get her."

We were going over the calendar again, juggling things around since I met with Judge Whittaker about the trial Ben had kept postponing. He's given me twenty-four hours to give him a date I'm available.

The door shuts quietly and I look up and find Camille in front of my desk, her eyes red and watery. I wonder if they will ever be dry again.

"Hey, Hank," she says softly. She dabs at her eyes with a wadded-up tissue.

I lead her to the couch, hoping the less formal we are the more she'll open up. "Let's sit and talk everything through before the detective gets here. How was your drive in?"

"It was fine. Silas brought me. My family is worried about me being alone since, you know, they haven't caught who did this."

I nod. "I get it. We hired a security guard here at the office for that same reason."

We spend the next hour going over everything Sullivan will ask her. A few minutes before one, we move to the conference room to wait for his arrival.

The conference room is a glass box that sits in the middle of our office, and I think it's the absolute worst design in history. The walls have this fancy feature that allows you to change the opacity with choices ranging from completely transparent to one way, where we could see out but no one could see in, to no visibility at all. This will be the first thing I change.

I hit the button on the panel and the glass turns a milky gray.

"Thank you, I was wondering if everyone was going to see us in here."

The groan escapes me before I can stop it. "I hate this room."

"Yeah, I'm not crazy about it either, but Ben was insistent. He thought the technology was cool."

I take a moment to study Camille. She looks rough. Her hair is pulled back and messy in a way that doesn't seem intentional. Her nails have been chewed down completely. But I'd be more worried if she didn't look like this. It's barely been seventy-two hours since she found her husband's body in their home.

"Remember, only answer what he's asking." I'm not sure why I feel the need to repeat this, but she nods like she understands the part I'm not saying out loud.

She draws in a deep breath and seems to fight tears. I lean over and squeeze her hand. "This is standard procedure. I know it will be hard to talk about it but I'm here for you. It's going to be okay."

Lila knocks on the door three times in quick succession then she opens it, allowing Sullivan to enter.

"Thanks for coming here for this. We appreciate it." We shake hands once he's inside the room.

He takes a look around before sitting in the chair across from Camille. "This is a nicer setup than that we've got at the station."

Lila is still in the doorway. "Anyone need something to drink? Coffee? Water?"

Camille and I both look at Sullivan. "No, thank you, I'm good."

"Okay, just let me know if you change your mind." The door clicks softly shut behind her.

"Mrs. Bayliss, first off, thank you for speaking with me today," Sullivan says.

"Of course. But please, call me Camille."

"Okay, Camille. Just answer what you can." Sullivan pulls out his recorder.

"Detective Sullivan questioning Camille Bayliss, wife of Benjamin Bayliss, regarding the events of October eleventh. Camille Bayliss's lawyer and Benjamin Bayliss's law partner, Hank Landry, is also present." He sets the recorder in the center of the conference table between us and gives Camille a small smile. "Okay, now that we've taken care of that, let's get started. I need to get a clear picture of your day on Sunday. You mentioned when we spoke at your home that you had been in St. Francisville for the weekend and returned midmorning. The call to 911 was received at 10:48 a.m. Was that the time you had planned to get home? Was it earlier than expected?"

"I originally planned to drive to Corbeau to attend Mass with my family but I wasn't feeling well so I decided to come home instead." She's twisting the tissue in her hands to the point it's about to fall to pieces, but at least it's in her lap where he can't see it.

I had warned her that the detective would want to get as much of what she said at her house on the official record, so the first twenty minutes of questioning was going back over everything she told him on Sunday.

Sullivan makes some notes even though he's recording this. "You mentioned you stopped for a drink before going back to the hotel Saturday night? Correct?" Sullivan asks, still looking at his notes.

She hesitates just a second and then says, "Yes. At Chantilly's."

He flips a few pages, checking his notes. "You stopped because you weren't ready to call it a night. Is that correct?"

Camille nods.

"Mrs. Bayliss, I need you to answer aloud, please."

She clears her throat. "Yes, that's correct."

"Thank you. And about what time did you arrive at Chantilly's?"

"Just after ten."

Her answers are a bit stilted but considering the subject matter and situation, I can't find fault with any of them so far.

"And what time did you leave Chantilly's?"

"Just before midnight."

"I spoke with the bartender on duty Saturday night, Ray Simmons. He said it looked like you met someone there. Sat with him at the bar the entire time. Can you tell me who that was?"

She coughs to clear her throat. "Yes, I met my brother, Silas, there. We had a drink and caught up since I haven't seen him in a while."

I was surprised when she mentioned this earlier when we were going over the case; otherwise Sullivan would see the shocked reaction I had upon hearing it. It was my understanding that she and Silas were not that close, and I can't help but think there's something here I'm missing.

"You were at Chantilly's with your brother, Silas Everett?" Sullivan's pen is poised over the pad while he studies Camille.

She nods then remembers the recorder. "Yes."

"Did you plan to meet him there? Was it a coincidence?"

Camille is blinking rapidly, which isn't good. It makes her look nervous and twitchy. Sullivan is seeing it too.

"I saw Silas at a charity event a few weeks ago and we made plans to meet for a drink since Corbeau is so close to St. Francisville."

This is the same thing she told me too, and I have to wonder if Sullivan is as skeptical about this as I am.

"Would it be possible for me to speak to your brother?"

I hold a hand up, stopping Camille from answering. "Just want to make sure we're on the same page. We're not opposed to you contacting Silas Everett, but my understanding is you need information from Camille about this past weekend, since she is a witness, not a suspect. Is that correct?"

I'm forcing his hand a bit here, but if he sees her as a suspect, I'm shutting this down immediately.

Sullivan leans back in his chair and looks at me. "Camille Bayliss is not considered a suspect. At this time."

That last part was deliberate. I nod to Camille to answer his question.

"He'll be here to pick me up when we're finished and he's prepared to tell you exactly what I just did."

It takes everything in me not to bang my head on the table. Phrasing it like that is about the worse way to put it when you're looking for someone to corroborate your story.

This is the tricky part. It's not just the anatomy of an alibi—having *someone* vouch that you were somewhere else when the crime was committed—but it's the psychology of it: that that *someone* is believable. A family member automatically brings skepticism, especially one who is "prepared," as she put it.

"Okay, I'll speak to him if he's out there when I leave; otherwise I will need him to come to the station." Sullivan looks up from his notepad. "Is there anyone you can think of who would wish your husband harm? Has he had a falling-out with a friend? Gotten sideways with a neighbor? Anyone from his past make a reappearance?"

She's gnawing on her bottom lip. First time she's really looked nervous about answering a question.

"No, no one that I can think of." I don't know how I know it but she's lying.

Sullivan nods slowly. He sees everything I do.

The detective puts his pen down again and pulls a picture from his bag, passing it to us. It's one the news stations have used several times when reporting on Ben's case. A Louisiana lifestyle magazine had done a story on Ben recently, and this photo they took of him in his home office was included in the article. In the image, Ben is leaned back in his chair, his feet propped up on the corner of the desk. When I first saw this picture, I thought he looked like a smug asshole. Not my favorite shot of him.

And now I'm really curious why Sullivan is showing it to us.

"We've all seen this picture," he says, leaning forward. "Mrs. Bayliss, could you look at the items on his desk."

Camille brushes the tears away then focuses on the picture. "What am I looking for?"

"I know this picture was taken back in the spring when this article was published, but would you say the decorative items on the front edge were still there when you left the house on Friday? Or was his desk staged like this for this photo shoot?"

I study the image. There are several things there that I recognize since I've been in that room multiple times. There's the gavel a judge gave him when he retired from the bench since Ben had won the last case he'd presided over. A brass set of scales his mom gave him when he graduated law school. And the wooden display box that holds a hunting knife.

"Those items are on his desk now. He's not one to put props out just for pictures." Camille's lower lip trembles when she asks, "Why?"

"Preliminary search results don't show any signs of forced entry. Our initial thought is that the assailant arrived after Mr. Bayliss and that he let them in the house. The only sign of a struggle was a chair that was flipped on its side. Usually when there's a robbery, you see signs of the intruder searching through drawers and cabinets and closets, and they aren't particularly neat and tidy when they do it. But the room wasn't disturbed nor was any other part of the house."

Camille grips the edge of the table while she listens, her eyes glued to him.

"There were several different injuries to Mr. Bayliss's body. We haven't gotten the full report from the coroner yet, but preliminary results look like Mr. Bayliss was stabbed multiple times in the chest. The gavel and scales were still on his desk when we arrived on the scene, but that display box was gone. And there were no signs of the knife anywhere. We believe it may have been the weapon used to kill him, but we won't know for sure until we get more details on the blade or recover it to see if the size matches his wounds."

Camille completely breaks down. Her face drops and her shoulders shake as she sobs. It takes several minutes for her to speak. "I . . . I can get you the . . . information on the . . . on the knife."

Sullivan looks at me but I wait for Camille to tell him how she has that information.

Finally, she pulls herself together enough to speak. "That knife was made by a local bladesmith in Corbeau. The handle was part of an antler from a deer Ben had killed. I had the knife commissioned as a gift for Christmas last year. The measurements and description of the blade are on the certificate I have in a file at home. I'll make sure you get a copy."

The public will lose their minds over this detail, and I can already see how quickly the narrative will spin that Camille killed him with a weapon she had custom-made for him.

"You're not going public with this, are you?" I ask.

He knows why I'm asking without having to say it.

Sullivan shakes his head. "No. We're keeping this detail out of the press right now. Especially since we don't know where the knife is."

Camille sinks down in her chair, her eyes glazed over.

"Did you and Ben have any marital problems?"

I start to object to this line of questioning, but Camille puts her hand on my forearm, stopping me. She clears her throat before answering. "No, we didn't. I mean, we had the usual arguments all couples do. I thought he spent too much time at the office and he thought I spent too much money, but nothing more than that."

It's a good answer. And true. I know how much Ben worked and often heard him complaining about the credit card bill.

But she's wrecked and I don't want her answering these types of questions in this frame of mind. "Sully, I think we're done for today."

CHAPTER 29

Aubrey

AFTER THE ALIBI
WEDNESDAY, OCTOBER 14

I put my laptop on the driveway as I consider the best way to destroy it.

Or, more specifically, get rid of everything that connects me to Camille and Ben, which is a lot.

The anxiety I felt leaving the Rosary came back with a vengeance this morning. Yesterday was mentally exhausting, so today I decided I'm tired of thinking about it and ready to do something about it, and protecting myself is the best thing I can do. I don't know much about computers, but I know erasing my search history doesn't mean it goes away for good. It seems like there is *always* a way to recover that data.

The cops have already been here once, so there's a good chance they'll be back. The laptop needs to go. I did one final search last night so I could assess just how screwed I was if Ben was killed while I was in St. Francisville and they showed up to ask me for my alibi.

For a rock-solid alibi, I would need to have proof that I wasn't where the crime was committed, had no opportunity to commit the crime, and bonus points if I had no motive to commit the crime. And the best proof comes in the form of credit card receipts, cell phone device location, vehicle location services, metadata from videos or pictures.

All of which I provided for Camille.

None of which I have for myself.

My phone sat untouched for twelve hours. I never considered what it would mean if it showed nothing. No movement. No activity. A complete dead zone. That in and of itself seems like a red flag.

Another form of proof that works is a witness who would testify they were with you when the crime was committed. All the legal sites I visited actually consider this the weaker form of evidence, since the witness's character comes into question, like whether they're a reliable witness or have anything to gain from giving the alibi.

I have this.

Kinda.

My housemates were with me in the earlier part of the day but what they were helping me do wouldn't make any of us look good. Any of them, especially Deacon, would lie and say I was home that night, but since I basically live with a house full of criminals, I'm not sure anyone would believe them. And I don't want to drag them into this in any more than I already have.

I can show proof I visited Angola. But there's a problem there too. First, Ben was still alive while I was there, so it doesn't really help. Plus, given that I was there to visit Paul and who Paul was to me and what I believe Ben did, it only adds to motive for me, not alibi.

And then there's the issue of Chantilly's. Silas Everett was there too, and he would one hundred percent say he was there with Camille, not me.

I'm so screwed.

"You look like you're up to no good."

I spin around quickly and let out a squeak of surprise when I see Deacon standing a few feet behind me.

"You scared me!" I decide to ignore his comment.

He comes closer and now we're both standing side by side, looking down at the laptop. "Do I even want to know what you're doing right now?"

"I'm being proactive. I've been googling Ben ever since Camille showed up at Doug's. I even mapped his address and which bus would get me closest to their house before I decided to confront her outside her Junior League meeting. So I'm going to destroy the laptop so no one ever knows. You know, in case someone comes looking." We both know that "someone" would be the cops.

Deacon is quiet next to me. I'm expecting him to tell me this is another dumb idea, but he surprises me. "How are you thinking you want to do it?"

I let out a laugh. "What I'm thinking is about all the ways the internet says people mess up trying to destroy stuff like this. It's harder than you think to get rid of *everything* on a computer. And now I've got that on my internet search history too."

He crouches down and studies it like it's some bomb ready to explode. "What if we lit it on fire?"

"I thought of that, but what I read said even if you burn it, there's still a chance of partial recovery. We would have to incinerate it. Like they do dead bodies when they're cremated." I turn to look at him. "You know anyone in the funeral home business?"

Now it's his turn to laugh. "No, sorry, can't help you there. What about water?"

I shrug. "Some sites say there could be partial recovery there as well. Apparently, retrieval technology is badass. I don't want to do anything where I risk partial recovery. And before you say it, I know I'm overthinking this. I should just go throw it in the river but I can't. That seems . . . too easy and therefore not good enough." I pause a moment, then add, "The only thing I found that seemed promising is to somehow shred the inner components, especially the hard drive, into itty-bitty pieces."

He looks at me, giving me a crooked smile. "Then we're going to need a big hammer." Deacon gets up then turns around, walking to his vehicle while I follow behind him.

"Do I want to know why you have a big hammer in the back of your car?"

He shakes his head. "No, you probably don't."

Deacon opens the back door and I spot a large toolbox next to a black duffel bag.

"I probably don't want to know what's in that bag either," I say.

He turns toward me. "You're really thinking the worst of me today," he says with a laugh. "I'm not driving around town collecting dead bodies."

"I don't know what you do!" I gesture to his overall physique. "But I do know you use this big body to scare the shit out of people and you know it too."

Deacon chuckles . . . actually chuckles at my description of him. "Okay, fair."

He grabs a hammer that's about three times the size of a regular one and walks back to where the laptop is waiting.

"Oh, I can do it. I wouldn't want you to be an accessory."

Deacon rolls his eyes. "An accessory? To what? An extreme amount of internet searches?"

"It's a thing," I mutter, grabbing the end that he's holding out to me. We've both got a grip on it for a few seconds before he lets go. The hammer immediately falls to the ground, taking me with it.

And there's that chuckle again. "You'll end up hurting yourself if you try to swing this as many times as you'll need to if you want that laptop in . . . what'd you say? Itty-bitty pieces?"

Leaving the hammer on the ground, I get up and brush the dirt off the hand that caught my fall. "You could've just said it was heavy."

Not going to lie, it's impressive watching Deacon completely destroy my laptop. We end up triple-bagging it in those thick, black trash bags so the pieces are contained. He's just started working up a sweat when he lifts the bag to give it a good shake. Hearing all those pieces rattle around makes me relax for the first time in days.

"Now what?" he asks.

"I was thinking I could sprinkle them in different trash cans around town."

The look he's giving me lets me know he's done humoring me. "How about we chuck it in the river. Let it wash away into the Gulf."

"Okay, yeah, that works too."

Dumping what was left of my laptop into the river is a bit anticlimactic, and I realize I could have thrown the thing in there whole and it would have disappeared all the same. So without overthinking it, I throw my phone in just as the last piece of laptop sinks under the water.

After we leave the riverfront, Deacon stops by the store and I grab a new phone. I really don't have the money for it but there's no way I can get by without one.

As we pull out of the lot, I turn to Deacon. "Can we make a stop before heading back to the house?"

Deacon and I pull through the gates and slowly make our way down the narrow, meandering lane, taking us deeper into the property, until we come to a dead end.

"Is this it?" Deacon asks.

"Yeah."

He puts the car in park. "Want me to wait here or come with you?" He hands me the flowers we just picked up from the grocery store.

"Wait here if that's okay. I won't be long." I take the flowers, then jump out before my mind lingers on how good he's been to me over the last few days. Even more so than normal.

I've been on edge all week and I know there is one thing I can do that might make me feel a little better.

The sun casts a gentle golden glow through the clouds, and a crisp breeze blows across the lawn and through the tree limbs, making them sway. I follow the sidewalk until it ends then step carefully through the grass. The bench is shaded by a lone pecan tree on the other side of the fence. I clear away the leaves and bits of shells and sticks before sitting.

There are prettier headstones and bigger headstones in this cemetery, but I think Mom and Dad have the best spot. They are in the very back, surrounded by others on three sides instead of four. I don't know why that feels important, but it does. Also, for most of the day they are protected from the elements. These branches seem to stretch further on this side of the fence, as if they know how special my parents were and deserve to be protected from the harsh sun when it is at its highest.

"I was going to wait until I knew the truth, one way or another, before coming back, but I'm scared that's never going to happen now," I whisper to them, holding the bouquet close.

The only response is the rattle of the cicadas in the limbs above me.

"I'm not giving up, but it may take a bit longer to get the answers we all deserve. I thought I had a good plan, but I just threw my laptop in the Mississippi River, piece by piece, so I guess I need a new plan." My quiet laugh is swept away by the gentle breeze.

I push off the bench and sit cross-legged in the grass at the base of their headstones, right between them. Needing to be closer. I bury my face against the soft petals and drag in a deep breath. The fragrance of my childhood. Roses were my mom's favorite.

I pull one free from the bunch and set it in front of Dad's tombstone before laying the rest in front of Mom's, then I put a hand on each granite slab.

"I can't believe you've been gone for ten years," I whisper, my voice catching as I try unsuccessfully to stop the tears. I trace the numbers on Dad's tombstone marking the day they died, him only an hour after Mom, and wonder for the millionth time if things would have ended differently had I been with them.

My parents had gone to Corbeau to attend the wedding of a distant cousin. I was supposed to have gone with them but they let me skip when I got invited to a concert in New Orleans with my friend and her family on the same night.

Ten years since another car ran a stop sign and T-boned my parents' car, changing my world forever. On that dark, empty road, that driver made a choice. They left. Fled the scene. No call for help even though later reports showed my dad didn't die instantly. Could he have been saved if he had gotten immediate medical attention? Not knowing the answer to that question has haunted me for a decade.

But my desperation to learn the truth may be my downfall. Maybe I should have left well enough alone and not chased Camille down, insisting she work with me.

I made the decision to use Camille to get to Ben when I approached her outside her Junior League meeting instead of letting this go, so it wouldn't be hard for someone to believe I did that so I could kill him in revenge.

A hand lands on my shoulder, making me jump.

"I didn't mean to scare you. I've been calling your name." It's Deacon. He's crouched in the grass behind me. "I was getting a little worried since you've been out here so long. You okay?"

Brushing the tears away, I say, "Sorry, got lost in my head a bit."

He gets up, moving away. "There's no rush. Take all the time you need. Just wanted to check on you."

I get up. "No, I'm ready. I've got to be at the bar soon so it's time to go."

I run a hand across the top of each headstone. "This may have been a setback, but I promise I'll find out what really happened to y'all that night."

CHAPTER 30

Camille

AFTER THE ALIBI
WEDNESDAY, OCTOBER 14

I'm trembling in the chair next to Hank when he finally ends the formal interview.

"Sully, I think we're done for today. You can see how hard this is on Mrs. Bayliss. If you have any other questions for her, we'll be happy to meet here with you again, but I'm going to have to insist we give her a break."

The detective clearly isn't thrilled this interview is getting cut short. Hank told me he would stop if it he thought we were drifting into territory he wasn't comfortable with and to just sit quietly and let him be the bad guy. I guess when Detective Sullivan started asking if Ben and I had marital problems, Hank thought it was moving into murky waters.

And he wouldn't be wrong.

I wait for the detective to throw some weight around and threaten subpoenas and all the other things you see on those cop shows, but he nods and starts packing up his things. He's got to have his own thoughts about why Hank chose to stop the interview, but I don't have the bandwidth to worry about that.

It's hard enough just to put one foot in front of the other right now.

My phone vibrates with a text notification from Silas. He's outside.

"Detective Sullivan, my brother is here if you want to talk to him." I'd rather get that part over with sooner rather than later so the detective can move on.

He straightens up and nods. "Yes, that would be good." Then he looks pointedly at Hank. "Any problems with him joining us in here or would that be too much for Mrs. Bayliss?"

It's a jab that I try hard not to react to.

Hank's got that smirk. The one that lets you know he thinks you're an asshole without saying it. "I think we can accommodate the few minutes it should take for you to speak with Mr. Everett." Then Hank looks at me. "Want to tell him to come on in?"

I nod, then send the text to Silas, explaining what he'll be walking into. A few minutes later, Lila is escorting him into the conference room.

Silas greets everyone in the room then sits down next to me. He reaches over and squeezes my hand. "You good?"

My eyes must be red and puffy so there's no hiding how emotional I've been. "Yes, I'm okay."

Hank leans forward to look past me at Silas. "The detective has a few questions for you."

Detective Sullivan has pulled the recorder back out and set it to record. He does the same opening, stating his name then Silas's while also mentioning that Hank and I are still present. Then he chuckles before addressing Silas. "Mr. Everett, I feel sure I know what your answer will be, but can you please tell me where you were on Saturday night?"

Silas settles back in his chair. He looks relaxed and I'm envious of his ability to hide his emotions so well. "Sure, I met Camille for a drink. She had told me she'd be nearby when I saw her at the fundraiser for the Tarver Braddock Foundation."

"And where did you have this drink?"

"Bar called Chantilly's."

The detective is back to taking notes while Hank and I sit quietly and watch their conversation.

"And what time did you leave?"

Silas's head tilts to the side while he thinks about his answer. "I think Camille left around midnight. I wasn't far behind her."

Detective Sullivan puts his pen down and looks at Silas. "And where did you go after you left Chantilly's?"

"Home."

"In Corbeau?"

Silas smiles. "That's the only one I've got."

"You didn't drive back to Baton Rouge?"

Silas's hand flinches slightly and I'm hoping I'm the only one who noticed it. "No. I did not."

Hank steps in. "I believe Mr. Everett has answered the question that solidifies where Mrs. Bayliss was on Saturday night. So unless there's anything else . . ."

The detective smiles. "Yes, this has established where both Mrs. Bayliss and Mr. Everett were between the hours of ten p.m. and midnight. My focus is more on the hours before that, from six p.m. to eight p.m., when the coroner has placed the time of death."

Oh shit.

We all react to this news in different ways. Hank seems visibly taken aback while Silas remains stiff. My tears start falling again.

An hour or so after I left our house someone came in and murdered Ben. I can't help but think about what Silas said to me in the car before he went into the bar. *I didn't get a chance to talk to him. I knocked but he never answered.* This has me questioning things I don't want to question.

But regardless, this puts him there in that time frame. And for me, it's when I was stalking Aubrey while she was parading around as me, even though I have nothing to prove that.

This is a nightmare.

Hank recovers first. "Sully, am I misunderstanding the purpose of this visit? We've been up front and transparent with you. It's clear where Mrs. Bayliss spent her time on Saturday and it was nowhere near Baton Rouge."

I may throw up. All over this table.

Then Silas adds, "If you're looking for an alibi for me, all you need to do is ask. I was at the farm working on one of the pecan shakers until I left to meet Camille. My wife, Margaret, can verify that if necessary. Just let me know the best way for her to convey that information to you."

Oh, God. Margaret had only left about an hour before me, so this doesn't bode well for any of us.

The detective holds up a hand, sensing the hostility coming from our side of the table. We're playing right into his hands, I know it. "I would be remiss in my duties if I didn't ask the hard questions." He looks at Silas. "Let me know a good time to speak with your wife."

Hank stands up. "Sully, my office will be in touch to set that up."

Silas looks almost surprised at Hank's unspoken offer to handle this for him.

Detective Sullivan gets the not-very-subtle hint that this interview is over. For the second time, he packs his things while Silas and I watch him.

We stay in our chairs while Hank walks him out. We're both silent, not willing to bring up anything while in this room. Finally, Hank returns and drops down in the chair across from us and looks at Silas.

"Your wife really going to be able to vouch for you during that time?"

Silas nods. "Yes, of course." Then he leans forward, resting his arms on the table. "Do you think Camille is at risk of being charged with Ben's murder?"

I'm proud I don't visibly flinch at his question.

Hank looks at me then back at Silas. "I don't believe so. She has a stack of receipts showing where she was during the window they'll be focusing on. I'm more worried Sullivan doesn't have any leads so he's looking for things that aren't there."

"Dad's not happy you're taking over this firm. Representing Camille."

I turn toward my brother. "Silas! Why would you say that?"

Hank just laughs. "Oh, your dad made it crystal clear how he feels about me. If there's anything productive you'd like to say, then please do. Otherwise, I have a full day ahead and talking about the things Randall Everett does and does not approve of is a waste of time."

Silas raises one eyebrow, while I just watch them in fascinated silence. "Want to know why Ben wanted you out?"

His question knocks Hank back in his seat as if Silas physically hit him.

Silas doesn't wait for his answer. "Ben thought he could dirty you up. And he was hoping since you came from the DA's office, you would know their weaknesses. Know which guys were on the take. The ones who could be swayed and used. He'd been relying on Foster for years but wanted someone who answered to him, not to Dad. So honestly, man, take it as a compliment he didn't want you anymore. For me, it makes me feel better that you're the one who has Camille's back now instead of Ben."

Speechless. Hank and I are both speechless.

"I'll add one thing then we'll get out of your hair," Silas says as he stands up. "Ben didn't get the amount of success he did, as fast as he did, without getting his hands very dirty and creating enemies along the way. You make sure Camille stays out of the detective's crosshairs and I'll make sure the promises Ben failed to keep don't come looking for you."

Hank is rigid next to me and I cover my hands with my face and groan.

Nightmare.

My absolute worst nightmare.

"Let's go, Camille."

Hank doesn't say anything as we leave and I wait until I'm in the car with Silas before I lay into him.

"What in the hell was that? Why are you threatening Hank? He's done nothing but try to help me!"

Silas is calm as he navigates through afternoon traffic. Too calm for what just happened in there. "He needs to know what he's up against. There's a mountain of shit he's going to have to deal with if he takes over that firm. And he either needs to man up and handle it or get the hell out of there and let someone else take over."

I sink back into the seat and close my eyes. "I can't believe this is happening. That any of this is happening."

"I should have told you the truth years ago. Maybe you wouldn't have been stuck marrying that son of a bitch had you known. I may have owed Ben but you never did."

"You pretty much got stuck with Margaret too, didn't you?"

He leans his head back against the seat but doesn't answer my question so I ask another one he probably doesn't want to hear. "Will she be able to cover for you?"

He glances at me quickly then his eyes are back on the road. "I didn't kill Ben."

I don't respond because I don't know if I believe him.

"Camille, Foster didn't just keep the video of what happened to Aubrey's parents that night. He kept bits and pieces of every single thing Dad asked him to do starting before either of us was born. He's been stockpiling evidence for years because he was afraid Dad was going to turn on him. And in his position, I would have done the same thing."

"What? What are you saying?"

"When he got his diagnosis and knew he was going to die, Paul Granger wasn't the only person he went to talk to. He basically went on tour, trying to make amends to people he felt he had wronged. He kept Dad's name out of it for the most part, because while he was scared of dying, he was still scared of Dad too. But word got back to us anyway. And I went to see him."

"What did he say?"

Silas rolls his eyes. "He pulled that bullshit you'd expect someone in his position to do. 'The evidence is in a safe place and if anything happens to me, it will be released to the public.'"

"Did you believe him?"

He shrugs. "Enough that I didn't push too hard. We waited for months to see what he was going to do, but in the end, he never turned it over like he threatened, because he knew he'd lose his power the second he did. That's why we're all scrambling now that he's dead, trying to figure out where he kept it."

I bite my lip and decide to tell Silas the one part I left out from last Saturday. "Aubrey said there's a video that shows the accident. That's what Foster has. And Ben believed Foster kept everything in the gun safe at his house. Ben went as far as getting a replacement key made and he was planning to go to Foster's house and get it the night he was killed."

Silas pulls over to the side of the road and puts his truck in park. "There's more you want to say. I can tell."

"I saw where he put the key. If he died that early in the day, I don't think he had a chance to go to Foster's, so it may still be there."

"Where is it?"

I describe what I saw through the camera I had set up. Finally, he asks, "Why didn't you tell me this on Saturday when I saw you outside Chantilly's?"

"Because on Saturday at Chantilly's I thought Ben was alive and he was going to Foster's and if I told you that, you'd have gone there too." I turn away and look out the window. "And I was afraid of what would happen if y'all were both there."

CHAPTER 31

Hank

AFTER THE ALIBI
THURSDAY, OCTOBER 15

Even though I promised Lila I was headed home, I need to swing by the precinct first and have a chat with Detective Sullivan.

As I make my way back to his cubicle, every cop and detective I pass takes the opportunity to give me shit for moving to the "dark side."

"Time for some new material!" I shout back.

A few of them laugh but one guy rolls his desk chair into the aisle when I get close. "Hank, sorry about Ben. Hated hearing what happened to him."

And there's that knife to the gut again. Grief is a nasty bastard. So is guilt, because I'm not mourning him as much as I should be. "Thanks, man. I appreciate it. And everyone's efforts to catch whoever did this. We're on the same side on this one."

He throws his fist up and I bump it with mine as I walk away. There's time for a few deep breaths before I reach Sullivan's cubicle and I'm able to push the pain and grief and sadness back into the place where I've buried them.

"They're never going to let you off the hook for switching sides," the detective says when I take the empty chair next to his desk.

"Yeah, I know."

"How you holding up?"

"You want the answer everyone hopes to hear, or you want the truth?"

He gives me a sad smile. "It's always the truth for me."

"Well, the truth is I don't know how I am. Between juggling both my and Ben's active cases and trying to wrap my head around everything in Ben's estate and keeping the office running and making sure Camille is okay all while grieving my friend . . . I don't know if I'm coming or going. I'm glad tomorrow is Friday so I can put an end to this week and hopefully catch up on some sleep."

Sullivan winces and I cough, clearing the emotion from my voice. "That may have been more truth than you were asking for."

"It's exactly how I'd feel in your position." He slides a large manila envelope my way, thankfully getting back to the business at hand. "The items that were on Ben that we can go ahead and release. Need you to sign off, verifying the contents and agreeing to take responsibility for them."

"Oh, sure." I open it up and pull the items out one at a time, initialing next to the item's name on the list stapled to the front. For the keys, there is a picture on the form with each one fanned out. I check each key to make sure it matches up.

"Looks like everything is here." I put it all back inside and sign the bottom of the form before pulling it off and handing it to Sullivan. "No phone?"

"Gotta keep it awhile longer."

I lean forward in my chair and lower my voice since there's not much privacy here. "Tell me you have a suspect."

He frowns and shakes his head. "I wish we did. Given that the knife is probably the murder weapon, this is looking more like a crime of passion than premeditation. Something went sideways that night and someone took advantage of it just sitting there."

I consider everything I've learned since Sunday. Although "crime of passion" only refers to a crime happening in the heat of the moment and not planned ahead, the word "passion" always throws people because of the sexual connotation associated with it. There are those who will hear that term connected with this case and immediately assume Camille did it, strictly based on that word. "You only know that knife is missing because of that picture from an article. It's reasonable to assume someone went in there that night knowing they had a murder weapon at the ready. Not sure you can rule out premeditation."

Sullivan laughs, shaking his head. "You damn defense guys always looking to make my job harder. That might be a hard sell to a jury."

"At least tell me you're clearing Camille for this."

He's surprised by the question. "I'm not clearing anyone at this point. I consider everyone a suspect." His pointed look tells me I'm not immune.

I roll my eyes. "Jesus, Sully, you saw her. She's wrecked."

He shrugs, lifting one eyebrow. "We both know being upset isn't a sign of innocence. All I can tell you is we haven't ruled anyone out at this point."

Now he's the one leaning closer to me. "I've been told we've gotten all the information we need from Mrs. Bayliss so there's no reason for another interview. We both know where that pressure is coming from."

That would be Randall's influence. Ben has been propped up all these years by his father-in-law and his connections so it makes sense Randall's stepping in to make sure Camille is protected.

"But since you're here of your own accord, may as well ask you about this." He leans forward, grabbing a piece of paper from one of the many files on his desk, then hands it to me. "Someone sent Ben a picture of Camille in a store in St. Francisville last Saturday."

Sullivan's voice is even, but it would be hard to miss the fact that he has thoughts about this and they probably aren't good for Camille. But with the pressure to back off her, there isn't much he can do about it.

I study the printout of the screenshot while also schooling my features. This isn't Camille. I can see why someone like Sullivan, who doesn't know her as well as I do, would think it is. In the image, the woman is turned to the side, talking to a woman behind the counter, her long dark hair covering a portion of the side of her face. The lighting is not great. The outfit is what I would expect Camille to wear. But it's not her.

"Who sent this to Ben?"

"Well, that's the tricky part. The contact doesn't have a name, just a three-digit number I'm assuming meant something to Ben. The phone number was traced back to one of those prepaid phones. Ben has a dozen contacts in his phone just like this. We've matched a few to PIs you guys use. And of course, very sparse on actual conversation. Paranoid bastards. Ben called whoever sent this almost immediately after getting it. Call lasted less than a minute. The picture and call were midafternoon, a couple of hours before time of death."

It feels like my heart is about to beat out of my chest. Ben would have recognized this wasn't Camille immediately, just like I did.

My head pops up and he's staring at me. Looking for my reaction to seeing this photo for the first time. That important moment that shows so much truth. There's a reason he's telling me this now. He used the excuse to pick up Ben's stuff to get me here, but this is the conversation he really wanted to have.

"So you're thinking Ben had one of his PIs checking up on his wife while she was out of town?"

His head bobs from side to side. "Yeah, that's where I'm leaning. Makes me think there was more trouble between them than what Mrs. Bayliss alluded to."

"I think you're right when you called us paranoid bastards."

I don't owe this detective my opinion. If he wants to try to prove that this means Ben and Camille were having problems, I'm not going to help him. I give him the paper back.

His smile falls. "I know this is tough for you, Hank. These are hard things to bring up but I gotta do it."

"I know you do," I answer. "Any other leads you can tell me about?"

Sullivan lets out a deep sigh. "You know I'm not supposed to get into this with you. But you've been on this side. You know how complicated pulling apart a life like Ben's is. The clients, the cases, the families who don't feel like justice was served when Ben got a not guilty verdict." He picks up his pen, twirling it around absently, deep in his thoughts on the challenges of this case. "We did run across something that's setting off some warning bells."

His words hang in the air. I stay relaxed in my seat even though I feel like I'm about to jump out of my skin.

"What's that?" I ask in my most bored voice.

"You know there was an open file on Ben's desk at the scene. We legally couldn't go through those files, but if the information is exposed, we're allowed to look at it."

I try to act like I don't know where this is going. "You'll have to remind me which file was on top."

"It was info on a woman named Aubrey Price."

I give him a hint of a frown. "Huh. Haven't gotten to that one yet. Why did it stand out?"

He pulls out another picture. "This is her."

It's a profile shot of her. I have no idea when or where it was taken, but when he drops it down next to the picture of "Camille" that was sent to Ben's phone, you'd have to be an idiot not to see the resemblance.

"Cute girl."

"Aubrey Price lives at the same house as the mechanics who restored that Mustang for Ben. The same car that was delivered the day he was killed."

I relax back in my seat. "Yeah? That's pretty wild."

The corner of his mouth quirks up. "You think that's wild, get this. Aubrey Price's parents were killed in Corbeau. The guy convicted for their deaths, Paul Granger, lived right down the street from Ben."

I throw my hands up in surrender. "Not gonna lie, Sullivan, you've got my head spinning with this. Seems like a weird coincidence, honestly." I laugh and it sounds a little too loud, even to my ears.

He holds my stare. "Hank, you're a good guy. Principled in a way that Ben wasn't."

This conversation needs to end. Immediately.

I nod, then get up from my chair. "Let me know if we can help out.

We've been going through his active cases to make sure nothing is slipping through. We want nothing more than Ben's murderer caught."

Sullivan nods and I take my leave.

Slamming my hand against the steering wheel several times does nothing to ease my frustration. I'm unsettled. Antsy.

Instead of heading home for the night, I decide to make a detour.

Two guys are playing pool at one of the tables and there's a booth with a couple toward the back of the room as well as a guy sitting on a stool about halfway down the bar. There's no sign of Aubrey Price, even though the file Ben had on her says she works every night except Sunday and Monday.

I choose the stool that gives me as much distance from everyone else as possible since it will be hard enough getting her to talk to me if she shows up. I don't want her worried about who could be overhearing our conversation.

Aubrey comes out of a door against the far wall carrying a tray of glasses.

Thanks to Scott, who gave me a summary on Aubrey and the other people who live in that house with her, I memorized the bullet points about each of them using the same techniques that helped me easily recall different football plays.

Aubrey Price, white, twenty-six. Employed as a bartender at Doug's for the last five years and longest resident in the house. Clean record, no arrests. Orphaned at sixteen when parents were killed by a drunk driver. Lived with her aunt and uncle on her mother's side until she was a legal adult. Never married, no sign of being in a relationship.

She sets the glasses down on the counter then wipes her hands on a bar towel as she walks toward me.

"What can I get you?"

"Ultra on draft."

She steps away to pour my beer then sets it down in front of me. "Anything else?"

"About five minutes of your time, if possible."

"For what?" she asks.

"My name is Hank Landry, Ben Bayliss's law partner."

This makes her take a step back. She scans the room, hoping, I'm sure, for some task needing her immediate attention, but there's nothing. Aubrey seems to resign herself to talking to me because I see her square her shoulders just before she turns to face me head-on.

"I'm also the executor of his estate, and I'm just trying to get a handle on Ben's things, which is an extremely difficult task while also mourning the loss of my friend and partner. There are some things I've learned that left me a little confused."

She raises just one eyebrow. "Was there a question in there somewhere?"

My laugh catches us both off guard but at least it cuts the tension a bit. "I have about a million questions but almost all of them are for Ben, and, well, I'm outta luck there. But yes, I do have a question. Why did you come to the Rosary for Ben on Tuesday?"

Her jaw goes slack, her eyes blinking rapidly. But she recovers from her shock quickly. "His wife took yoga from my housemate Serenity. She wanted to go but not alone, so I agreed to meet her there. But Serenity being Serenity, she flaked off and didn't show."

I've underestimated her. I expected her to mention Shane and Eddie, which would lead me to asking about the Mustang.

"That it?" she asks.

"One more, if you'll allow it. Were you, by chance, in St. Francisville last Saturday?"

There's a split second of pure shock that crosses her features before she hides it away. Then she tilts her head to the side while she studies me. "That's a pretty random thing to ask me."

I shrug. "As I said earlier, Ben isn't here to answer my questions. It feels like I'm missing something. I'm just trying to make this make sense."

"Well, welcome to my world. I've been trying to get things to make sense for a really long time." She glances at the wall clock behind the bar. "And that's your five minutes."

I tip my head toward her. "That's fair. I appreciate your time."

She walks away while I sip on my beer, deciding it was a terrible idea to come in here and tip her off that I may know things that I really don't know. But if there's one thing I'm sure of, the woman in that picture on Ben's phone was Aubrey Price. And her name has been swirling around Ben's since Camille found his body on Sunday morning. There's a lot Camille isn't telling me.

Aubrey makes sure not to come anywhere near me for the next half hour, and I realize I've gotten everything I'm gonna get out of her. I wanted some indication I'm thinking in the right direction and her reaction has given me that.

I throw a twenty on the bar to cover my beer plus a generous tip and head outside. I'm only a few steps past the front door when a guy follows me.

And because Scott is thorough, he included photos with each housemate summary, so I while I didn't notice him inside, I recognize him now.

Francis Deacon: mixed race (father is white, mother is Cuban), thirty-two years old. Goes by Deacon. Sealed file from juvie. A couple of arrests since turning eighteen. Some petty theft, resisting arrest, and a handful of charges for fighting. Nothing since he started working for a bookie named Chris Ricci, first cousin on his dad's side. Never married, no sign of being in a relationship.

He steps in front of me, blocking my way.

"Excuse me," I say, stepping to the right so I can move around him, but he mirrors my move. I put my hands in my pockets, showing him I'm no threat, although we both know he could whip my ass easily. "Look, man, not sure how I've pissed you off, but I'd really like to get out of here and call it a day."

His arms are crossed in front of him and he doesn't seem to have any intention of letting me pass. "Why are you here?"

"Stopped in for a beer?" Pretty sure he's not going to buy that.

"Try again."

Thought so. "I'm guessing you know who I am and who my partner was so we'll skip that part. I had a few questions for Aubrey Price and decided to stop in and ask her. That okay?" I'm too tired to play any more games. "Do we have a problem?"

"Does Aubrey?"

Pulling my hands loose from my pockets, I hold them out to my sides in a form of surrender. "I've got zero problems with Aubrey. I'm trying to figure out what the hell was going on with *Ben*." I let that hang in the air a minute then add, "You work for Chris Ricci, right?"

His right eye flinches just slightly. He takes a small step toward me and I'm proud of myself for not backing up.

"I promise you I'm not dumb enough to get on your bad side, man. Glad Aubrey's got someone looking out for her. I'm not your enemy. Or hers. All I'm trying to do is wrap my head around what Ben was doing."

A small smile flashes across his face and that worries me more than the fierce look I was getting. "You want to know what your buddy Ben was up to? Maybe you should ask his wife? Pretty sure she'd be able to answer all your questions."

Now I take a step back because I was not prepared for him to bring Camille into this. "Camille Bayliss is devastated by the loss of her husband and has willingly cooperated with authorities in hopes that his killer is found as soon as possible." He can say whatever he wants to me but I'm not going to let him sit here and malign her character.

He laughs. "Well, look at you. You're pretty protective of her. Maybe more than someone should be over their dead partner's widow."

We're done here.

But Deacon isn't finished. "If you know anything about Chris Ricci and the people in his employ, then you know we don't hesitate protecting one of our own."

We stare at each other for a few tense seconds. "Message received."

Before I can step around him, Deacon adds, "I get you're in a tough spot and trying to figure shit out. I only mention his wife because, like you, I'm trying to protect someone I care about."

I hesitate a second or so then pull out my wallet. "My card. With my cell number. If . . . *something significant* happens, give me a call."

CHAPTER 32

Aubrey

AFTER THE ALIBI
FRIDAY, OCTOBER 16

I groan when we pull up the driveway and see all the people still filling the backyard. I'm home a few hours earlier than normal. Doug messed up the schedule, had too many of us there and needed one of us to take off early because it was too crowded behind the bar. I'm usually the last to offer to do that since I need the money, but it's been a long-ass week.

But it's Friday night and I forgot Serenity planned to use the backyard to throw a birthday party for her boyfriend, Frank. The small space is packed with people and the party doesn't show any signs of slowing down. I should have just stayed at work.

"This is more people than she said it would be." Deacon throws the car in park and goes to get out but my hand on his arm stops him. He's given me a ride home every night this week, and I'm not gonna lie, I'm getting a little spoiled.

"It's his birthday. If everyone else in the house is okay with it, I'm fine with it too." The crowd and noise won't bother Deacon so he'd only be forcing Serenity to end Frank's party early for me.

"No one else's window is within feet of where she set up the keg."

Unhooking my seat belt, I lean close and give him a hug. "Thank you for the ride. So much better than walking."

He tugs on the back of my shirt before I make it out of the car. "Hold up." Deacon opens the center console and pulls out a single key. "Here's the key to my room I promised. Stay in there tonight. You won't hear them up there. Use the tub again if you want."

"I'm definitely taking you up on the tub again but I'm sure the crowd will be gone by the time I get out, so I can stay in my room. I'd hate if you got off early and you couldn't get some sleep because I was in there."

He laughs and leans a little closer. "If I'm being honest, finding you in my bed wouldn't be unwelcome."

My cheeks heat and I duck my face into my shoulder. The huge, goofy smile is still in place when I look back up at him, which makes me blush even harder.

I've been alone for so long. So scared to let anyone in. Let anyone get close in case I lost them like I lost my parents.

But then I realize I've already let Deacon in. I'm already past the point where I would be devastated if something happened to him. I'd say it snuck up on me but it didn't. It's been growing slowly but steadily since he first moved in. This past week just highlighted how often I turn to him and how rock solid and there for me he is without question.

His hand slides into mine, our fingers lacing together.

The second his skin touches mine, I know I'm not alone in my feelings, even if I've only just recognized them for what they are.

There must be something in my expression that makes him think he's overstepped because he starts to pull his hand away. I tighten my grip, trapping him. "I probably look like I'm freaking out or not open to whatever this is but I am. I'm just not very good at letting people get close. And I don't know how to thank you for everything you've done for me. And not just this week. You don't think I know you're the one who refills my laundry detergent and makes sure there's food in my cabinet? It's not fair though. You've been so good to me and I haven't done anything as nice for you."

There's surprise but then also something else in his gaze. Maybe it's relief that I'm finally seeing what he's been trying to show me. He slides his free hand across my cheek, into my hair. "You've trusted me with your biggest secrets. Looked to me when you needed someone. I think we're pretty even."

We stay like this for a few seconds until he slowly pulls his hand away from my face then unlinks his fingers from mine. "I better go. I'm close to bailing on work and going inside with you but Chris would kill me. Stay in my room. I'd love nothing more than to find you in there when I get home."

Emotion clogs my throat and words fail me, so I can only nod. He watches me until I turn the corner and disappear from view.

I've gone from dreading the night to suddenly looking forward to it.

I unlock the exterior door to my room so I can get my things before going to his. Heading to the bathroom first, I load my caddy up with bath and hair stuff then move to the closet to grab some pjs.

Just as I shove my hand in the top drawer, I feel something sharp. "Ow!" I pull it out and my finger is bleeding. Carefully, I move the clothing aside piece by piece until I see it.

I don't realize I'm screaming until Shane and Eddie rush into my room. Shane skids to a stop next to me. "What's wrong?"

Eddie looks in my bathroom as if he's searching for an intruder then pulls my curtain back to check my window.

My injured hand is balled against my chest and I'm trying to slow my breathing.

Shane leans closer to look into my dresser then at me, confused. "What the hell is that?"

Eddie moves in to see for himself. "Shit. That's a big fucking knife." He grabs a pair of sleep shorts and uses it as a barrier between his hand and the hilt, then holds it up for inspection.

"Is that dried blood?" Shane asks.

I feel like I'm either going to pass out or throw up when I see the engraving on the blade: BWB.

The program for the Rosary had Ben's full name. Benjamin Wyatt Bayliss.

BWB.

"No. No, no, no . . ."

Shane steps back. "Holy shit. That knife looks like the same one that was on Ben Bayliss's desk."

"Those are Ben's initials!" I take a step back, tripping over my own feet. "Someone's trying to set me up!" I press myself against the wall, my hand on my heart as if I can stop it from racing.

"Oh, shit," Eddie says, holding the knife higher to inspect it.

Shane grabs Eddie by the shoulder, pushing him to the door. "We need to get that out of here. Like right now."

Eddie has the sleep shorts and knife still gripped in his hand and moves it behind his back when he leaves my room. Shane is directly behind him, shielding it from view. I'm right on their heels. No one at the party pays us any attention as we move across the yard to the garage, walking straight to the car the guys started working on after finishing with Ben's Mustang. It's elevated a couple of feet off the ground and all the tires are off to the side.

"Pull the oil pan off," Eddie says. Shane drops down on the little roller board thing they use to slide under the car. In a minute or two he is sliding back out, the pan resting on his chest and stomach. Eddie drops the knife and my sleep shorts in the pan, which is partially filled with oil. It only takes a few seconds for them to sink out of sight.

"Okay, put it back."

Oh my God.

Once Shane is out from under the car, Eddie hustles us all out of the garage.

"Sit," Shane says.

I find an empty folding chair not far from the keg. Eddie fills up cups for all three of us while Shane pulls two more chairs closer, putting them on each side of me.

My blood is pounding and my hands are trembling so bad that beer is spilling over the edge of the cup. "I can't sit out here. I need to find out who was in my room. Who would do this to me."

I go to get up but Eddie puts a hand on my leg, holding me in my seat. "No, we're waiting right here. There will be time for that later but not right now."

Shane puts his arm on the back of my chair, his hand resting on my shoulder. "The only reason you plant something like that in a place where it would easily be discovered is so the cops find it. You're not supposed to be here. You should still be at work. So there's a good chance the cops will arrive before you're scheduled to be home."

"You think the cops are going to show up here?" My voice is shrill.

Shane nods. "Yeah, I do."

Eddie says, "And we're going to be shocked when that happens since all we're trying to do is enjoy our housemate's boyfriend's birthday party."

The wait is excruciating. It's only about an hour before my normal shift ends and I don't know what we're going to do if we pass that time and no one has shown up. But almost as soon as I start to think the guys have overreacted, the wail of sirens has us all turning around.

The driveway is only wide enough for one car, but the noise tells us there is definitely more than one out front.

Half a dozen cops flood the backyard. The music is turned off while we all stare at them.

One of the cops steps forward. "I need everyone to stay right where you are. We're looking for Aubrey Price."

The three of us stand and I raise my hand slowly. "I'm Aubrey Price."

He moves toward me, a piece of paper extended. "We have a warrant to search your premises."

There's no need to fake being shocked, because even though the guys told me this was likely, I'm absolutely floored this is happening. I take the paper from him but don't look at it. "I don't understand. Why do you need to search my room?"

"It's all listed on the warrant, but to summarize, we are searching for a hunting knife that matches the description of the one missing from the Bayliss home."

"This is crazy! I don't have anyone's knife!"

Eddie puts a hand on my arm. "Aub, it's best to just let them do what they need to do."

Serenity moves closer. "I don't know why y'all are here but this is bullshit."

Shane shakes his head at her then whispers softly, "Don't give them any reason to arrest you, okay?"

It looks like she's about to go off on them, but Frank slides an arm around her and whispers something in her ear. Whatever he says seems to settle her down.

The cop looks at Eddie, Shane, and Serenity. "Are you the other residents?"

They nod and Serenity adds, "There's another one but he works nights."

Eddie asks, "Does the warrant cover the search of the entire house or just Aubrey's space?"

"Just the space Miss Price has access to, which is her unit and any common areas. We will not enter any of the other units. The property management company supplied us with a detailed plan of the house. Miss Price will need to remain out here but the rest of you are free to go back to your own units. You just have to stay out of the common areas."

"We'll stay out here with Aubrey until you're done," Shane says.

We were able to hide the knife, but we didn't check to see if there was anything else planted in my room, waiting to be found.

Tears form and spill over. I bat them away only for them to quickly be replaced. I hate crying. Hate it. But now that I've started, I can't seem to stop.

Shane pulls me back to the chairs we were sitting in when the cops arrived, Eddie following close behind.

Frank's party breaks up, everyone deciding it's time to go home after a few of them are questioned by the police. No one wants to be caught up in whatever this is, but Frank stays, pulling up chairs for himself and Serenity next to us. I'll be forever grateful to them for sticking with me.

Cops come in and out of the house, but thankfully, no one goes into the garage. Shane and Eddie pay an extra hundred dollars a month in rent for it so it should not be considered a common area.

Deacon is aware of what's going on since Shane called him, but we decided if things go sideways here, he's more help to us if he's not involved. We may need someone available to bail us out of jail.

Close to one a.m., the cop who spoke to us earlier exits the house, followed by the half dozen who showed up with him. He approaches where we've been waiting patiently.

"We have executed the search and it came up empty. If you have any questions, you can call the number on the paperwork I gave you when we arrived."

We just look at him.

When he realizes we aren't going to say anything, he adds, "You are free to enter your unit, Miss Price."

He turns to leave and yet we still don't move. Not until every single cop is gone.

When it's just us, I call Deacon. "They're gone."

"I'll be there in five." The line goes dead.

Serenity motions for Frank to follow her back to her place above the garage. "Fill us in tomorrow. We're headed to bed." I appreciate Serenity getting Frank out of here because we wouldn't be able to speak freely in front of him.

The rest of us move to the kitchen, where we wait for Deacon.

Eddie drops the copy of the warrant on the table. "I'm going to walk through the house to make sure they didn't break anything. At some point, everyone else needs to check their rooms to make sure the cops didn't go where they weren't allowed."

Shane pulls a couple of beers from the fridge, offering one to me, but I decline.

I scrub my hands across my face, wishing I could wipe away the evidence of how badly this has upset me, but I start crying again the second Deacon walks through the back door.

He sees me immediately and slides into the chair next to mine. "Are you okay?"

I nod and he wraps an arm around me, pulling me in close.

"What the hell happened?"

Eddie catches him up on everything. Deacon is absently playing with the ends of my hair and I sink into him even more while I listen to them bat around their theories.

Finally, Deacon says, "Let's talk to Serenity in the morning about a list of people at the party since one of them could have planted the knife. Not much else we can do tonight. Until we figure out who did this, the house stays locked up tight. No one but us in or out. Everyone good with that?"

We all nod.

Shane and Eddie head to their room and then it's just Deacon and me in the kitchen. I can tell from how tense he looks that he's pissed. He shifts me to the side so he can pull his wallet out of his back pocket and pulls out a business card and props it against the saltshaker so he can read the number.

"Who are you calling?"

"That lawyer, Hank, who showed up at Doug's last night."

"Why are you calling him?"

He finishes putting the number in and hits the call button. "He said to call him if something significant happens and this feels pretty fucking significant."

Despite the late hour, Hank Landry shows up forty-five minutes after Deacon called him. While we waited, Deacon peeked in my room, but neither of us went in any further. We wanted him to see it exactly as the cops left it.

We meet Hank in the front yard after he texted Deacon that he was parked on the street in front of the house.

Things are tense. We're not friends. We're not working together. But somehow we've found ourselves connected to Hank in a weird way.

"Show me where they searched." It's all he says as we lead him around the house to the backyard, taking him to my exterior entrance so we don't wake up Shane and Eddie.

His shoulders stiffen when he sees the mess left behind in my room. "Did they give you a copy of the warrant?"

I hand him the document the cop gave me, and Deacon and I stand quietly next to him while he reads through it.

After he's finished, he glances around the room. "And they said the search was unsuccessful?"

I nod.

Hank walks through the room, stopping near my dresser, where the knife was planted. Obviously, we left that part out.

Deacon gets antsy and rights the mattress over the box spring then picks up the sheets and comforter to remake the bed. I appreciate the effort but I'm not sure I'll ever be able to sleep peacefully in here again.

"What is all of this?" Hank asks.

I have to step around a pile of clothes to see what he's referring to. "Shit," I mumble when I move closer. "Those are the letters and gifts an inmate at Angola named Paul Granger has sent me over the last several months. The police must have spread them out like that because they were in my drawer."

Each letter is unfolded and stacked on top of the dresser, next to the leather goods he makes and sends with each one.

Hank's head tilts to the side. "Gifts?"

Hank not asking who Paul Granger is tells me he's way more aware of what's going on than he let on at the bar last night.

"He makes leather goods and sells them at the craft shows Angola has on Sundays in April and October."

Hank picks each one up, inspecting all the items. There's a wallet, a couple of bracelets, a jewelry box, and the bookmark.

He moves on to the letters and reads each one carefully.

"He makes a good case," I say.

Hank ignores my comment and instead says, "All the letters are handwritten except this one. When did you get it?"

"Hold on." I shuffle the letters around and match them up. "This one came with the wallet, which also had a Saint Jude prayer card in. He's the patron saint of lost causes. Paul is kinda dramatic like that. The bracelets came separately with these two, and the typed one came inside the jewelry box. That's the last one I got."

"And the bookmark?"

I shake my head. "No letter with that." I'm not about to tell him I visited Paul in person last weekend.

Hank looks everything over then takes a step back. "I'm not sure what you want me to do about any of this."

"You showed up at Doug's last night for a reason." Deacon has been silent up until now. "You know more than you're saying, which I get. The cops thought a knife missing from the Bayliss house was in this room. Just know that if Aubrey is in their sights, so is Camille Bayliss. But I think you know that already."

Hank lets out a deep breath. He looks tired. Beat. This hasn't been an easy week on him either.

Deacon takes a step closer, his voice dropping to a whisper. "There's no saving one without saving the other."

The grim look on Hank's face tells me he's not convinced that's the case.

"Ask Camille why I was at the Rosary," I blurt out. "Why I was in St. Francisville." It's a risk saying this to him, but the fact that a killer broke into my room and planted a murder weapon makes it worth it.

He turns to me, his eyes scanning my face as he seems to consider what he wants to say.

"I think it's best if I leave. If you need legal counsel, my office can recommend someone."

And then he's gone.

"Shit," Deacon says.

"Was calling him the right thing to do?" I sink down on the bed.

"Who the hell knows? But I do think he's a stand-up guy. And I don't think he'll let you take the fall for this if it means Camille gets in trouble too." Deacon moves closer, pulling me to stand. "Let's do this, get what you need from here and bring it to my room. We'll get you settled in there. I can stay in here tonight if that makes you more comfortable."

"Okay."

We dig around for my phone charger, my favorite pillow, some pajamas. My room is a complete disaster. My sadness turns to anger. Not only was I violated by whoever planted that knife but also by the cops who tore apart my room. Once I have everything I need, we walk upstairs to his room. I crawl in his bed while he plugs in my charger.

"What do we do?" I should probably correct that to *What should I do*, but he doesn't seem phased.

"Not much tonight. Try to get some rest and we'll make a plan tomorrow. I'm going to take a quick shower and then I'll head down to your room."

I watch as he gathers some clean clothes from his closet to take into the bathroom with him, and in that instant, I'm not only angry about someone trying to pin Ben's murder on me, I'm angry someone took away a night with Deacon that I was looking forward to. It's the worst possible time to start something with him, but the one thing I've learned is not to wait for what you want because you never know how long you have to get it. He's being delicate with me, which is really sweet. But it's not what I want right now.

Without overthinking it, I throw off the covers, shed my clothes, and join Deacon in the shower.

CHAPTER 33

Ben

TEN YEARS AGO

We're both quiet on the ride back to Corbeau. Margaret spent a few hours at the townhouse with Silas yesterday then left to go home. I ordered us a pizza and we watched a baseball game and spoke only a few words to each other. Before this weekend, Silas and I got along fine. He's a couple of years younger than us so it's not like we were close, but we could easily hold a conversation.

I glance at Silas. "The silence is getting old."

He's leaned back in the passenger seat, staring out of the window. "I know you think I should be appreciative that you're lying for me but I didn't ask you to, my dad did."

"So you don't want me to?"

He shrugs. "It doesn't matter what I want. You're stuck doing it and I'm stuck letting you. Neither of us really ever had a choice."

Laughing, I say, "How sad for you that your dad is making sure you don't go to jail for drunk driving and God knows what else. We still don't know what happened to whoever you hit." He flinches at my words.

That accident wasn't picked up by the Baton Rouge news stations so we still haven't heard if anyone was hurt.

"Whatever my dad is doing is for him and the family name, not me. You're stupid enough to think you've got some power over him now. And he'll let you think that as long as it keeps you in line. What he really did was figure out your price, which was pretty low, honestly. Whatever happened to the people I hit is on you too. Plus whatever happens to Paul Granger, because they will bury him for this."

"Whatever. Paul should have been in jail years ago. You forget, he's from my side of town. He's a drug dealer who doesn't care about the quality of his product or the people he poisons with it. Only reason he's free is because the people on your side of town would have to admit their kids are addicts. Probably save some lives by getting him behind bars."

He grunts, taking issue with my assessment of Paul. He can do his own digging and he'll find out I'm not exaggerating.

"You'd rather go down for what happened? Really? I've seen how you live and you wouldn't fare well behind bars."

Silas finally turns around. "No, I don't want to go down for it but that doesn't mean I don't feel like fucking shit for what I did. And for those people I hit. And for Paul, even if he does deserve to be in jail."

We pull into their driveway. It's long enough that you can't see the house from the road.

Mr. Everett had called before we left Baton Rouge and told me to drop Silas off but not come in, adding that someone would stop by my house later for my statement.

There's a cop car in the driveway, telling us Foster is already here. Silas straightens but there's no hiding the look on his face. It's fucking pitiful. "You need to pull yourself together. If you're struggling so bad, get your daddy to hire a shrink you can talk to."

Silas rolls his eyes and jumps out of the car the second I come to a stop.

Instead of driving straight home, I pull into Margaret's driveway. I'm telling myself I just want to talk to her, but really, I'm not ready to face Mom. Mr. Everett had forwarded me an email this afternoon detailing the steps he plans to take for her next week. As soon as I sign my witness statement, Mom will be debt-free and entering a treatment facility where she will get help with her depression and the subsequent alcohol addiction born from it.

Margaret's driveway is empty as expected, since her parents work weekend shifts and she doesn't have a car. She had to borrow her friend's car to come check on Silas yesterday. I knock and ring the doorbell but no one comes to the door.

It takes some effort to get through the overgrown shrubbery on the side of her house. I'll be covered in scrapes and scratches from the branches by the time I get close enough to knock on the glass.

Luckily, her curtain is parted enough that I can see inside. She's on her bed, an open laptop in front of her and headphones on, which is probably why she didn't hear me knocking.

I wave my hands around and finally get her attention. Without meaning to scare her, I do just that.

Margaret takes her time coming to the window. Once it's raised, she says, "Why are you here?"

I push her back just enough that I can crawl inside. "You climbed in mine so I can climb through yours."

She turns around, grabs the blanket from the end of the bed, and wraps it around her shoulders.

"Just wanted to check on you. Make sure you're okay."

She rolls her eyes then drops down on the bed again, waiting for me to get to the point of why I'm here. "You're checking to see if I'm going to keep Silas's secret, which is now your secret since you're covering for him. You don't care about me." She pulls the blanket tighter. "Did you hear the couple in that car died?"

My stomach flips. Shit. Silas will not handle the news well and now I'm thinking that's why Mr. Everett didn't want me to come inside when I dropped Silas off. I bet he's doing damage control.

I feel bad but remind myself that there's nothing I agreed to that would have stopped their deaths. This is on Silas. Not me.

Margaret bites down on her bottom lip while her eyes get glassy. "I didn't think the wreck was that bad. We were barely hurt."

"It's okay to talk about it if you want. Obviously, I'm not saying anything."

"Have you talked to the police yet?"

I shake my head. "No, Silas is talking to them right now. They're supposed to come to my house later. Have you given your statement?"

"Foster came by yesterday."

She picks at the material at the edge of the blanket. We're silent again and it's awkward.

"Well, if you're okay then I guess I'll go. But call Silas. He's not handling this very well at all."

"Okay, I will," she says, then pushes her hair out of her face. "Mr. Everett went from trying to keep me away from Silas to calling me family. Did he call you that too?"

I lean back against her doorframe. "Yeah. Nicest he's been to me since I first starting dating Camille."

"Yeah, me too." She plays with the ends of her hair, twisting it around her finger. "It feels different, doesn't it. I've been hanging on to Silas by the tips of my fingers and now it feels like I've got a good hold on him with both hands. Mr. Everett will do whatever it takes to make us happy now that we're keeping Silas's secret."

The same thought has been floating around my head for the last couple of days.

"But that doesn't mean he won't take advantage of the first opportunity to get rid of us. It's not like we'd be the first choice for either of his kids if he had his way," she adds.

Yeah, I was thinking that too. "We need to stick together. I've got your back if you've got mine."

"Silas and Camille are stuck with us now, though. Not too bad for two white-trash kids from the south side of Corbeau." And for the first time since Saturday night, her mouth turns up in a smile.

CHAPTER 34

Camille

AFTER THE ALIBI
SATURDAY, OCTOBER 17

Silas and I pull into the garage at my house and I'm frozen in the passenger seat. We're in my car since the opener is programmed directly to it. This is our only way inside, since I've become a little too dependent on the keypad lock on the door in the garage and don't carry a house key anymore.

"I don't know if I can go in." The police were done days ago, but it took a while to get a cleaning service that specializes in crime scenes here and there's no way I was coming back until they were done.

Technically, I'm free to move home, but my parents think it's too dangerous since the police still haven't made an arrest. But honestly, I'm not sure I could stay here even if Ben's killer is caught.

Silas puts the car in park but doesn't cut the engine. "You don't have to. I can run in and get it."

He starts to get out but I stop him. "Wait. Just give me a minute."

"Whatever you need," he says as he settles back in his seat.

"I just feel like if I don't go in now, I'll never be able to."

A mix of emotions rolls through me. Even though I know Ben isn't on the floor of his office, that's all I picture when I think about going inside. The ache in my chest flares when faced with walking into the house he loved. The house he spent so much time perfecting. The house that has always felt more his than mine.

I don't want to be one of those people who sugarcoats all the bad times with someone just because they're gone, but grief has a funny way of making the good moments we shared shine brighter in my memory. The misgivings and concerns that drove every single action I made last weekend seem minor now.

I give myself a few minutes to center myself in reality, mentally listing all the reasons I snuck back here and climbed in the attic to spy on Ben exactly a week ago. Those rose-colored memories can't hold up against the fact that we're here to find the key to a dead cop's gun safe so we can retrieve evidence that Ben was going to use against my brother. It's a horrible way to think about it but the only thing that grounds me.

"Not trying to rush you but we only have a small window of opportunity to get into Foster's house while his wife is out this afternoon."

Silas created a situation where Mrs. Foster would be away from home. The Corbeau Police Department will be honoring Kevin Foster today by having a small reception and presenting his wife with a plaque. I'm impressed Silas was able to throw that together in a couple of days.

"Okay, I'm . . . I'm ready."

He wastes no time getting out of the car while I'm moving at half speed. I follow him to the door and tell him the four-digit code to unlock it. Silas bounds into the kitchen once it's open, while I'm still stuck in the garage.

He's back by my side when he realizes I didn't enter behind him. "You do not have to do this."

"Yes I do."

He holds out his arm and I clutch it like my life depends on it. Slowly, he pulls me through the door.

A strong antiseptic smell hits me the second we're inside. He leads the way to the kitchen, and there's a stillness in the air as if the house knows it's been abandoned.

That stupid mum is still sitting on the counter, the same one I felt so smug that I had already bought when Ben questioned why I was at the feed store. How naive I was to be worried about him catching me in a lie. The tiny flowers are withered and dead from lack of water, as if this house has sucked the life out of everything inside it.

I move to the small desk where I pay bills and keep my calendar and pick up the glass jar that holds all my pens and markers. I dump the whole thing out and sort through them until I find the key.

"Just where he left it."

Silas is driving us back to Corbeau. We left the house as soon as we retrieved the key. He asked me if I wanted to grab any clothes or other items, but I couldn't bring myself to go any further inside than the kitchen.

I twist the key in my hands and think about how drastically my life has changed in the last week.

"Was Ben killed over this?"

It takes a while for Silas to answer me. "That's my guess. When Ben first came to Dad and me to tell us about Hank getting Paul's file, he was freaking out. Worried how it would look if the truth came out now. How it would hurt his practice. Dad lost his shit though and was less worried about Paul and more about how much other evidence Foster had been stockpiling over the years. Paul Granger's case would blow back on me and Ben, but everything else would destroy Dad."

I can only imagine how pissed Dad was. "So what did Ben do once he realized that?"

"He turned on us immediately. You could see it in his face. Almost hear the thoughts rolling around in his head. How much control he'd have over us if he got to it first."

The trees pass by in a blur as I stare out the window and process everything Silas is telling me. I'm embarrassed about how naive I've been. How my entire family knew more about my husband than I did.

I can't look at Silas when I admit, "I always felt like Ben and I were better than Mom and Dad. Superior to them. I mean, I knew Ben wasn't perfect and pushed the line of what was legal, but I had no idea how far on the other side of it he really was. Or that Dad was helping him. I feel so stupid."

"Don't feel like that. I'm glad you didn't know. I was relieved you were blissfully unaware. Ben's problem is he didn't understand what becoming a member of this family meant. Dad wanted to control him like he did us. At first, he was okay with it because Dad made sure he got some big clients and won those cases. But then Ben realized you couldn't just take the parts you wanted, you were stuck with all of it. Ben would have made the most out of having this wealth of information to hold over all our heads."

Looking at Silas, I ask, "Did Dad have him killed?"

Silas shakes his head. "He wouldn't have done that before we had possession of those files. Before he was sure Ben didn't have a copy stashed somewhere."

It's a cold answer, especially since it's about my husband.

"So who killed him?"

He shrugs. "Honestly, I don't know. Foster wasn't just confessing his sins, he was outing anyone who helped him, because he's definitely had help over the years. Maybe whoever helped Foster got wind of what Ben was up to that day. Was worried about how he'd use that information against them. Or there's a chance it wasn't about this at all. Maybe it *was* something to do with one of his cases. Maybe he was messing around with someone else and their husband found out. Hell, Camille, I really don't know."

Shivers roll through me as I consider his words. We're back in Corbeau, headed to Foster's. The closer we get to his house, the more my thoughts switch from what happened to Ben to what we're about to do.

"We're just going to pull into the driveway and walk inside?" I ask.

"I offered to take you back to Dad's."

"And I told you I'm seeing this through."

Silas is trying to act like this isn't affecting him but from that white-knuckle grip he has on the steering wheel, I know it's taking a lot to hold himself together.

He nods to the back seat. "That's what the gift basket is for. We'll leave it on the doormat so if someone says they saw your car here, Mrs. Foster will think we were just dropping this off."

I pick at my nails, which are already destroyed. "But she'll know we were here."

He nods. "That's the point. You don't try to hide it, you embrace it. Answer the question before they can ask it."

"Something is wrong with you that your mind works like that."

He chuckles but it sounds sad. "Dad's had a long time to groom me."

Silas pulls over at a gas station not far from Foster's house. "Why are we stopping here?" I ask.

He pulls his phone out. "Just making sure Mrs. Foster is at the ceremony in town." He sends a text then we wait a few minutes until we get a response. "We're good to go."

My heart is racing when we pull into the driveway. The Fosters' house is just out of the city limits on a small plot of land, so at least the neighbors aren't on top of one another. It's a modest house considering how much money he's had to have made doing all Dad's dirty work over the years.

Silas parks and says, "Grab the basket."

I do what he says and follow him to the carport door. "How are we getting in?"

"Foster kept a key on a hook in the storage closet."

Silas opens the closet door in the carport and a few seconds later he's got a house key in his hand.

"Not very smart for a cop," I mutter.

"It's Corbeau and everyone knew who he was connected to. No one was breaking into his house."

"Except you."

He raises one eyebrow. "Yeah, except me."

I set the gift basket and card down on the mat in front of the door then follow Silas inside. It feels so wrong walking through the house, knowing his widow will come back and hopefully have no idea we were here. We only have to look into a few rooms before we find the safe. It's huge. So much bigger than I'd thought it would be.

"It's almost as tall as I am." The gun safe looms in the corner of a small office next to a recliner that looks at least twenty years old.

"Well, yeah, it's made to hold half a dozen hunting rifles."

Dad has a whole room that is reinforced for stuff like this, so I've never seen this kind of safe. It feels like I'm walking up to a bomb that needs to be defused.

Knowing there's a good chance Ben was killed because of what's behind that door makes me queasy.

And scared.

Silas pulls off the circular mechanism that houses the digital lock and lets it hang by the red and blue wires that power it. A small keyhole is visible underneath.

"This is the backup in case the electronics fail." Silas takes the replacement key and slips it inside. We both hold our breath when he turns it in the lock. There's a click and then Silas turns the wheel and we hear the bolts slide back into the door.

He takes a deep breath and then pulls it open.

It's completely empty.

Not a single thing inside.

Just as I start to say something, we both hear a noise coming from the front of the house. We barely have time to spin around before someone enters the room in a rush. Silas pushes me behind his back, sandwiching me between him and the open safe door.

"What the fuck are you doing here?" Silas yells.

My heart is racing as I peek around him and see that guy who always seems to be within a few feet of Aubrey Price. The housemate, Deacon.

"Guessing for the same reason you are," he says.

And then I notice both of them are holding guns, pointed at each other. I had no idea Silas even had a weapon on him.

They stare at each other a long moment while I grip the back of Silas's shirt. Finally, Silas says, "I know who you are. You keep a pretty close eye on Aubrey Price. You kill Ben for her too?"

I peek over his shoulder so I can see his reaction to that question.

He gives Silas a smirk I can't decipher. "I could ask you the same thing since you're the one who's been having some trouble keeping your brother-in-law in line."

Aubrey still believes that Ben was responsible for her parents' deaths in some way. She can't know it was Silas. Ben is already dead. What would happen to Silas if the real truth came out? The danger he would face was not only legal; I'm realizing it could also be life-threatening. No matter what Silas did, he's still my brother and I don't want him to get hurt.

It feels like we're in a standoff that won't end until someone gets hurt, but then suddenly Deacon lowers his hand, letting the gun hang at his side. "From that empty safe behind you, seems like we're both too late or it was never here to begin with."

Silas's shoulders tense but he doesn't lower his weapon. "Unless you tell me how you came to be here, this won't end well for you."

"I work for Chris Ricci. Know him?"

From the jerk of Silas's head, it's clear to both of us that he does.

Smiling, Deacon says, "Good," then nods toward the front of the house. "Got one of my guys outside. If I don't walk out of here, it won't end well for you either. But I'm happy to talk as soon as you get your gun out of my face."

Silas hesitates a few seconds then lowers his arm. "Start talking."

"Ben trusted the wrong guy. Hired a PI to help him get the key to that safe right there. Same guy that owes Chris a shit ton of money. So who do you think he was loyal to?"

It was clear when I was watching Ben that there was more to his plans that day than we'd anticipated. It shouldn't be surprising to hear that Aubrey knew more than she had led me to believe, but it still knocks the wind out of me.

"That's fair. But how in the fuck did you know we'd be here now. Today."

He shrugs. "Let's just say we took advantage of the access to Camille's car when we had it."

Silas spits out a curse and I lean close, asking him softly, "What does that mean?"

"Means they put a tracker on your car when Aubrey was driving it around."

Deacon gives us the short version of their plan B, meaning he planned to show up here, like this, last week to surprise Ben, but obviously Ben never made it. He's been watching my car ever since.

"Ben went to a lot of trouble to get a key for an empty safe," Silas says.

"So what now?" I ask.

"My plan is to walk out of here and go break the news to Aubrey it wasn't here." And then Deacon turns and leaves.

Silas and I stand there staring at the empty doorway.

"What the fuck," Silas mumbles, relaxing for the first time when he hears the front door shut.

"This means Dad is wrong. If Foster sent it to Aubrey, Deacon wouldn't have shown up here looking for it."

Silas leans his back against the safe and closes his eyes. "If it's not here, where the fuck is it?"

CHAPTER 35

Hank

AFTER THE ALIBI
SUNDAY, OCTOBER 18

A sk Camille why I was at the Rosary.

The entire weekend, that one sentence has plagued me. Haunted me. Kept me up at night.

I send Camille a text telling her I need to talk. My phone rings less than a minute later.

"Hey," she says when I answer. "What's going on?"

"Hey, checking on you. How are you holding up today?"

It's Sunday and exactly a week since she found Ben. I imagine it's a rough day ending a rough week, so I'm not jumping right into questioning her about Aubrey Price and St. Francisville.

"I'm better than I thought I'd be, but that bar was pretty low. I think the fact that I'm wearing regular clothes and not the pajamas that were welding themselves to my skin is a good sign." Her words are light but there's still a heaviness to her voice.

"That is a good sign."

"Is there something you wanted to talk to me about or were you just calling to make sure I got out of bed this morning?"

Camille is a weakness for me. More than I would have admitted when Ben was still alive. Funny how Deacon picked up on it before I did. And he was right when he said I was trying to protect her. But I can't do that if I don't know the truth. "I got a weird call Friday night."

"Oh. What was it?"

"The police conducted a search on a house for Ben's hunting knife."

"What? Where?"

"The owner of the residence called me after the search was completed and came up empty. Her name was Aubrey Price."

Her gasp tells me everything I need to know.

"I don't understand. Why . . . why would she call you," she says.

I'm quiet for a moment then say, "Camille, I can't help you if you don't let me in."

Emotion spills out of her in a sob. It's gut-wrenching. She cries for several minutes and I hate myself for bringing her further down today than she already was.

Finally, she seems to pull herself together. "I can't talk right now but . . . but are you free later?"

"Yes, I'm available whenever you need me. Do you want to talk at your parents' or somewhere else?"

"Not here! But I don't want to drive my car . . ."

"I can pick you up. I have something I need to do around lunch and then I can head that way."

"Okay, Hank. I'll see you when you get here." And the call ends.

Glancing at my watch, I think through what I need to do between now and then.

It's time to have a conversation with Paul.

To outsiders, the Angola Prison Rodeo must seem too ridiculous to be real. Every Sunday in October, the prison that houses the most dangerous criminals in the state of Louisiana opens its door to folks of all ages.

There are the usual events you expect to see at a rodeo: bull riding and barrel racing, but there are some that are unique to Angola. There's convict poker, where the inmates sit at a poker table in the middle of the arena then a wild bull is released and runs straight through their card game. The person who stays seated the longest wins. And then you have one event called wild cow milking, which is exactly what it sounds like.

The inmates who sign up, risking life and limb, have their reasons, I guess. Any prize money is deposited in their commissary account, which they can use to purchase such luxury items as a new toothbrush, an extra blanket, or even specialty foods. And I'm assuming the bragging rights to winning Angola's version of the chariot races come with their own benefits. Plus, prison life is stagnant. Every day is the exact same. I would think getting to break that routine while you train to ride a bull would be enticing.

The inmates who have creative skills get to take part as well. They have a chance to peddle their wares from behind a twelve-foot-high fence that is topped with razor wire. Their products, everything from belts and bags to wooden signs to jewelry to clothing, will be laid out on tables on the other side of the fence. They are free to haggle with customers for the best price for their handmade creations and it's a safer way to make some money.

While most will make their deals from behind the fence, the ones who have exemplified model behavior are rewarded with a level of freedom they haven't had since being incarcerated. Those inmates will be under a different shed, where they sit behind their table with no fence separating them from their customers. This is where Paul Granger will be, which I discovered after reviewing Paul's file again this morning.

I've been to this rodeo once before, in college. A big group of us drove over and spent the afternoon watching the absolute chaos and mayhem of the events. Didn't walk through the arts and crafts part, though.

It's not uncommon for friends and family members of inmates to buy a ticket for the day and spend their entire time next to them while they conduct their business. I figure I can use that same model to get a few minutes to talk to Paul, off the record of course.

There are guards everywhere, armed to the teeth, but the process to get in is relatively easy. No bags on me so all I have to do is empty my pockets and walk through the metal detectors. Then I'm inside.

The air is thick with the scents of grilled hamburgers and hot dogs, popcorn and churros. The open-air sheds are long but the shade is welcome since the temperature is still in the nineties even though it's mid-October.

Every inmate behind every table is turned toward the main gate, hopeful either that someone special has shown up to spend the day with them or about the possibility of a big sale that will fatten their account to last until the craft show opens again in the spring.

I've met with Paul once so I know who I'm looking for, but by the third aisle, I'm thinking he's not here. He could have gotten into trouble and they wouldn't let him participate today. Or he sold everything in the earlier shows and is out of inventory. I worry momentarily that this is a wasted visit.

Then I spot him. I head to his table, but a family of five beats me there.

"Oh, I love these! Did you make all this yourself?" The mom of the group is picking through the leather goods he has laid out on his table in front of him.

I take this time to study everything he's selling. He hasn't noticed me yet since he's giving the group in front of him his full attention.

Paul had just turned thirty when he was locked up, and there's no reason to believe he possessed this skill prior to that, so not only did he learn a new craft but he has perfected it. There are braided leather bracelets and necklaces, wide cuffs and belts in every size, and some cool bookmarks. I spot several items that match the ones he gifted Aubrey. The stitching is nice, as are whatever tanning techniques he uses to get the finished color he does. Outside these gates, he could sell these pieces for ten times what he charges in here.

"The leather comes from the cows here after they're butchered for our food. They weren't killed for their hide, which I think is important. Everything is handsewn. You won't find better quality anywhere else." He is right to be proud of his work.

He haggles with the dad over a bracelet his daughter wants until they finally agree on a figure only slightly less than the original amount.

Once that family moves on, Paul turns his attention to me. It's clear he recognizes me instantly.

"What are you doing back?" He has a deer-in-the-headlights look. I'm sure he's heard of Ben's murder, which would make my visit worrisome.

"Your work is beautiful."

A smile stretches across his face at my compliment and he relaxes a bit. "Thank you. Not much else to do in here." Then his guard is back up. "Why are you here?"

"Honestly? I've got a couple of questions I hope you'll answer."

"About my case?"

I shake my head. "No. About Aubrey Price."

He takes a step back. "Why, because she came to visit me?"

Not what I was expecting him to say. "When did she visit you?"

His face scrunches up like he's trying to decide if I'm tricking him in some way, so I say, "Look, I'm trying to help her out. She may be in some trouble."

Paul's face drops. "Oh, shit. No, they can't get to her too."

"Tell me what you can so I can help her." I may be exaggerating our relationship a bit but she opened this door when she called me about the cops searching her house.

"She was here last Saturday. First time she came to see me."

Last Saturday. The day Ben was killed.

"Was this a planned visit?"

He shakes his head. "No. She just showed up."

"Did she say why?" It's like pulling teeth getting an answer out of him.

"Yeah. She had questions just like you."

We stare at each other and I wait for him to add more but he doesn't. "Can you tell me what she wanted to know?"

All he does is shrug.

"I'm not going to waste your time or mine. You can be up front with me now, and if there's some way I can help you with your case, I will."

It takes a little longer before he finally gives it up. "Same thing you wanted to know when you came to see me the first time. Wanted specifics on the new evidence."

"So Aubrey was aware of that too."

He nods.

"And did you tell her what it was exactly?"

"Yeah. May as well tell you too. It's a video from a surveillance camera. But before you ask, no, I never saw what was on it."

I think back to Ben's handwritten note in his file on Aubrey and Paul. "Did Kevin Foster come see you in early June? Was he the one who told you about the video?"

Paul's eyes get big, and it's the only confirmation I need that "Chief" and Kevin Foster were the same person.

"Yeah, it was him."

"Did he give you any information other than telling you about the existence of a video?"

"He said the driver was at my house that night. Should be easy enough to match them to that list of people."

I know what list he's talking about. Same list I asked Scott to do a deep dive on.

Paul grips the edge of the small table. "Maybe you can call Foster, talk to him. But don't tell him I told you his name! I mean, I didn't have to, you already knew it. Just don't want to scare him off from helping me."

My mouth turns down in a frown. "Paul, I'm sorry to be the one to tell you this but Kevin Foster died over a month ago."

Paul's face pales and he sits back on the wooden chair behind his table. "I'm never gonna get out of here now."

I lean forward. "Look, there's a good chance what he had wouldn't hold up in court. I'd have to prove chain of custody and a lot of other things. But after looking back at your case, I'm not even sure we need it. There's enough there that I think an appeal would be possible."

His mouth drops open as he stares at me. "You'll take my case?"

I hold a hand up. "I'm looking at it very closely. I'm not promising I can get you out of here but if I think there's a true path forward, I will take it."

He jumps up and tries to hug me but I catch his hands between mine and we do an awkward sort of double-fisted shake.

"I can't thank you enough!"

I nod and say, "One last question before I go: Tell me about the last note you sent Aubrey. The typed one. Something about how you hoped she had more luck than you did?"

His brow furrows in confusion. "What are you talking about?"

I reach down and pick up one of the jewelry boxes similar to the one in her room last night. "You sent it with one of these."

Paul is shaking his head before I finish. "I sent her a wallet and some bracelets because those fit in a flat envelope. Gave her the bookmark when she was here last week. I wouldn't have sent her one of these. Shipping is too expensive 'cause it needs a box. Plus they don't let us use computers so you can only send handwritten letters."

My mind is spinning. Aubrey believes that jewelry box and letter were from Paul, and there wasn't any reason for her to lie about that. But if it wasn't from him, who was it from?

"You keep a list of who buys your stuff?" I know it's a long shot while I'm asking it.

"No, almost everything I make is sold at one of the craft fairs to people walking up."

"Almost everything. When else do you sell things?"

Paul laughs. "No, this is the only place I sell things. I got permission to give stuff as gifts to people who come visit me."

I let out a loud sigh. I feel for Paul, I do, but he makes helping him very difficult. "Is there anyone you've given a jewelry box to as a gift?"

"Yeah, gave one to Foster." He picks up one from the table. "Looked a lot like this one."

Holy shit. Paul didn't send that jewelry box to Aubrey, but Foster could have. That's why the letter was printed instead of handwritten. "I think Foster sent the box to Aubrey with a letter. The one she has looks just like that one. But why would he have just sent her a letter?"

His face lights up. "Maybe he gave her the video!"

I shake my head. "No, she said it was empty other than the letter." She would have known if there was a USB drive or some other device that would hold digital files inside.

"Did she check the compartment at the bottom?"

"What compartment?" Last night, I looked over the jewelry box very closely and I didn't see a bottom compartment. Paul sees my confusion and flips the box over.

"There's a small tab underneath here. Just give it a tug and the bottom opens up. It's a space where you can keep stuff you don't want anyone else to find. I showed Foster when I gave it to him so maybe he put it in there?"

I glance around to see if anyone is watching us. I feel like running out of here, hauling ass back to Aubrey's for another look at that jewelry box, but I don't want to give Paul any false hope.

"Let me do some research and I'll be in touch soon."

"Thanks, man, I appreciate it. It'd be nice to get out from behind these bars before I'm dead."

CHAPTER 36

Aubrey

AFTER THE ALIBI
SUNDAY, OCTOBER 18

Last night was rough and emotional. I was already at my breaking point from finding that knife in my drawer and the police search shortly after on Friday night. But when Deacon got home yesterday and told me what happened at Foster's house, it was more than I could handle. It felt like that was my last chance to find out the truth about who caused my parents' deaths, and now I'll never know.

Deacon is making us grilled cheese sandwiches while I'm trying to coax at least two cups of coffee out of the machine before it dies.

"Please, please, please, just a little bit more." The thing spews and sputters, and I hold the cup up, making sure to catch every single drop that shoots out of the few nozzles that actually work.

Once our food is plated and we each have at least half a cup of coffee, Deacon and I sit at the kitchen table. His chair is as close to mine as he could get it, his hand wrapped around my thigh, anchoring me to him. I'm all for it.

I woke up in Deacon's bed for the second morning in a row, with my back against his front, his arm wrapped around me. The first thing he said was, "You're going to spoil me, waking up like this."

Same, Deacon.

The two of us talked all morning. We discussed whether or not Foster really had what he said he did, and if so, what he did with it. Also, we went over every possible scenario of who would want to frame me for Ben's murder. Sadly, we didn't come up with much.

Thankfully, Shane and Eddie had removed the knife from the oil pan early Saturday morning and disposed of it. I didn't ask what they did with it and I don't want to know. I'm just relieved it's gone.

Serenity breezes in the room wearing a colorful caftan. "Morning, you two."

"Hey, Serenity," I say.

She stops and looks at me. "Oh, sweetie, are you okay? I know it's been a helluva week but you look like you could use one of my smoothies."

I can't shake my head no fast enough. Last time she talked me into trying one of her concoctions, I was higher than I've ever been and didn't sleep for three days. "No, no, I'm good. But thank you!"

"Okay, well, you let me know if you change your mind."

She moves to the coffeepot and starts to make a cup when Deacon asks, "Did you have a chance to ask Frank for a list of people who were here Friday night?"

"Yes! He scribbled the names down on a piece of paper in my unit last night when he got in from work. Let me go get it."

Deacon stops her just before she steps outside. "Hey, we're keeping things locked down around here for a while until we figure out what's going on. You good with that?"

"Sure. But I have my usual group coming here for yoga this afternoon." Serenity gives me a small smile. "But if that makes you uncomfortable then we can figure out somewhere else to go."

"No, your group is fine to still come here." Serenity holds a yoga class in the backyard every Sunday afternoon, weather permitting.

"There's no one new in the group, is there?" Deacon asks.

She shakes her head. "No. Same ole bunch that's been coming for years."

"Thanks, Serenity."

And then she's gone.

I take a final sip of my coffee and say, "It's going to take me all day to get my room back in order." I've avoided it until now.

"We don't have to tackle that today. You're welcome to stay in my room for the foreseeable future. In fact, that's the way I would prefer it."

I lean against him. "Can I get my room straight and still stay in yours? Because that mess in there is all I can think about."

He stands up, lifting me with him, then carries me down the short hall to my room. "Let's knock it out and then head upstairs for a nap."

We've been working for a couple of hours and there's still so much to do. Deacon is a huge help with the big stuff but I'm the only one who can sort through everything.

"I'm starving," Deacon says. "That grilled cheese didn't make a dent."

He's standing in front of the bed in the only clear spot on the floor. "Are you hungry? I can go pick something up."

My lap is full of socks that I'm trying to sort into pairs. "I could destroy a cheeseburger right now."

"Done." He pauses before leaving the room. "Eddie and Shane are in the garage if you need them. And Serenity and her group have their asses up in the air in the backyard so hopefully that will scare anyone off who tries to come in here."

I throw a sock at him. "I'm going to tell her you said that."

He laughs. "I'll tell her myself." He walks to the exterior door, but only to check it to make sure it's locked before leaving through the interior door. It's that little bit of thoughtfulness that makes me weak in the knees for him.

A moment later I hear his car crank and back out of the driveway. Getting up from the floor, I decide to take a break while I wait for him to get back. I'm making myself some tea when Frank comes in the back door.

"Mind if I sneak in a load of laundry?" he asks.

"Not at all."

He sets the basket down on the kitchen table and starts sorting his clothes into piles. And from the variety of colors, some of Serenity's stuff is mixed in, which is really cute.

I drop our lunch plates into the sink and glance out the window. "Serenity had a pretty good turnout today."

Frank laughs. "I gotta admit, I'm surprised some of those older ladies can bend their bodies like that."

"You should try it! You did just have a big birthday so you may want to stay limber in your old age."

"Ha, ha, very funny."

My phone rings and I hesitate a moment since I don't recognize the number, but ultimately answer it.

"Hello?"

"Aubrey, this is Hank Landry."

"Oh, hi."

"Listen, this is gonna sound strange, but can you grab that jewelry box Paul Granger sent you?"

That was not what I was expecting him to ask me. "Sure, hold on." I walk back to my room and grab it off the top of my dresser. I glance around the room, and it's covered in clothes with nowhere to sit, so I bring it back to the kitchen table. "Okay, I got it."

"Turn it upside down."

"Hold on. Let me put you on speaker." I hit the button and put the phone on the table. "Can you hear me?"

"Yeah."

Frank comes back out of the laundry room, puts his empty basket on the table, and watches me flip the jewelry box over. "Okay, what am I looking for?"

"There should be a small tab in the corner. Might be tucked in the seam."

I feel around the bottom edge and run across a bump near one corner. "I may have found it but I'm not sure there's enough sticking out for me to grab. How did you know about this?"

It's a few seconds before he answers me. "Went to Angola today to talk to Paul. He had another box like that. Apparently he likes to put secret compartments in some of the things he makes."

"Oh, wow . . . Okay."

I work the little piece but can't get any movement.

"Here, use this." Frank has a pocketknife in his hand and pulls out the small set of tweezers.

"Thanks." I take it from him and it does the trick. Just a few tugs later, the bottom pops open and something falls out, bounces across the table. "Oh shit! There was a USB drive in there!"

"Aubrey, Paul didn't send you that jewelry box, but he did give Foster one just like that when he visited him."

"What?"

"If it's okay, I'm coming there. I'd like to see what's on the drive."

Part of me wants to hang up on him. I don't think he'd be on my side if there's anything on here that could harm Camille or her family, but then he didn't have to tell me about the compartment. He could have just figured out how to take it from me.

My voice cracks when I ask, "Is this what I think it is?"

"I believe it could be. Can I please come there and view it with you?"

"Yeah, okay." And then I end the call before he can say anything else.

I stare at the drive. My hand shakes as I pick it up.

Ben was killed because of this. The murder weapon planted in my room because of this.

So many people are searching for this.

And I've had it for weeks.

Frank's eyes are big as saucers.

"I'll explain everything later but I don't know how long I have until he gets here and I want to see what's on this thing before he does. My laptop . . . broke. Do you have one I can use?" I ask him.

He nods. "Uh, yeah. Let me go get it."

I examine the jewelry box again while I wait for Frank to come back in case there's something else I'm missing. Probably need to give the other items Paul sent me a good look-through too.

It doesn't take Frank long to get back. He puts his laptop on the table next to me and I hand him the drive. He examines it a second. "Shit, this is a USB. Mac only has a USB-C port. I need a converter to load it. Hold on, let me go get it from my bag."

He turns toward the door and heads back to Serenity's unit.

It feels like my whole body is vibrating from nerves. Am I about to see how my parents died?

I don't know if I can handle that.

But I also feel like I've waited so long for the truth that I have to watch it.

Deacon comes in the back door a few minutes later, a white bag in his hands. "Hope you're hungry!" Then he looks at me. "What's wrong?"

I hold up the jewelry box. "Hank went to Angola to talk to Paul. Paul told him there was a secret compartment in the bottom so I pried it open and there was a USB drive inside."

He looks around the table. "Where is it? I can grab my laptop."

Shaking my head, I say, "No, Frank's got his. Went to get a converter so he could load it."

Deacon turns to the window over the sink. "Frank left. Passed him when I was turning onto our street."

"What!"

I run past him, out the door into the yard. Frank's truck is gone.

And so is the USB drive.

CHAPTER 37

Camille

AFTER THE ALIBI
SUNDAY, OCTOBER 18

I'm eyeing the clock, counting down until the moment Hank gets here to pick me up. I've got all my things packed and ready, because when I leave, I'm not coming back. This week has been hard enough on its own, but being back in my parents' house is sucking the very life out of me.

It's as if the distance I've managed to create over the last ten years has evaporated completely. Dad insisted we all go to church together, sitting in the same pew we've all but owned since I was a baby. Then family lunch after at home.

Mom has carried the conversation throughout the meal with meaningless small talk. "We'll probably just do leftovers for dinner," she says. "Hate for all this food to go to waste."

Everyone is picking at their food because no one really wants to be here except my parents. Dad is reveling in having everyone home together like my husband's murder isn't what brought me here. Their mourning period is over.

"I have other plans for dinner," I say.

Dad perks up. "I'm not sure it's a good idea for you to be seen out to dinner a week after your husband was killed."

His words hit like a slap across the face. Of course the first time he mentions Ben's death, it's used as a weapon.

I tighten my grip on my fork. "Hank is picking me up. There are a lot of things we need to go over and I don't want to put it off any longer."

Silas throws me a questioning look but I ignore him. Margaret is steadily sipping her glass of wine, ignoring the judging glances Mom throws her way. Drinking at Sunday lunch is completely frowned upon in her opinion.

"Y'all can discuss whatever you need to here," Dad says, looking at me pointedly.

Before, I would have given in and done exactly as he wanted, but I refuse to slide back into my old role any more than I already have.

"No. We've already made plans and I'm not changing them."

We have a silent standoff of sorts across the table. Finally, Mom breaks the tension. "Everyone has been so kind to drop off food this week. The fridge is bursting. I'll send a few things with you to give to Hank since we'll never eat it all." Then she looks at Margaret. "You can take some to your house too."

Margaret nods but doesn't look up from her plate.

The rest of lunch is quiet, and Margaret leaves the second our plates are removed from the table.

I can't wait to get out of here even though I know I can't go back to the house I shared with Ben. Yesterday proved that. Silas keeps telling me that it's only because the grief is so new and finding Ben like that is still so fresh, but he's wrong. There would never be enough time to make that house feel like a home.

Silas offered for me to stay with them but that's basically like staying here since their house is on the property, a golf cart ride away. Plus, I can't even stand to look at Margaret right now. I have no idea if he told her I know everything and I don't care.

Once I'm settled in a hotel, I'll tell my parents I'm not coming back because I know if I mention it before I leave, Dad will throw up every obstacle he can to keep me here.

I've decided to come clean with Hank and tell him everything. He's bound by privilege to keep my secrets, but I think he would anyway because he's my friend. While I trust Silas with my life, he's wrapped up in this in a way that dictates his actions. But I'm not. I need someone to talk to who isn't connected to any of it.

Silas can tell I'm planning something but he hasn't said anything. I talked to him before church about Hank's call and the search of Aubrey's house. His reaction . . . or lack of it . . . tells me this was not news. He's been weirdly quiet all day but also glued to his phone. Whatever he's got going on, I have no desire to know what it is. Before, I was furious that Ben, Silas, and Dad had kept so much from me, but now I would welcome that ignorant bliss.

I'm putting the last bit of leftovers away when Silas appears at my side. His expression is strained.

"What's wrong?" I ask him.

"I need a favor."

I dry my hands off on a rag and throw it in the sink. "Okay."

He nods for me to follow him. Mom has disappeared to some other part of the house and Dad is half asleep watching the Saints game on TV. Neither of us speaks as we move across the yard to the shop on the other side of the driveway. It's a big metal building where most of the equipment is stored but it also houses a small office where Dad and Silas take care of farm business.

We enter the shop, the only light coming from the few windows on the left side of the building. Just before we go inside, Silas stops. "My guy found the video. Aubrey had it this whole time. He's here with it and it's . . . unsettling to think about watching it but I need to see what's on it. I just thought if you were here . . ."

He's scared. Scared to see what he did all those years ago. And while he's struggling with that emotion, it's actually a relief to me to see it. It means he's human. It means Dad hasn't completely ruined him.

"Of course I'll watch it with you."

He gives me a brusque nod but I catch the relief in his eyes before he opens the office door, allowing me to enter first. I was expecting the room to be empty so I'm surprised by the man sitting on the couch.

My hand flies to my chest. "I'm sorry, you startled me."

He tips his head but doesn't say anything. Silas shuts the door behind us. "This is Frank. He works for me."

"You were the one watching Aubrey?"

Frank looks at Silas, who has sat down in the chair behind the desk. He motions for me to take the one in front of it. "Frank found a way to get close," Silas says cryptically.

Turning to face Silas, I ask, "That's how you knew Aubrey's house had been searched by the cops, isn't it?"

He nods. "Yeah, Frank was keeping me posted."

I drop down in the chair next to Silas's desk.

"Does Dad know you got the video?"

He shakes his head. "No. Not yet. I've got to figure out how much of this I'm going to tell him. His idea of fixing problems tends to be a bit more nuclear than I'm comfortable with." He pauses a moment, swiveling slowly toward Frank. "Okay, let's have it."

Emotions I can't put a name to rush through me as I watch Frank pull a USB drive from his pocket, handing it to Silas. "I wouldn't have found it if I hadn't been there when Aubrey got a call from Hank Landry."

I sit up straighter at the mention of his name. "What do you mean?"

"Apparently, he went to the Angola Rodeo today and had a little chat with Paul." Frank fills us both in on Hank's call to Aubrey.

I don't know how I feel about Hank calling her about this.

Silas inserts the drive into the port on the side of his laptop while Frank moves to the door. "I'll be outside." And then he's gone.

I get up from the chair and stand behind his so I can have a clear, unobstructed view. His mouse hovers over the device name but he doesn't click on it. Putting a hand on his shoulder, I give him a gentle squeeze. Finally, he opens it up and we're looking at a list of folders. All of them are labeled with dates going back over twenty-five years.

"Oh my God. You weren't kidding."

Silas doesn't say anything, just clicks on the file name with the date that corresponds with Aubrey's parents' deaths. There are two files. A video file and a Word document. His fist clenches as the internal fight wages inside of him then he clicks the video file. It's dark and grainy.

"Where is that?"

"The parking lot of the convenience store on Maple." He points to the right side of the screen. "The accident happened right here."

There is no movement for several seconds. The only thing visible is the empty intersection lit by a lone streetlight.

And then it happens so fast. A car, presumably Aubrey's parents' car, enters the screen from the left side just as a truck runs the stop sign at the intersection. We both jump when the two vehicles collide even though there is no sound on the video.

"Oh my God." Even in black and white, it's difficult to watch knowing the outcome.

The two vehicles spin in a full circle, and when they stop, the driver's side of Paul's truck is visible to the camera, the front end embedded into the passenger side of Aubrey's parents' car. It's easy to see why her mother died instantly. Nothing happens for a few seconds.

I don't realize I'm crying until Silas hands me a tissue from the box on his desk.

The driver's-side door opens. Slowly. I glance at Silas. He's staring intently at the screen, his jaw clenched.

A person falls out of the driver's seat. I'm expecting to see Silas, ten years ago, but it's not him. It's a female. Long blond hair. She's disoriented. And then she turns toward the store, giving us a clear shot of her.

"That fucking bitch."

"Is that . . . is that Margaret?" I ask. "Was she driving?"

"It seems she was." His voice is hard and I can almost feel the anger rolling off him.

We watch as Margaret seems to get what's happened. She goes back to the driver's side and leans in. It takes a few minutes, then she's pulling someone else out of the vehicle. Silas.

He falls on the ground the second he's more out of the truck than in.

It takes her another minute or so to wake him up. She uses her shirt to wipe away the blood on his face. Once she's gotten him on his feet, he stumbles around. He appears drunk and is probably suffering from a concussion. He seems to gather himself and looks toward the other vehicle. Takes a couple of steps in that direction. But Margaret grabs his hand, pulling him away. They disappear out of the bottom corner of the frame.

At least Silas attempted to check on them but she didn't hesitate running from the scene without a single glance to see if anyone was hurt.

There is no movement from Aubrey's parents' car. Silas told me her dad, who was driving the car, didn't die upon impact. He bled out. And he has lived with the regret of not getting him immediate medical attention.

Silas's mouth is set in a hard line. "The first thing I remember is falling through the window at Ben's house. She was freaking out. Ben was confused. She started talking about the accident. I just assumed I had been driving. Said something like—*You shouldn't have let me drive like this.* And she never corrected me. All these fucking years she allowed me to believe I was the driver—that I killed those two people."

The video ends abruptly. Silas makes a few keystrokes and the document is open. It's a typed letter from Kevin Foster.

> To whom it may concern regarding the case of Paul Granger:
>
> I went to the Sip and Save on Maple Road in Corbeau, Louisiana, in the early morning hours after the accident that killed Henry and Vanessa Price to pull any of the surveillance video that might have recorded the accident. The store was just opening and the young man working handed over the tapes without issue. I didn't look at what was there until I got home. At this point, Paul Granger had been arrested. Randall Everett was led to believe his son was

driving the car and I let him believe I had covered for him even though the real driver was Margaret Wilson. I knew Randall Everett would pay for my silence to protect his son, but not his son's girlfriend. I take full responsibility for Paul Granger being incarcerated even though he was innocent of this crime. Now I'm facing death and will have to answer to God for my cowardly and greedy decisions. I'm hoping by setting the record straight, God will see how sorry I am and have the grace to forgive me and let me into heaven.

1 John 1:9: *If we confess our sins, he is faithful and just to forgive us our sins and to cleanse us from all unrighteousness*

Silas leans back in his chair, his eyes closed, as he takes a deep breath in, holds it, and then lets it out slowly. He looks like he's ready to explode. "Makes sense now why Margaret went to see Ben. She wasn't worried about me, she was worried he was going to find out it was her behind the wheel."

"I know you're not okay and I get why," I say. "But I'm worried about what you're about to do."

He shakes his head. "Don't worry about me."

I wait for him to say something else, but he doesn't. "I'm leaving this house and I don't think I'm ever coming back."

He nods but doesn't open his eyes. "I don't blame you."

"I'm going to tell Hank about last Saturday. About St. Francisville and Aubrey."

Another nod. "Where will you go if you won't stay here?" He knows I won't go to the house I shared with Ben.

I shrug. "Not sure, but I'll figure it out. Hank is picking me up in a little while."

Silas lets out a deep breath. "We found that tracker on your car and removed it. There's no reason why you can't drive it."

I shake off his words. He thinks I'm being silly but I can't explain why all of it feels so tainted . . . my house, my car . . . everything. I change the subject. "You're going to tell everyone it was Margaret?"

Silas sits up abruptly then ejects the drive, putting it in his pocket before he gets up from his chair. "No. I'll take care of Margaret."

He opens the door and Frank is waiting outside. Silas turns back to me before he leaves the office. "Go back to the house and wait with Mom and Dad until Hank gets here."

Silas is going to his house to confront Margaret, taking Frank with him. I don't want to be anywhere near that, but I don't really want to be around my dad right now either. They take off while I sink down in his desk chair and try to wrap my head around what I just saw.

A few minutes go by and I decide to call Hank and ask him to come get me now. I don't want to be here anymore. Leaving the office, I walk back through the shop since my phone is in the kitchen.

"He saw it, didn't he?"

Margaret's voice startles me and I twist around to see where it's coming from. My hand presses against my chest, my heart racing underneath it.

She steps out from behind some metal shelves that hold fertilizer and other chemicals they use on the farm.

"What are you doing hiding in here?" Just looking at her makes my blood boil. If she hadn't let my brother think he was guilty of her actions all those years ago, how different would each of our lives have been? Ben wouldn't ever have gotten under Dad's thumb. I wouldn't have been offered up to him as the prize for his loyalty. Silas wouldn't have been stuck with her either.

"Saw Frank when I was leaving from lunch. Followed him in here instead. There's only one reason he'd be here. Silas told me you said there was a video so I'm guessing y'all found it."

The audacity of her talking about this like it's nothing. "You mean the video that shows you were driving Paul Granger's truck that night and not Silas? The video that proves you killed them but let my brother believe he was a murderer all these years?"

She storms closer. "You don't get to just show back up here after all these years and act like you give a shit about Silas. You have no idea what *he* had to do make sure *your* husband was successful and that you had everything you wanted!"

Margaret pivots and tries to leave the shop but I'm on her before she gets too far away. "Oh, hell, no. I don't know where you're going but we're not done." I grab her by the back of the shirt and jerk her back.

She loses her footing and slips, taking me down with her. "Get off of me!"

Margaret pushes me away and slips free then gets to her feet while I'm still on the floor.

"Did you kill Ben too, you murderer? I know you were at my house that day!"

This stops her cold. She turns around and looks down on me. "No. Was I worried about what Ben would do if he discovered he covered for me instead of Silas? Yes, of course I was. That's why I wanted to talk to him. To see if he knew. But I didn't kill him."

I glare at her with narrowed eyes. "Why would I believe a liar like you?"

Margaret screams and lunges for me. I only have a few seconds to cover my head before she's on top of me. "I've always hated you! You've turned your back on this family yet they all still worship you!"

She tries to pull my hands away but I hold firm. I twist, trying to roll her off me, but she's got me pinned down. I move one hand away from my face so I can push her. Her eyes are wild, the ditzy blond facade long gone, and I worry about how far she's going to take this.

She grabs something from the shelf next to us and raises it above her head.

And then the world goes dark.

CHAPTER 38

Hank

AFTER THE ALIBI
SUNDAY, OCTOBER 18

For a moment, I thought I was going to have to cancel my plans with Camille, thinking I'd be tied up at Aubrey's. But a very terse conversation with Deacon changed that. After hearing about what happened today at their house, it's clear Frank was a plant, because the second he got his hands on that drive, he was gone.

I have my suspicions about who he works for.

Camille hasn't answered any of my calls, which is also concerning. I'm a couple of hours earlier than she's expecting me but my gut tells me something isn't right.

Pulling up to her parents' place, I park between the house and a big metal building. When I get out of the car, I see the shop door is wide open, the wind causing it to bang on the side wall. I decide to secure it before heading to the house. The second I get to the opening I see Camille on the ground and I'm running full speed to get to her. Blood pools beneath her head and the scene is so reminiscent of how Ben was found that I'm terrified Camille has somehow met the same fate.

Dropping down next to her, the first thing I do is check for a pulse. The relief is sharp when I feel the steady beat of her heart, but the volume of blood oozing from the wound on her head scares the shit out of me. Part of me is afraid to touch her in case there's a chance I could do more damage, but the other part knows she needs medical attention immediately and we are miles from the nearest hospital.

Checking quickly for any other visible wounds, I scoop her up and jog toward the exit. Silas and another man are just coming in when I get to the door.

"What the hell happened?" Silas yells.

"Found her like this. She's bleeding and unconscious."

He doesn't ask any other questions, just runs to my truck since it's the closest vehicle, while the other guy ducks back inside the shop. Silas opens the back seat door and helps me get her inside. "Hold on to her. I'll drive."

Silas gets in the driver's seat and cranks the engine. Then the other guy is back, with a stack of shop towels. "These are brand new, never been used." He passes them to me then gets in the passenger seat. Within seconds we are speeding down the driveway to the blacktop road.

I apply one of the towels to the wound, putting pressure on it. Camille doesn't even stir.

Silas throws the guy with him his phone. "Call the doc and tell him we're on the way."

He looks familiar but I can't place him.

"I know it may take a little longer to get there but we need to take her to Baton Rouge."

Silas nods. "We are. Just making sure my guy is there though."

That sounds shady as shit but I don't argue. Only thing that's important right now is getting Camille help.

Finally, it dawns on me where I know the guy in the passenger seat from. The report Scott made me on all of Aubrey's housemates. Other than Deacon and the two guys who restored the Mustang, the only other person who lives there is Tammy Simpson, aka Serenity Woods. She teaches yoga and claims she can see not only your past lives but also your future. She's also been arrested multiple times for passing fake checks, forgery, and fraud. Married and divorced four times, the last marriage ended prior to her moving in that house two years ago.

But one of the pictures Scott included from social media showed her with a new boyfriend. The guy sitting in the front seat.

"You're Frank, Tammy's boyfriend."

He throws me a look. "She prefers to go by Serenity."

I look at Silas. "You planted him there to watch Aubrey."

He doesn't answer me, which is fine because it wasn't really a question.

Before I can ask him anything else, Silas says, "We'll talk about this later, Hank. After we make sure Camille is okay."

Silas is sitting in the hard plastic chair while I'm pacing a hole in the rug in front of him. It was a scene straight out of one of those medical TV shows when we pulled up at the hospital. Whoever Frank called to alert we were on the way was more than ready for us.

Within seconds, Camille was whisked out of my arms, on a gurney, and disappearing through the sliding glass doors with at least eight people tending to her.

They've got her behind a closed door now, checking her out, while we wait. Frank has disappeared to God knows where. Silas hasn't said a word, just sits with his arms crossed while he stares at the wall across from him.

Me, I can't sit. I can't stand still. The only thing I can do is walk back and forth and back and forth.

About half an hour later, the door opens and I grind to a stop while Silas pops up from his chair and moves closer to the doctor coming to talk to us. They shake hands and it's clear this is "his guy."

"How is she?" he asks.

The doctor spares me a glance then gives all his attention to Silas. "She's going to be okay. Got hit on the head pretty hard. Needed a few stitches so we called in someone from plastics to make sure it won't be too noticeable when it heals. She's got a concussion. Camille was pretty foggy when she came to, but we ran some tests and don't think there will be any lasting damage. We want to keep her for at least twenty-four hours for observation, then she can be released as long as someone is available to watch her closely over the next few days. She will have to follow concussion protocol."

From my football days, I'm very aware of what happens after someone has a concussion. Lots of rest, especially mental rest, which means limited screen time. And after our conversation this morning, I know she doesn't want to be at her parents' house.

"I can watch over her."

Silas and the doctor both turn to look at me.

I didn't really mean to blurt it out like that but it doesn't mean my offer isn't genuine.

Silas turns back to the doctor. "When can we see her?"

"I can let you go in now. Just remember she needs rest and as little stress as possible."

Silas barely lets him finish before he's walking past him into the room. I'm close behind him.

Camille looks small in the hospital bed. There's a bandage covering the wound on her forehead. Her eyes are closed but she must hear us enter because she says in a weak voice, "Am I dead?"

Silas lets out a relieved laugh. "No, but I should kill you for scaring me like that." He goes to one side while I take the other. She opens her eyes, clearly surprised at seeing us both here together.

"How are you feeling?" I ask her.

"Like someone hit me on the head."

Silas leans close, all playfulness gone. "Who did this to you?"

She licks her lips and has to clear her throat before she can manage to get the words out. "Margaret."

This knocks me back while Silas doesn't seem surprised his wife attacked his sister.

But he does seem to be struggling with wanting to be here with her and also wanting to track down his wife.

"I can stay with her if there's something you need to take care of."

He stares at me long enough that I know he's weighing his options. Then he looks at Camille. "I won't be long." He squeezes her hand, then leaves the room.

Camille shifts in the bed until she's turned slightly my way. She winces at the movement.

"Do you need anything? Water? Pain meds?" The curtains are drawn and the overhead lights are off. The only light in the room is coming from the variety of monitors next to the bed.

"No. I want you to tell me what happened. How did I get here?"

I give her a quick rundown of how I found her and the ensuing events. She takes in everything I tell her with watery eyes.

Pulling a chair close the side of the bed, I sit so she doesn't have to look up at me. "Camille, it's time to trust me and tell me what's going on."

"Oh, Hank. It's so bad." Once she starts, the words just tumble out. Everything leading up to last Saturday when Aubrey Price spent the day as her, the same day Ben died, then the events of this week, including Silas's right-hand man, Frank, and the USB drive he showed up with this afternoon.

I lean back in my chair, my hands running through my hair as my mind tries to process what she's telling me. Half of this story is new information, but the other half I already knew. And it's colliding in the most mind-blowing way. When I get somewhat of a grasp on what she's told me, I fill in a few holes she has, telling her about my visit to Aubrey's house and the bar where she works as well as my conversation with Paul today.

"But why would Margaret attack you like this?"

"Silas thought he was the one driving Paul's truck all these years, only to find out this afternoon that Margaret was the driver."

"There is a video that shows this?"

"Yes, I watched it this afternoon with Silas."

I wait for her to say more but she doesn't. "And? What's he going to do, because I don't see him going to the cops."

"I told you my family isn't like other families. They tend to take care of their own problems."

These hospital chairs fold out into beds but that's a very generous description of the surface I'm currently lying on. The nurses checked on Camille half an hour ago and she's finally drifted off to sleep.

The door opens and I shield my eyes from the crack of light from the hallway. It takes me a few seconds to see it's Silas.

He shuts the door and walks to the edge of Camille's bed. "How is she?" he whispers.

"Seems a little better. Had a nasty headache a little while ago but the meds seem to have gotten it under control. Do I even want to know what you've been doing?"

He's been gone for hours.

"Looking for my wife, who seems to have disappeared."

"Say no more." Because honestly, the less I'm dragged into this, the better.

"Did she tell you everything?"

I nod. "She did."

Silas watches her for another long moment.

I pull the lever, converting this bed back to a chair. "She doesn't want to go back to Corbeau. I've got plenty of room at my house and can work from home for the next few days so I can make sure she follows the concussion protocol."

Silas doesn't say anything, just nods again.

I'm not sure how long we stay like this, quietly watching Camille in the dark. Finally, he turns to me. "I can stay if you need to get home. Your truck is outside." He tosses the remote and I catch it in midair.

"Thanks, but I'm good. Hopefully, I can take her with me in the morning."

Silas moves to the door. "I'll come by your house tomorrow to check on her. Bring her things from Mom and Dad's so she has some clothes. And then we probably need to have a conversation."

I nod. "Yeah, I've got a couple of things I want to go over with you."

Scott just emailed me the list of people who were at Paul's that night and one in particular stuck out.

CHAPTER 39

Ben

TEN YEARS AGO

It's painful waiting for the cops to show up for my statement. It's been two days since I dropped Silas off at his house.

The couple who died were from Baton Rouge, and left a teenage daughter behind. It's all anyone in town is talking about.

Paul's arrest was as swift as expected. The police keep reminding everyone of all the other crimes he's been arrested for and suspected of over the years in a full-on PR move so absolutely no one listens to him when he says he's being framed.

It's not long after I get home from work on Tuesday that there's a firm knock on the door, and I know it's time. Nerves race through me but I steel myself for what I have to do. I open the door to find Chief Foster along with another guy. He looks a few years older than me and he's wearing regular clothes.

"Hey, Ben," Foster says. "Can we have a few minutes of your time?"

I nod and invite them in then glance at Mom to see how she's handling their arrival. She's been sober the last few days but it won't take much to have her reach for a bottle.

Foster sees Mom, giving her a smile. "Sorry to bother you but we're working through the hit-and-run case from last weekend. The suspect threw a bunch of names out of people who had been at his house and could have taken his truck that night," Foster says. He gestures to the guy next to him. "My nephew, Nathan. He's staying with me this summer and starting at the police academy this fall. Thought it would be good experience for him to observe. We don't usually have such a big case, so I didn't want him to miss out on this opportunity."

My mom's hand flies to her chest. "You don't think Ben was at that Granger boy's house, do you?" Then she turns to me. "Are you buying drugs from Paul Granger?"

I roll my eyes. "No, Mom. I wasn't there."

Foster jumps in quickly when it looks like Mom's about to start crying. "Mrs. Bayliss, Paul didn't give us your son's name. But he did give us Silas Everett's name. I spoke to Silas on Sunday and he said Ben picked him up from Paul Granger's when his friends left him and then they went on to Baton Rouge. We're just following up and making sure that we've got the correct information."

Mom relaxes with a heavy sigh. "Well, y'all almost gave me a heart attack. And yes, Ben and Silas were in Baton Rouge this weekend. My Ben was showing him around campus since Silas will be headed there this fall."

Foster nods, pleased at her answer. "I just need a written statement from him for the file. And from you too, if you're willing, since you can verify that's where both boys were."

"Oh! Sure, happy to do my part."

Shit, Mom thinks she's helping solve this case when she's actually providing Silas a stronger alibi than I am. And now there's no way I can back out.

Foster turns to his nephew. "Pull out two witness forms for Mrs. Bayliss and Benjamin."

He does as requested and Mom and I take a seat at the kitchen table. He puts the forms down in front of us while Foster gives us each a pen from his chest pocket.

"All you need to do is fill out the top with your name, address, phone number, then in the open space below write your statement. Ben, in your own words, say that you picked up Silas Everett from Paul Granger's house and then the two of you drove to Baton Rouge and spent the weekend there. Mrs. Bayliss, if you'll just verify that both Ben and Silas Everett spent the weekend out of town, that would be all we'd need from you."

I haven't gotten into law school yet, but I'm pretty sure the investigating officer isn't supposed to tell us what to write on our witness statements. He's not even trying to make this look legitimate.

Mom signs her name along the bottom of hers and slides it across the table. "Now that's cleared up, anyone want some coffee?"

Foster smiles at her. "I'd love a cup."

I finish up my statement, rereading it to make sure the details Silas and I agreed on are right. Then I sign it and hand it over.

And just like that, it's done. Mom and I deliver Silas an alibi on a silver platter.

Mom turns to Foster's nephew. "Do you want coffee? And forgive me, I didn't catch your name."

He smiles at her. "It's Nathan Sullivan, but you can call me Sully."

CHAPTER 40

Aubrey

AFTER THE ALIBI
MONDAY, OCTOBER 19

Mondays are the one day of the week I have the house to myself. Deacon has been by my side since Friday night. He's been beating himself up about the fact that the moment he left me, Frank was able to steal the USB drive. Serenity is struggling with this as well. She's not so much heartbroken as she is pissed off Frank used her to get close to me.

Even though Deacon tried to stay home today, Chris needed him at work, so I forced him out of the house. Same with Shane, Eddie, and Serenity. No one needs to lose their day job because I'm sad my safe space doesn't feel that safe anymore.

I've gotten texts from all four of them throughout the morning, which helps, but they can't keep this up. With Frank gone and the USB drive with him, I'm trying to convince myself to give up trying to find out what happened to my parents. We all agree that my pushing for the truth is what put me on Ben's killer's radar, and I need to get out of that spotlight.

So I gather my laundry and get a load going, then make a grocery list that I can text to Deacon for him to pick up on his way home. I'm going to fake normal until it feels . . . normal.

I'm folding my towels when the doorbell rings, and I scream as if someone jumped out and scared me. I take a few deep breaths then slowly make my way to the door. I swallow my sense of dread when I peek through the side window to see who's here.

Opening the door, I try to hide the panic coursing through me.

"Can I help you?" It's the same detective who showed up here the night Ben was found dead.

He flashes his badge like he did the first time. "Detective Sullivan. I had a few follow-up questions I needed to ask you if you have a moment."

"Um . . . okay." Before I can even think about how to handle this he starts walking inside, forcing me to take a few steps back. He shuts the door and we're standing just a few feet apart in the foyer. He's too close. This feels wrong.

"I need to ask you about a man who has spent a significant amount of time here. His name is Frank West."

I take a step back. "Why are you asking me about him?"

"I had a chance to go over all the information the officers who served the warrant on Friday night collected. The event taking place in the backyard was a birthday party for him thrown by your housemate, correct?"

I nod.

"Do you know Mr. West well?"

I don't like where this is going. "Detective, I'm not sure if I'm the one you need to be speaking with about Frank."

He takes a step forward, closing the distance between us once again. "Miss Price, it will be so much easier for you to answer my questions now than if I have to take you down to the station."

I know a threat when I hear one. This isn't right. Whatever is happening right now isn't right.

"I don't really know him."

His eyes squint. "So you're unaware he is employed by Silas Everett?"

There is no faking the shock at hearing this. We weren't sure who sent Frank here. "No! I . . . no. I told you I don't really know him."

His mouth twists. "But you do know Silas Everett, then? By your reaction, it's clear that name means something to you."

Shit. I need this to end. Right now. And there's only one way I know to do that. "I want a lawyer."

He laughs. Actually laughs at me. "No. We're not doing that."

My mouth hangs open. "You can't tell me no."

He takes another step forward. "I can tell you anything I want." He reaches for me so quickly I can't react. He twists my arm until it's behind my back and pulls me in close. His mouth is close to my ear. "Listen and listen good. Seems like we've all been looking for the same thing and something tells me you got it or at least know where it is."

"I don't know what you're talking about!" Tears are running down my face.

"Your boyfriend, Deacon, just randomly showed up at a dead man's house in Corbeau, I guess? A lot of people were eager to get a look inside an empty gun safe there. And then there's Frank West, who has been here for months but now he shows up back in Corbeau, which makes me think his job here is done."

I struggle in his grip but don't say anything.

"Camille Bayliss is currently in the hospital. Did you know that?"

I try to shake my head but he's holding me to him so tightly I can barely move.

His mouth gets so close that I can feel his lips on the edge of my ear. "And Silas is having a little trouble locating his wife, from what I understand. So my guess is, he's finally seen the video and there was some blowup. Bet you didn't know that little blond bitch was the one who killed your parents."

My knees go weak and I almost fall to the ground, but the detective's other arm wraps around me. "How do you know that?" Is he just saying this to screw with me? Get me to admit to something? Or was Margaret really the one driving Paul's truck?

He ignores my question. "You've got one minute to tell me what I need to know or I will make sure you go down for Ben Bayliss's murder. And I'll bring all your roommates down with you."

Panic spreads through every part of me. But also anger.

I'm pissed. So freaking pissed off! "Seems like you already tried that. Too bad those cops didn't find the knife you planted."

I don't know what makes me say it. I wasn't a hundred percent sure he was the one who did it, but when his hand goes around my throat and he starts to squeeze, I know I'm right. This is Ben's killer.

"Ben made the same mistake you're making now. I offered him a pretty good deal. All he had to do was stop looking. Give up his search. But he turned me down, just like you are now. I may have underestimated you before but I won't do it again," he whispers in my ear.

I struggle against him but he's still crushing me so close to his body that I can't move. I kick at his shins and stomp on his feet but his hold around my neck doesn't loosen.

"Tell me what you know and I'll let you go."

He's going to kill me.

"You're not going to get away with this," I say, trying to stall him until I figure out how to get free.

He laughs. "First on the scene controls it. Learned that years ago. Works even better when you create it. I could strangle you right now and make everyone believe your boyfriend did it."

I claw at his hands hard enough that I have to have drawn blood.

Just as I start to see spots, I slip from his grip and hit the ground. There's a scuffle happening behind me but I'm on my hands and knees trying to catch my breath. I'm gasping for air and I'm so dizzy I fall over. When I can finally sit up and turn around, I find Deacon and the detective twisted into a heap on the floor. Before I can even think about how to help Deacon, a shot rings out and I scream.

It's a long few seconds before either of them moves. Finally, Deacon untangles himself and the detective flops on the ground, blood blooming from the center of his chest.

I run to Deacon and throw myself at him, sobbing. "Oh my God! I thought it was you. I thought you were the one who got shot!"

He squeezes me tight. "Are you okay? I was so scared I wouldn't get here in time."

I nod against his neck. "How did you know he was here?"

"Frank called and warned me. He and Silas will be here any minute and then we'll figure out what the hell we're going to do."

Deacon moved us to the kitchen so I wouldn't have to look at the dead body in the foyer. Both of us sit shell-shocked at the table. All Deacon could tell me was that Frank called him and said he needed to get over here as fast as possible.

I don't know how much time passes before Silas and Frank are at the back door. Frank lets himself in, just like he has for the last several months. By the way Deacon is looking at him, I'm not sure if he wants to punch Frank or hug him.

"The only reason I'm not kicking your ass is because you saved Aubrey's."

Frank nods. "That's fair."

Deacon quickly fills them in on what happened, then they all go look at the scene. I stay at the table.

When they get back to the kitchen, Deacon sits down next to me while Silas and Frank stand near the sink. "How did y'all know he was here?" I ask.

Frank runs a hand through his hair. "I have one of those doorbell cameras hooked up on the porch. Shows the front yard and driveway." He ducks his head, seemingly embarrassed to admit he was spying on who was coming and going.

I can't even be mad, honestly.

Silas finally sits down across from us. "Hank is actually the one who tipped us off. He had gone back through Paul's file, looking at the list of people who had been at his house that night. Was shocked to see Nathan Sullivan's name there. He did a little digging and discovered he was Foster's nephew. Apparently, he had spent the summer with Foster in Corbeau before going off to the police academy and had made friends with some of the locals, including Paul."

I'm shaking my head. "I don't understand."

"After Hank told me Sullivan was on that list, I went through some of the more recent files on that USB drive. And there was Sullivan's name. I would have discovered it eventually but Hank helped us get there a little quicker.

"Sullivan was Foster's go-to when he needed help to carry out whatever Dad wanted outside Corbeau. Dad liked to keep his hands as clean as possible so he only ever talked to Foster about what he wanted done. He trusted Foster to handle things and didn't get into the weeds of how he did it, so we never knew about the connection. Foster may have been a big deal in Corbeau, but he wouldn't have had any pull here in Baton Rouge."

I tell them everything the detective said to me about Ben, including how he planted the knife in my drawer. "He killed him because Ben wouldn't stop looking for those files."

Silas shrugs. "There was no way for Foster to confess his sins without forcing Sullivan to confess his as well."

I take a deep breath and look directly at Silas. "He told me your wife, Margaret, was the one driving Paul's truck that night my parents were killed."

He seems surprised but recovers quickly. Silas frowns when he says, "Yes, that's what the video showed. I had no idea she was the one driving until I saw it yesterday." It looks like he wants to say more but he doesn't.

So I push. "I thought Ben was the driver. Why else would he try so hard to get that video from Foster unless it showed that?"

"The truth of what happened to your parents wasn't the only file on that drive. Ben wanted information that he could use to his benefit. That's all I can tell you."

"So what happens now to Deacon?" I ask.

Silas pulls out his phone. "We gotta call this in but trust me to take care of it." He steps away to make the call.

I knew this couldn't be avoided, but calling the cops has always been the absolute last resort. They don't show up looking to help people like us. They show up looking to blame us. And all I can think is Deacon killed a cop. There's no way he's not going to jail.

When tears start rolling down my face, Deacon pulls me onto his lap, holding me close.

Shane and Eddie rush through the kitchen door but stop cold when they see Frank sitting at the table.

"You son of a bitch," Shane says, lunging for Frank, but Eddie holds him back.

Deacon throws his hand out, stopping the chaos that has erupted. "We have a much bigger problem."

Just as Deacon finishes filling them in, Silas rejoins us.

He doesn't look happy that Shane and Eddie are here. "Not sure it's a good idea to have so many people involved in this."

Deacon shrugs. "I called them as soon as I got off the phone with Frank to see if they were closer to home than I was. Told them Aubrey was in trouble. And we don't have any secrets in this house."

I can tell Silas doesn't want to say anything in front of the guys but we're so past that. "Look, we're all in this shit together so just tell us what's about to happen."

Silas gives Shane and Eddie a long look, then turns to Deacon. "A friend of mine on the force, not Dad's, will be here shortly. Tell him the truth. That you walked in while Sullivan was choking Aubrey and you knocked him off her. Sullivan pulled his gun and you fought over it. It discharged and struck him in the chest."

"Sure, man. And he'll believe me, no problem."

"He will." Then he gestures to me. "With those bruises blooming all over her neck and the blood under her fingernails, it'll be clear what Sullivan was doing to her and how she was trying to fight back."

"They're going to wonder why Sullivan was choking me, right? They're going to want to know how we're connected. It's not like we can tell them he tried to frame me for Ben's murder but we got rid of the knife before the cops showed up."

Shane and Eddie share a look that Deacon interprets immediately. "You didn't get rid of it, did you?"

They glance at Silas before looking back to Deacon. They both shake their heads no. Shane says, "It's in a safe place. We both thought there may be a chance we'd need it. That we could plant it somewhere advantageous if necessary."

My mouth drops open as I consider what this means.

"I could suggest the perfect place to put it," Silas says, as if he's reading my mind.

Without another word, Shane and Eddie sprint out of the kitchen.

"Having the knife found at Sullivan's obviously helps, but I don't see how you connect Sullivan killing Ben to him showing up here today to hurt Aubrey," Deacon says.

Silas leans back in his chair. "Honestly, that's going to be easier than you think. Paul Granger has always said someone partying at his house that night took his truck after he passed out and was the one who hit Aubrey's parents. And he was right. Detective Nathan Sullivan was on the list of potential drivers and his uncle was the first cop on the scene. It's easy to connect the dots that Foster covered for his nephew. And everyone will believe that because it makes sense." Silas looks toward Sullivan's body in the foyer. "And neither of them can deny it since they're both dead."

Deacon and I stare at him, taking it all in. But he's not finished.

"Hank has already been to Angola to talk to Paul about his case. Won't take much for Hank to get on board and confirm he and Ben, both, suspected Sullivan."

Deacon's head tilts to the side as if he doesn't believe it will be that easy. "And why would Hank do that?"

"Hank's going to have his hands full with taking over the firm now that Ben's gone. It'll sure make it easier if Ben died trying to get an innocent man out of prison, especially when everyone finds out it was a dirty cop who put him there. He'll have clients lining up at the door."

I'm shaking my head. He's right, this seems too easy. "But how does this connect to me?"

He frowns, regret clear in his eyes about what he's going to ask me. "You're going to have to say Foster told you Sullivan was driving the truck that night when the police question you today. He went to Paul to clear his conscience, but you'll need to say he came to see you too. And it's not a complete lie. He sent you that drive. He wanted you to know the truth."

I'm chewing on my bottom lip as I consider what he's saying. "This is too easy. Too perfectly wrapped up. As if you've already known all of this before now and had time to work it out."

"It works because it is pretty damn close to the truth. We're just putting Sullivan in the driver's seat of that truck." He's frustrated I'm questioning this, questioning him.

"And no one ever finds out your wife killed my parents."

Silas leans forward, his arms resting on the table. "I will deal with Margaret, but not publicly. And that's going to have to be okay." Then he nods toward Deacon but keeps his eyes on me. "That's the only way I can make sure Deacon doesn't go to jail for killing a cop. If it comes out Margaret is involved, I can't help you."

My anger starts to rise about the fact that he'd put conditions on helping us, that my lie will protect his wife after what she did to my parents, but then I look at Deacon and I know I'm not willing to risk his freedom. Letting the world know who killed my parents doesn't bring them back.

"You think that's all it will take? Me telling the cops Foster told me his nephew was driving Paul's truck."

He nods. "Yes. You were the last loose end Sullivan needed to tie up after killing Ben. He tried to silence you. But thankfully, Deacon showed up in time to protect you."

Deacon pulls me close, whispering in my ear, "Don't agree to anything you don't want to. We didn't do anything wrong. I *was* protecting you. We can get through this without Silas's help."

I pull back so I can look at him and cup my hands around his face, kissing him softly. "I love that you are giving me that option. And thank you for saving me. Now it's my turn to save you." I turn to face Silas. Lines you couldn't imagine crossing disappear when someone you love is at risk. I will do whatever it takes to protect Deacon like he protected me. "You have a deal as long as it keeps Deacon out of trouble."

CHAPTER 41

Camille

AFTER THE ALIBI
MONDAY, OCTOBER 19

The doorbell rings and Hank gets up from his makeshift desk on the kitchen table. We're at his house and he'll work from here the next few days while I'm recuperating on his sofa a few feet away. I was released from the hospital this afternoon to Hank's care and he offered for us to stay at my house, thinking I'd be more comfortable in my own bed, but when I said I was never going back there, I meant it. In fact, I told him to put it up for sale the second Ben's estate is settled.

Hank has gone above and beyond to make sure I feel not only comfortable but safe, and I'd be blind not to notice his feelings run deeper than friendship. But that's not a conversation or a situation I'm ready for, and he seems to understand that as well. He knows I need a friend more than anything else and he seems happy to fill that role.

Hank comes back in the room with Silas right behind him.

"How's the patient?" Silas sits in the chair next to the couch and hands me a white paper bag. "Brought you some of those macaroons you like."

"Thank you. I'm just glad to be out of the hospital. Hank is an excellent nurse even if he's following those protocols a little too closely."

Hank laughs. "You're not getting any extra screen time no matter how bratty you act."

Silas tries to smile but it doesn't reach his eyes. He looks stressed.

"What happened?"

He takes a deep breath and runs a hand over his face. "There was an incident today at Aubrey's. It's just about to hit the news so I wanted to come over and tell you both about what happened." He looks pointedly at Hank. "Do we need to sign some shit to make it formal so this is covered under attorney-client privilege?"

"I think we're pretty far past that. To make it official, you're my newest client. Welcome to Bayliss and Landry Law Firm. Consider yourself covered."

He nods, then says, "Detective Sullivan is dead. Deacon killed him protecting Aubrey."

"What!" I sit up so fast a sharp pain slashes through my head.

Hank moves next to me on the couch. "No sudden movements like that. Lean back."

Once he gets me settled again, he looks at Silas. "Start at the beginning."

And he does. Hank and I are speechless as we take in everything Silas tells us. By the time he's done, Hank is slumped next to me as if the weight of what he just learned is too heavy to bear.

"You didn't know Sullivan back then?" I ask.

"No, but I was only there a couple of times since I spent most of the summer working on that ranch in Texas."

"You really think you can pin Aubrey's parents' deaths on him?"

"Hank, you know the only thing stopping one side from winning a case is the fight the other side puts up. The other side isn't gonna put up a fight on this one. Represent Deacon and make the case Sullivan was driving Paul's truck that night, and Sullivan's recent actions were the result of trying to stop the truth from coming out. You will win. And that should pave the way for Paul's appeal."

"Sullivan's death is going to send shock waves through town, especially when it comes out he was the one who killed Ben," I say.

"Yeah, we're all going to have to weather the storm. Going to talk to Dad after I leave here, and I don't imagine it's going to be an easy conversation. With Foster and Sullivan dead, it's time for things to change. I'm going to suggest he take a step back and let me take over. He's going to put up a helluva fight, but if he doesn't agree, I'm walking away from the business. He won't let that happen."

Hank's forehead creases. "Does you taking over mean you're going straight?"

Silas shrugs. "*Straighter.* It's gonna get a little dirty before we're clean. Just like with this Sullivan business. He may not have killed the Prices but he did kill Ben, so in my opinion, I don't have a problem with him being guilty of both. Aubrey wants Deacon's freedom, as well as Paul's, and this is the easiest path for both."

"What does Aubrey know?" I can't imagine what she's going through right now.

"Mostly everything. Sullivan told her Margaret was the driver. Didn't think she needed to know any more than that."

Hank runs a hand across his face. "This is going to be a nightmare for the firm. The media is already unrelenting and this is only going to add more fuel to that fire. They're never going to stop talking about Ben."

"That asshole is actually going to look pretty good by the time it's all done," Silas says, shaking his head. Then in a high-pitched whiny voice, he adds, "Poor Ben was just trying to free an innocent man from prison until the dirty cop killed him."

I lean my head back against the couch and close my eyes. "Silas. Please. This is so wrong on so many levels."

Silas shrugs. "Honestly, this is the first time things have felt right."

We all sit quietly for a moment while we digest everything that's happened. Hank will struggle with this in his own way, but I know going forward, the firm will be better having him in charge.

I turn to Hank. "Can I have a few minutes alone with my brother?"

Hank stands up immediately. "Of course. I'll be outside if you need me." He's probably more than happy to get away.

There are a couple of things I need to talk to him about so I start with the easiest one first. "I'm going to buy that house Aubrey lives in and make some repairs. I drove by it before I approached her that first time and it's in pretty rough shape. I'll get Hank to draw up the paperwork for me to gift it to her. She can sell it if she wants or stay there and collect the rent from the others . . . her choice, but at least it will give her some options."

Silas's head tilts to the side as he considers what I'm saying. "Let me pay for the repairs."

I nod. We both need to make reparations to her for what our family has done.

And now for the harder part of this conversation.

"Have you found Margaret?" I ask.

He tenses at my question. "Not yet."

"What are you going to do?"

"Camille, you've gotten a glimpse behind the curtain, but I promise, you don't want to pull it all the way back. You need to let me handle this my way."

"I don't want you to do something you're going to regret."

Silas laughs but it sounds sad. "I have so many regrets I'd never be able to count them all. For ten years I thought I was a murderer who got away with my crime while someone else paid the price. I've lived with that guilt. I've stuck close to Dad, not because I wanted to be like him but so I could get in front of another incident like that one. I knew I couldn't go back and change anything, but I could stop it from happening again. Sacrificed my life because I thought I deserved it. I've done the time, Camille, so I may as well be guilty of the crime."

His words make me sad, because even though Silas has tried his hardest, he's already turned into exactly the person our father groomed him to be.

CHAPTER 42

Aubrey

AFTER THE ALIBI
THURSDAY, OCTOBER 22

The door chimes and I yell, "Welcome to Doug's," then drop the bottle of vodka when I see Silas Everett walk into the bar.

Doug hears the bottle shatter in the sink and rushes to my side. "You okay?"

I nod because words have left me. Completely left me.

The last time I saw him was three days ago when there was a dead cop in my house and he was making me promises I wasn't sure he could keep. To say I've been on edge since then is an understatement.

But so far, things have happened the way he said they would. The detective's death has been on every newscast, but then so has Paul Granger's case. The two were linked together from the first moment and it's the only thing people are talking about.

Silas sits on the barstool at the end, closest to the door. Movement from the back of the room catches my eye, and I watch Deacon put his pool cue down and head this way. He has barely left my side.

Deacon takes the stool one over from Silas. The two men look at each other and nod but don't exchange words, then Silas turns his attention to me.

"Go take his order and I'll clean this up," Doug says as he picks up pieces of glass and throws them in the trash.

It feels like I'm wading through mud as I walk to that end of the bar. Why is he here? When he left the house on Monday, there shouldn't be any other reason for us to ever have contact. While I appreciate everything he's done for Deacon, his wife killed my parents and she's still roaming free.

I don't say anything when I stop in front of them.

"Miller Lite?"

I reach down into the cooler in front of me and pull out a beer, setting it in front of him. He picks it up and points the neck of it at Deacon. "Can I buy you a beer?"

Deacon shakes his head. "No. I'm good. But I would love to know what brought you in today."

Silas takes a swig then sets it down in front of him.

"Just having a beer. It's been a shitty couple of weeks. My wife, Margaret, hasn't been herself lately." Hearing him say her name is like a punch to the gut. I glance at Deacon, but he hasn't looked away from Silas. "Really, she's been fighting the same demons for the last ten years. We just discovered she did a terrible thing when she was young and naive, and she's struggled with that guilt all these years."

I'm so confused. Why is he saying this?

"I got word today that the DA isn't going to fight Paul Granger's appeal. Shouldn't be long before he's free." He takes a drink of his beer and wipes his hand across his mouth while studying me.

I'm standing here staring at him with my mouth hanging open. Is this what he came here to tell me? That Paul is getting out of prison soon? Hank has already let me know that.

Deacon leans toward him. "What the fuck is this about?"

Silas holds his hands up. "Just stopped in for a beer and a little conversation." He throws a $100 bill on the bar. "Well, I've got to be going. Like I said, Margaret has been having a really hard time. I'm afraid she's started drinking again. I sure hope she doesn't get behind the wheel of a car. That would be tragic."

Oh, shit. What is he saying? Deacon looks at me and then back at Silas. He's struggling to understand as well.

Silas gets up from his barstool just as his phone rings. "I'm sorry, I need to take this. Hello? Yes, this is Silas Everett."

We watch him as he listens to whatever the caller is saying. His head bows, his hand covering his eyes.

"I'm on my way."

He ends the call, looking straight at me. "It's just as I feared. If you'll excuse me, that was the Corbeau Police Department. Poor Margaret has been in a fatal accident." He pauses a second or two, then adds, "It may not be the justice you wanted, but it's the only justice possible." Then he turns and walks right out of the bar.

Neither of us moves.

He's struck us both dumb.

"Did what I think just happened . . . happen?" Deacon asks.

"He made sure I knew the person who killed my parents just met the same fate." I try to figure out how I feel about this. I wanted Margaret to be held responsible for her actions, but I never said I wanted her dead.

Is her death really justice for me? For my parents?

I'm not sure.

I'm not sure about anything.

The only thing that feels certain is it's the justice Silas felt like she deserved, which leaves me feeling strange. Curious and unsettled. Like a piece of this puzzle is still missing.

Did Silas think that by meting out his own form of justice he would sever this connection between us? We're still irrevocably linked together. Connected forever in a twisted, ugly way.

Because if Silas Everett is ever questioned as to where he was when his wife died, Deacon and I are now his alibi.

ACKNOWLEDGMENTS

Even though this is my eighth book, it was the hardest one to write. And it took a village to get it done, so there are a lot of people to thank!

First, a huge thank-you to my agent, Sarah Landis. I am so lucky to have you in my corner and grateful for our friendship. Without your unwavering guidance and support, this book wouldn't be what it is today.

Thanks to everyone at Sterling Lord Literistic, especially Szilvia Molnar and the foreign rights team. I'm thrilled *Anatomy of an Alibi* will be published around the world!

I'm so happy my books have found such an incredible home at Pamela Dorman Books in the United States and at Headline in the UK! Pamela Dorman, Jeramie Orton, Natalie Grant, and Sherise Hobbs—y'all are the dream team of editors and I'm so grateful to have your expertise! To Jane Cavolina, thank you for the cold read when I needed it the most. And thank you to everyone at Viking, especially Brian Tart, Andrea Schulz,

ACKNOWLEDGMENTS

Patrick Nolan, and Kate Stark, for all the support you've given me and my books. And to everyone behind the scenes who worked on *Anatomy of an Alibi*: Tricia Conley, Tess Espinoza, and Diandra Abernethy for managing editorial and production; Chelsea Cohen, senior production editor; Jason Ramirez, Lynn Buckley, and Ervin Serrano for the beautiful art; Claire Vaccaro and Nerylsa Dijol for the interior design; Mary Stone and Anna Brill for marketing; and Rebecca Marsh, Carolyn Coleburn, and Becca Stevenson for publicity. I appreciate all of you!

To Megan Miranda, Elle Cosimano, and Julie Clark, thank you for being the absolute best critique partners and friends a girl could ask for. I can't imagine doing this without you.

I'm so fortunate to have so many people cheering me on. Thank you to all my friends and family who read early drafts and listened when I needed to talk something through and for generally being the absolute best.

To my husband, Dean, and our sons, Miller, Ross, and Archer, thank you for being my biggest supporters. I love y'all so much and am so thankful for you every day.

A special note: In this book, Ben and Camille attend a charitable event in support of the Tarver Braddock Foundation. This is a real organization started by friends from my hometown to celebrate the life of their son, Tarver. The Tarver Braddock Foundation's mission is to spread love, laughter, and happiness through random acts of kindness. I invite you to check it out at www.tarverbraddockfoundation.org and maybe do a random act of kindness in Tarver's name.

RAISING READERS
Books Build Bright Futures

Dear Reader,

We'd love your attention for one more page to tell you about the crisis in children's reading, and what we can all do.

Studies have shown that reading for fun is the **single biggest predictor of a child's future life chances** – more than family circumstance, parents' educational background or income. It improves academic results, mental health, wealth, communication skills, ambition and happiness.[1]

The number of children reading for fun is in rapid decline. Young people have a lot of competition for their time. In 2024, 1 in 10 children and young people in the UK aged 5 to 18 did not own a single book at home.[2]

Hachette works extensively with schools, libraries and literacy charities, but here are some ways we can all raise more readers:

- Reading to children for just 10 minutes a day makes a difference
- Don't give up if children aren't regular readers – there will be books for them!
- Visit bookshops and libraries to get recommendations
- Encourage them to listen to audiobooks
- Support school libraries
- Give books as gifts

There's a lot more information about how to encourage children to read on our website: **www.RaisingReaders.co.uk**

Thank you for reading.

---

[1] OECD, '21st-Century Readers: Developing Literacy Skills in a Digital World', 2021, https://www.oecd.org/en/publications/21st-century-readers_a83d84cb-en.html

[2] National Literacy Trust, 'Book Ownership in 2024', November 2024, https://literacytrust.org.uk/research-services/research-reports/book-ownership-in-2024